ALSO BY MELISSA MARR

DARKEST MERCY

melissa marr

YA
Fic
Marr, M

HARPER

An Imprint of HarperCollinsPublishers

Library of Congress Cataloging-in-Publication Data
Marr, Melissa.
Darkest mercy / Melissa Marr. — 1st ed.
p. cm.
Sequel to: Radiant shadows.
Summary: The political and romantic tensions that began
when Aislinn became Summer Queen threaten to boil over as
the Faery Courts brace against the threat of all-out war.
ISBN 978-0-06-165925-6 (trade bdg.)
ISBN 978-0-06-165926-3 (lib. bdg.)
ISBN 978-0-06-205954-3 (international edition)
[1. Fairies—Fiction. 2. Fantasy.] I. Title.
PZ7.M34788Dar 2011   2010033584
[Fic]—dc22   CIP
                                                                   AC

11 12 13 14 15   LP/RRDB   10 9 8 7 6 5 4 3 2 1

First Edition

To Anne Hoppe,
for loving Donia even more than I do,
for faery wings and temp tattoos,
for putting the "good parts" at the end of the letter,
for arguing and for not arguing,
and for skipping your tea one Saturday morning
to fall for these characters

ACKNOWLEDGMENTS

Once upon a time, I walked into what was reputedly "the worst bar in town" to listen to the blues. I said, "I like it here," and a woman offered me a job. I wasn't looking for a job, but I said yes. Years later, the Scramble Dog is still in my memories and heart. If you're out there—Richard, Debbie, Rob, Taz, Swift, Kyote, Andy, Johnny, Becky, Sarge, Little Dave, Thumper, Grandpa, JW, August, and many of the rest of you—thank you for smiles, stories, dances, music, thrills, and rides. You're not characters in my books, but sometimes I see your shadows in the background of my faery courts. I hope you're all happy wherever you are.

Over the years, a lot of folks touched my life in wonderful ways, so thanks to: Cheryl, Dave, and Dawn for being here through everything; Gene for many things; Alison, Kara, Jeep, Adrian, Janice, and Scott for pool halls, parties, and dances; Scott K. for being so real; Byron C. for bad habits and good poetry; Ingrid and Robin for conversation, music, and bars; Jeanette, Richard, and Erica for faith and fabulousness; Hunter for ivy vines and intensity; Matt, Harm, Brian, and Stacy (from Raleigh-Durham) and Derrick and Ken (from Seattle) for table dancing, exhibitionism, and the unexpected. I'm grateful to have your fingerprints on my life.

This time, I'm not going to list any of you in my *today*. You know who you are, and you know I think my life is better because you're in it.

But, as always and ever, the daily debt of gratitude is to Loch. I'll never figure out how you keep from locking me in an attic somewhere when I'm lost in the story or in a mood, or how you know what I need before I do. I love you.

PROLOGUE

Niall walked through the ruins of the tattoo shop. Shards of painted glass crunched under his boots. The floor was strewn with vials of ink, unopened needles, electric apparatus he couldn't identify, and other things he'd rather *not* identify. The Dark King had known rage before, known grief; he'd felt helpless, felt unprepared; but he'd never before had all of those emotions converge on him at once.

He paused and lifted one of the mangled bits of metal and wire from the floor. He turned it over in his hand. Only a year ago, a tattoo machine—maybe this one—had bound Irial to the mortal who had brought the former Dark King and Niall together again after a millennium. Irial was the constant, the one faery that had been a part of Niall's life— for better and worse—for more than a thousand years.

Niall stabbed his bloodied hand with the broken tattoo machine. His own blood welled up and mingled with the drying blood on his hands. *His blood. Irial's blood is on my*

hands because I couldn't stop Bananach. Niall lifted the broken machine in his hand, but before he could stab himself a
second time, a Hound grabbed his wrist.

"No." The Hound, Gabriel's mate, Chela, took the
machine. "The stretcher is here, and—"

"Is he awake?"

Mutely, Chela shook her head and led him toward the
living room, where Irial lay.

"He will heal," Niall said, trying the words out, testing
the Hound's reaction to his opinion.

"I hope so," she said, even as her doubt washed over him.

Irial was motionless on the litter. The uneven rising and
falling of his chest proved that he still lived, but the pinched
look on his face made clear that he was suffering. His eyes
were closed, and his taunting grin was absent.

The healer was finishing packing some sort of noxious-
smelling plants against the wound, and Niall wasn't sure
whether it was worse to look at Irial or at the bloodied ban-
dages on the floor.

The Hound, Gabriel's second-in-command, lowered her
voice. "The Hunt stands at your side, Niall. Gabriel has
made that clear. We will fight at your side. We will *not* let
Bananach near you."

Niall came to stand beside Irial and asked the healer,
"Well?"

"He's as stable as can be expected." The healer turned to
face Niall. "We can make him comfortable while the poison
takes him or we can end his suffer—"

"No!" Niall's abyss-guardians flared to life in shared rage. "You will *save* him."

"Bananach stabbed him with a knife carved of *poison*. He's as good as d—" The rest of the words were lost under the Dark King's roar of frustration.

Irial opened his eyes, grabbed Niall's hand, and rasped, "Don't kill the messenger, love."

"Shut up, Irial," Niall said, but he didn't pull his hand away. With his free hand, he motioned for the waiting faeries to approach. "Be careful with him."

Niall released Irial's hand so that the faeries could lift the stretcher.

As they left the tattoo shop, Hounds fell into formation around Niall and the injured king, walking in front, flanking them, and following them.

The former Dark King's eyes closed again; his chest did not appear to rise.

Niall reached out and put a hand on the injured faery's chest. "Irial!"

"Still here." Irial didn't open his eyes, but he smiled a little.

"You're an ass," Niall said, but he kept his hand on Irial's chest so that he could feel both pulse and breath.

"You too, Gancanagh," Irial murmured.

Far too many miles away from Huntsdale, Keenan leaned against the damp cave wall. Outside, the desert sky glimmered with stars, but he wanted to be home, had wanted to be home since almost the moment he'd left. *Soon.* He'd needed to be away, needed to find answers, and until he did that he couldn't go back. Being on his own was unheard of, but despite the challenges, he was certain he was doing the right thing. Of course, he'd been certain of a lot of things. Surety was not a trait he lacked, but it did not always lead to wise choices.

He closed his eyes and let sleep take him.

"Is this what you freely choose, to risk winter's chill?" Sunlight flickered under his skin, and he reveled in the hope that this time it would not end, that this time, this girl, *was the one he'd been seeking for so long.*

She didn't look away. "It's what you *want."*

"You understand that if you are not the one, you'll carry the Winter Queen's chill until the next mortal risks this? And you agree to warn her not to trust me?" He paused, and she nodded. "If she refuses me, you will tell the next girl and the next"—he moved closer—"and not until one accepts, will you be free of the cold."

"I do understand." She walked over to the hawthorn bush. The leaves brushed against her arms as she bent down and reached under it—and stopped.

She straightened and stepped away from the staff. "I understand, and I want to help you . . . but I can't. I won't. Maybe if I loved you, I could, but . . . I don't love you. I'm so sorry, Keenan."

Vines wrapped around her body, became a part of her, and as they stretched toward him, his sunlight faded.

He dropped to his knees . . . and was once more in front of another girl. He'd done this for centuries: asked the same words of girl after girl. He couldn't stop, not until he found her. *He saw her, though, and he knew that this girl was different.*

"Is this what you freely choose, to risk winter's chill?" he asked her.

She glared at him. "It's not what I want."

"You understand that if you are not the one, you'll carry the Winter Queen's chill until the next mortal risks this? And you agree to warn her not to trust me?" He held his breath for a moment, feeling the sunlight flare in his body.

"I don't love you," she said.

"If she refuses me, you will tell the next girl and the next"—he moved closer—"and not until one accepts, will you be free of the cold."

"I do *understand, but I don't want to be with you for eternity. I don't want to be your queen. I'll never love you, Keenan. I love Seth." She smiled at someone who stood in the shadows, and then she walked toward the hawthorn bush—and kept walking.*

"No! Wait." He reached down, and his fingers wrapped around the Winter Queen's staff. The rustling of trees grew almost deafening as he ran after her.

Her shadow fell on the ground in front of her as he stood behind her. "Please, Aislinn. I know you're the one. . . ."

He held out the Winter Queen's staff—and hoped. For a moment he even believed, but when she turned and took it from his hands, the ice filled her. Her summer-blue eyes filled with frost, and it crawled over her body.

Aislinn screamed his name: "Keenan!"

She stumbled toward him, and he ran from her until he couldn't breathe in the freezing air from her continuing screams.

He fell to his knees, surrounded by winter.

"Keenan?"

He looked up.

"No. You can't. Say no. Please say no," he pleaded.

"But I'm here. You told me to come to you, and I'm here." She laughed. "You told me you needed me."

"Donia, run. Please, run," he urged. But then he was compelled to ask, "Is this what you freely choose, to risk winter's chill?"

She stared directly at him. "It's what I want. It's what I've always wanted."

"You understand that if you are not the one, you'll carry the Winter Queen's chill until the next mortal risks this? And you agree to warn her not to trust me?" He paused, hoping she'd say no before it was too late.

She nodded.

"If she refuses me, you will tell the next girl and the next"— he moved closer—"and not until one accepts, will you be free of the cold."

"I do understand." She smiled reassuringly, and then she walked over to the hawthorn bush. The leaves brushed against her arms as she bent down and reached under it.

"I'm so sorry," he whispered.

She smiled again as her fingers wrapped around the Winter

*Queen's staff. It was a plain thing, worn as if countless hands
had clenched the wood.*

*He moved even closer. The rustling of trees grew almost
deafening. The brightness from her skin, even her hair, intensi-
fied.*

*She held the Winter Queen's staff—and the ice did not fill
her. Sunlight did.*

She breathed his name in a sigh: "Keenan."

*"My queen, my Donia, I wanted it to be you." His sunlight
seemed to fade under her brightness. "It's you . . . it's really you.
I love you, Don."*

He reached for her, but she stepped away.

*Her sunlight grew blinding as she laughed. "But I've never
loved you, Keenan. How could I? How could anyone?"*

*He stumbled after her, but she walked away, leaving him,
taking the sunlight with her.*

Keenan was still reaching for her when he opened his
eyes. The cave where he'd been sleeping was filled with
steam. *Not frost. Not ice.* He let the sunlight inside him flare
brighter, trying to chase away the darkness where his fears
and hopes played out in twisted dreams.

Not so different from reality.

The faery he'd loved for decades and the queen he'd
sought for centuries were both angry with him.

Because I've failed them both.

CHAPTER 1

Donia walked aimlessly, taking comfort in the crisp bite in the air. The promise of it made her want to draw it deeply into her lungs. She did, releasing the cold with each breath, letting the lingering breath of winter race free. Equinox was fast approaching. Winter was ending, and letting loose the frost and snow soothed her as few things could of late.

Evan, the rowan-man who headed her guard, fell in step with her. His gray-brown skin and dark green leafy hair made him a shadow in the not-yet-dawning day. "Donia? You left without guards."

"I needed space."

"You should've woken me at least. There are too many threats. . . ." His words dwindled, and he lifted his bark-clad fingers as if to caress her face. "He is a fool."

Donia glanced away. "Keenan owes me nothing. What we had—"

"He owes you everything," Evan corrected. "You stood against the last queen and risked all for him."

"One's court must come first." The Winter Queen lifted her shoulder in a small shrug, but Evan undoubtedly knew that she was walking because she missed Keenan more and more. They didn't discuss it, and she'd not descended into foolish melancholia. She loved the absent Summer King, but she simply wasn't the sort of person to fall apart over heartbreak.

Rage, however . . . that is another matter.

She forced away the thought. Her temper was precisely why she couldn't settle for only half of Keenan's attention.

Or heart.

Evan motioned to the other guards he'd brought out with him, and they moved farther away, all but three disappearing into the night at his command. The three who remained, white-winged Hawthorn Girls, never wandered far from her side if at all possible. *Except for when I leave without telling anyone.* Their red eyes glowed like beacons in the poorly lit street, and Donia took a measure of comfort in their presence.

"I would be remiss if I didn't remind you that it's too dangerous for you to be out alone," Evan said.

"And I would be a weak queen if I wasn't able to handle myself for a few moments alone," Donia reminded her advisor.

"I've never found you weak, even when you weren't a queen." He shook his head. "Summer Court might not be powerful enough to injure you, but Bananach is growing stronger by the day."

"I know." Donia felt a flush of guilt.

Faeries from all of the courts had been slipping away, and Donia knew that they were joining Bananach. *Can she form her own court?* The mortality of the newer monarchs caused more than a little unease, and War had made sure to nettle to heighten the tension. Likewise, worries over the interrelations between courts caused traditionalists to rally around Bananach. Niall wasn't openly sympathetic to the Summer Court, but his centuries advising them made his faeries ill at ease. Her whatever-it-was with Keenan had a similar effect on some of her court, and Summer's attempts at imposing order on their court made faeries who were used to freedom chafe.

Donia wished that a new court was what Bananach sought, but the raven-faery was the embodiment of war and discord. The odds of her settling for a peacefully created court—if such a thing was even possible—weren't high. Mutiny and murder were far more likely goals for Bananach and her growing number of allies.

War comes.

Once the others were out of sight, Evan announced, "I have word of trouble from the Dark Court."

"More conflict?" she asked, as Evan led her around a group of junkies on the stoop of an abandoned tenement building. When she'd walked with Keenan over the years, he'd always sent a cloud of warm air to such mortals. Unlike him, she couldn't offer them any comfort.

Keenan. She felt the fool for being unable to stop thinking about him. *Even now.* Every other thought still seemed to lead to him, even though he'd been gone for almost six months. *With no contact.*

She exhaled a small flurry of snow. In almost a century, she'd never gone very long without seeing him, or hearing from him, even if it was nothing more than a letter.

"Bananach attacked the Hounds two days ago," Evan said, drawing Donia's attention back to him.

"A direct attack?"

Her guard and advisor shook his head. "Not at first. One of the Dark King's halflings was caught and killed, and while the Dark King and the rest were mourning, Bananach attacked them with her allies. The Hunt is not reacting well."

Donia paused mid-step. "Niall has *children*? Bananach killed his *child*?"

Evan's lips curved into a small smile. "No. Neither Niall nor the last king has children of his own, but the *former* Dark King always sheltered his court's halflings. His fey—*Niall's fey* now—are amorous creatures, and the Hounds mate with mortals far more than any other fey. It is an old tradition." Evan paused and flashed a faux-serious look at her. "I forget how young you are."

She rolled her eyes. "No, you don't. You've known me most of my life. I'm just not ancient like you."

"True."

She waited, knowing he wasn't done. His patterns were a familiar rhythm by now.

"The Dark has a regard for family that is unlike the other courts." With a slight rustling of leaves he moved closer. "If Bananach is killing those dear to Irial . . . the court will be unstable. Death of our kind is never easy, and the Hounds, in particular, will not deal with pointless murder. If it were in battle, they would accept it more easily. This was before the battle."

"Murder? Why would she kill a halfling?" Donia let frost trail in her wake, giving in to the growing pressure inside. It was not yet spring, so she could justify freezing the burgeoning blossoms.

Evan's red eyes darkened until they barely glowed, like the last flare of coals in an ashy fire. He was watchful as they moved, not looking at her but at the streets and shadowed alleys they passed. "To upset Irial? To provoke the Hunt? Her machinations aren't always clear."

"The halfling—"

"A girl. More mortal than fey." He led Donia down another street, motioning for her to step around several more sleeping vagrants.

She stopped at the mouth of the alley. Five of Niall's thistle-clad fey had captured a Ly Erg.

When Donia stepped into their field of vision, one of the thistle-fey slit the Ly Erg's throat. The other four faeries turned to face her.

She formed a knife of her ice.

One of the thistle-fey grinned. "Not your business."

"Does your king know—"

"Not your business either," the same faery said.

Donia stared at the corpse on the ground. The red-palmed Ly Erg was one of those who often lingered in the company of War. They were all members of the Dark Court, but the Ly Ergs gravitated to whoever offered access to the most fresh blood.

Why are they killing their own? Or is this a result of factions in the Dark Court?

The murderous faeries turned their backs to leave.

"Stop." She froze the metal fence they were about to scale. "You will take the shell."

One of the thistle-covered faeries looked over his shoulder at her. The faery flashed teeth. "Not your business," he repeated again.

The Winter Queen advanced on him, icy blade held out to the side. It was a sad truth that the fey, especially those of the Dark Court, responded best to aggression. She raised the blade and pressed it against the dominant faery's throat. "I may not be *your* regent, but I am a regent. Do you question me?"

The faery leaned into her blade, testing her resolve. Some residual thread of mortality made her want to retract the blade before it was bloodied, but a strong faery—especially a queen—didn't fold under challenges. She willed serrated edges to form along the blade and pressed it hard to the faery's skin. Blood trickled onto the ice.

"Grab the body," the faery told the others.

She lowered the blade, and he bowed his head to her. The thistle-fey held their hands up in a placating gesture, and then one after another they scaled an unfrozen section of the aluminum fence. The rattle of the metal joined the growing din of traffic as morning broke.

The last faery heaved the corpse over the fence, and then they ambled off with the body in their hands.

Beside her, Evan said quietly, "Violence is here, and conflict is growing. Bananach will not stop until we are all destroyed. I would suggest that you speak to the Summer Queen and to the Dark Kings. Divisiveness will be to our detriment. We need to prepare."

Donia nodded. She was tired—tired of trying to bring order to a court that couldn't remember life before Beira's cruel reign, tired of trying to find a balance between discipline and mercy with them. "I am to see Aislinn soon. Without Keenan . . . *between us*, we are communicating better."

"And Niall?" Evan prompted.

"If Bananach is striking Irial's family, she is either testing for weaknesses or has found one already." Donia whistled, and Sasha came toward her, the wolf appearing from the shadows where he'd waited. "We need to find out who the girl was before I seek out the Dark King. Summon one of the Hounds."

Evan nodded, but his expression darkened.

"It is the right course of action," she said.

"It is."

"The Hunt is not all bad."

Evan snorted. The rowan had a long history of discord with the Hounds. Her advisor did not, however, object to her plan. She took comfort in that. The tranquility of Winter was pervasive in her fey. Typically, they could consider the situation, weigh the possibilities, and bury their tempers under the cold. *Most of the time.* When those tempers came screaming to the surface, the winter fey were a terrifying force.

My *terrifying force.*

As comforting as it was to have such a strong court, the pressure was daunting. She'd never thought to be sole monarch of a court. Once when she was still mortal, she'd dreamed of joining Keenan, ruling at his side. Barely a year and a half ago, she'd expected to die at Beira's hand. Now, she was trying to function in the role into which she'd been thrust. "Some days, I am not ready for what approaches."

"No one is ever ready for War," Evan said.

"I know."

"*You* hold the most powerful court. You *alone*. You can lead the way to stopping Bananach."

"And if I can't, what then?" She let her defenses drop for a moment, let her fears show in her voice.

"You can."

She nodded. She could if she didn't let her doubts get in the way. She straightened her shoulders and peered up at Evan. "If I allow another early spring, Summer will grow stronger, closer to an even balance with our court. I will speak to Aislinn. You will find out what you can about the Dark and send word to the Hounds. Sasha and the Hawthorn Girls will see me home."

"As you wish." With a fiercely proud look, Evan nodded and walked away, leaving her with the wolf and the trio of Hawthorn Girls, who were silent but for the whirring of their wings.

Chapter 2

When he'd left Huntsdale, Keenan had spent the first month wandering, but after centuries of leading his court, he could only remain unoccupied so long before the reality of being Summer King became too pressing. Violence seemed more inevitable by the day, and the Summer Court was not yet strong enough to face conflict, so Keenan had used the last five months pursuing alliances—with no success yet.

His meetings with various solitaries, especially those in the desert, hadn't gone well, but Keenan held hopes for those in the ocean. Over the past several months he'd shown himself at the ocean and then withdrawn. This time, he was staying until they spoke to him.

Entice and retreat. Appear and retreat. Approaching the solitaries was in many ways no different from the seduction he'd used on countless mortal girls over the centuries: they required strategies fitting to their personalities. With court faeries, he had to observe protocol. With various solitaries who functioned in pack mentalities, he had to demonstrate those traits they valued. In the desert, that meant strength and manipulative negotiation; at the ocean, that meant temptation and feigned disinterest.

A green-skinned merrow opened his whiskered mouth in a faux yawn, flashing serrated teeth at Keenan, and then resumed staring silently. The water fey weren't often likely to ask questions, not finding themselves interested in land dwellers' dramas, but with patience, their curiosity could be piqued. Keenan had counted on that.

With their volatility, they were closer in temperament to his court than any others, but water creatures were unpredictable in a way that perplexed even the regent of the most impetuous court. Whether river fey, lake fey, or ocean fey, they had moods that were as fluid as the water in which they existed.

Keenan walked on the beach. *Waiting.* The water lifted in well-formed waves; the sky was purest blue; and the air was mild this far south. If he looked at the water with only a mortal's gaze, he'd see colorful fish darting in crystal-clear water. Shells drifted and skittered over the sands, pulled and pushed by the waves, and the Summer King took pleasure in the beauty of the sea. It was a welcome respite: in nine centuries, he'd never had time to be anything other than the Summer King. When he hadn't been trying to tend a weakened court, he'd been seeking or romancing the mortals he hoped would be his missing queen. Once he'd found Aislinn, he'd needed to be there while she adjusted, and then he'd needed to be there while she was mourning Seth's abandonment—both to help her and to encourage her affection for her king and court.

It was what any monarch would do.

The Summer Court needed a queen who was tied to her court and king first. Her divided affections had weakened them in a time when they should be growing stronger. If Seth had stayed in Faerie, Keenan had no doubt that his court would be strong, with two monarchs who, if they were not truly in love as he had hoped they would be, were fond of each other.

It could've been enough.

Instead, they were facing an even more complicated dilemma. He was drawn to his queen—and she to him—on such a level that ignoring their connection was impossible. He'd been guiltily grateful that she clung to her mortal lover; it had given Keenan one night with the faery *he* loved and couldn't have, but when Solstice ended, so had the dream of being with Donia. The second Winter Solstice since Donia had been queen had passed while he was away, and the inability to run to her that day had made him despondent. *She is not mine . . . and neither is my queen.* The boy Keenan had thought would be a brief distraction to his newly found queen—a distraction that allowed Keenan time with Donia—had become a faery. Worse still, he was now protected by an angry Dark King and the dangerous High Queen. Keenan wasn't sure how one previously mortal boy had become such a problem.

Between Seth and the external threats the court faced, Keenan was more afraid for the future than he had been when his powers were still bound. Then, he'd had a single threat: Beira. Now, his court was headed toward dangers from too many directions. Bananach had grown stronger, as had Niall's Dark Court. Even Sorcha's High Court, which stayed hidden away in Faerie, had still managed to cause complications. Keenan had heard enough to know of her recent instability.

Over Seth.

The water edged closer as the tide came in, and Keenan stepped away from the lapping waves. In doing so, he moved toward a rocky outcropping. The sand under his bare feet wasn't as soft now, but it wasn't yet covered with the sharp-edged black mussels.

"What do you seek here?"

Even though he'd hoped to gain conversation with the water fey, the suddenness of the faery's appearance startled Keenan. He lifted his gaze to an indent in the rocky alcove beside him, where a slender salt faery hid. Her salt-heavy hair hung in thick ropes to her thighs, covering much of her translucent body; the exposed skin glistened with the crystals that gathered there when she left the water for more than a few moments. One partially webbed hand was splayed out on the rock, as if to hold herself upright.

She didn't move any nearer, but her proximity was already enough to unsettle him. The touch of such fey would leave even him weakened. For many, a salt faery's embrace was fatal. For regents, it was merely debilitating. Her position had placed him securely between her and the water, where other equally unpleasant faeries lurked.

"I'm seeking allies," he told her. "My court, the Summer Court—"

"Why?" Her gaze darted toward the water and then returned to him abruptly. "Land concern is not our concern."

"War has grown strong, and she—"

"The *bestia*?" The salt faery shivered delicately, and the motion sent a glittering shower to the sand and rock around her. "We do not like the winged one. She is not welcome in our waves."

"Yes," Keenan said. "The *bestia* . . . she's found her wings again. They are solid now. She flies well and far."

After flicking her salt-crusted hair over her shoulder, she stepped closer to him. "You falter."

Keenan reminded himself that retreating at this point would be a mistake. Even the water fey chased. *And running would put me in the water.* He let the sunlight that resided in his skin rise up. He'd rather not strike her, but if she reached out, he wasn't sure that he'd be able to resist.

"You are strong, and"—he gestured to his right, where the waves lapped very near his feet—"your kind are unsettling."

The faery smiled, revealing sharp teeth. "We mean you no death this moment."

The fear he felt rolled over him as a wave surged up his legs, drenching him to the thigh. "And the next moment?"

Instead of answering, she pointed to the alcove where she'd been waiting. "You will stay here while I tell them— unless you trust me to take you under the waves?"

"No." Keenan went to the fissure and leaned against the rock. His objection wasn't merely a matter of trust: water folk didn't think like land dwellers. She was as likely as not to forget that land dwellers needed air, and he couldn't convince anyone to ally with his court if he were unconscious.

"I'll stay on the shore," he added.

The salt faery stepped into the water and dissolved. The foam that lingered where she had just stood scattered as the next wave receded. The transition between solid and fluid was instantaneous and complete. The salt faery was gone.

He climbed higher on the rock. Being within reach of the water seemed unwise, especially while the tide was coming in. As he climbed, he donned his usual mortal glamour, lightening his copper hair to a mortal hue that was almost common, dulling his eyes to an only slightly inhuman shade of green, hiding the sunlight that radiated from his skin. The illusory image gave him an oddly comfortable feeling, like slipping into a favorite jacket. The glances of the mortal girls on the beach were a welcome balm on his still injured pride.

In front of him an unnatural wave rose up. Mortals pointed, and Keenan repressed a frown. Coexisting with mortals meant learning what was too extreme for them to explain away. A single twenty-foot wave in an otherwise tranquil sea was definitely too extreme.

Atop the wave sat a figure. He'd call it a faery, but beyond that he knew no words to fit it. Bits of gray skin and solid black eyes were obvious, but the faery's body was cloaked under strands of kelp that were crossed and layered in a great fibrous mass. The mortals didn't see the faery; of that, Keenan was sure. *There are no screams.* On either side of the towering wave a kelpie pranced. The horselike beasts slashed the water with their hooves. At their touch the sea frothed. If he were easily intimidated, their entrance would be impressive, but he'd grown up under the watch of an overly dramatic mother—one who wielded Winter—and he was the embodiment of Summer. It made him difficult to impress.

He waited while the sea stilled and the kelpies departed. The center wave delivered the creature to the rock where Keenan sat. In a blink, the amorphous water fey was a lithe mortal-shaped faery. Keenan couldn't say for sure whether it was male or female, only that it made him think of both dancers and warriors. The faery folded its legs and sat beside him.

"We do not speak to your sort. Not out here. Not often. Not as this," it said. The voice rose and fell as if the sound of the water rolled into the words. "Why do you ask for speech?"

"War comes. Bananach . . . the *bestia.*" Keenan fought an unexpected urge to stroke the creature's bare leg. It shimmered as the water at the horizon does when the sun seems to vanish at the end of the day.

The faery turned its head, so Keenan was staring directly into its eyes. The depths of the ocean were in those eyes, the deepest waters where all was cold and dangerous and still and . . . *Not tempting.* He forced his gaze away. "If she wins, your faeries will die too."

"Mine?"

Keenan folded his hands together to keep from reaching out to the faery. "You are not just another faery. You're a regent, an alpha, one who commands."

"You may call me Innis," it said, as if that answered the question implicit in his statement. Perhaps, for Innis, it did. "I will speak for those of the water."

Innis' words seemed to fall onto Keenan's skin, dripping down his forearm as if they were tangible things. His skin felt parched, too hot, painful almost.

Heat that strong needs quenching, needs water.

"I knew your parent," Innis said.

"My . . . parent?" Keenan fisted his hands, hoping that the movement would keep him from touching Innis. "Which? The last Winter Queen or the Summer King? Beira or Miach?"

"I do not remember." Innis shrugged. "Your forms are all alike. It was pleasant."

Keenan stared out at the rolling waves before him. The shimmering surface was mirrored in the flesh of the faery beside him. It was an odd similarity. He had sunlight inside him, but he also had traits other than light. Innis was as if water had taken form.

He glanced at the faery, and as he did so realized that Innis now faced him. They'd been side by side at the edge of a rock a moment before.

"You moved . . . or something." Keenan struggled not to back away from the water faery. "How?"

"You looked at the water. I am the water, so now you look at me." Innis stared at him as it spoke, and the faery's proximity made the air taste like brine. "We do not want to be dead."

"Right." Keenan let sunlight fill him, remind him what he was. "We don't either."

"The flesh creatures?"

"Yes. Faeries who live on the land."

"You speak for all of you?" Innis had his hand now. "On the not wanting to be dead?"

"I think so." Keenan forced the words to his lips. "I am the king of a court. The Summer Court. I want to be allies."

For the span of no more than six waves crashing, Innis was quiet. Then it said, "We have swallowed the sun. It does not shine after a while, and we left it on the sand then." Innis sighed. "It faded."

"My father?" Keenan tried to clarify.

"No. There were other summers." Innis shrugged again. "We would not like the winged one here. Your War. It pollutes."

"So, you would be an ally? You would help stop her?" Keenan prompted.

"I do not think drowning the *bestia* would be pleasure." Innis stroked wet fingers over Keenan's leg. "I believe I would enjoy seeing you drown, though."

"Oh." Keenan felt a decidedly conflicted thrill of pride and surge of terror. *I do not want to die.* He forced more sunlight into his skin, trying to chase the clammy dampness away. "If I ever want to drown, I could . . . I would come here. Is that good?"

Innis laughed and waves surged over the rock, covering them both, tearing Keenan's breath away and filling his throat with salty water. He tried not to panic, but when he attempted to stand, to get his head above the water, hands wrapped around his neck. Lips pressed to his, and kelp slipped into his open mouth. His chest ached, and his eyes couldn't focus.

I could find you pleasurable, flesh creature. Innis' words were in his mind as surely as its arms were around his neck and its tongue was in his mouth. *I will be your ally. I will take the* bestia *into our world if she touches the waves. We will fight for you in exchange for an open vow. Yes?*

An open vow, he thought. The mutability of such a vow was reason enough to refuse, but the Summer Court needed powerful allies and he'd had no luck in his other attempts to negotiate with solitary fey. He nodded.

The water receded then, leaving him sprawled on the rock, choking and gasping.

Innis stood over him. Its body was neither solid nor fluid. It held a form, but the form was as a wave when it was above the ocean: water temporarily given the illusion of solidity.

Once Keenan spat the water from his throat and mouth and had stopped gasping, he looked up.

Innis leaned closer. "I will watch for the *bestia*, flesh creature. If the *bestia* makes you dead before I can truly drown you, I will be angered. Do not allow that. You will speak my name to the water when you need aid. In return—"

"In return, my word that I will repay what service you offer in equal measure." Keenan forced himself not to think about the dangers of such a vow. *My court is not strong enough to defeat Bananach. Some dangers are unavoidable.*

The water faery nodded. "The terms are binding and accepted. I would have a token of faith to seal the vow."

A wall of water rushed toward them.

"I do not want to drown today," Keenan said.

"Just a little," Innis suggested.

For a moment Keenan wondered at the possibility of not-living. *It should not appeal to me.* He'd stolen scores of girls' mortality. He'd made them into faeries while everyone and everything they knew faded away; he'd convinced them to risk everything for him. *To be my queen. To free me.* He couldn't have done anything differently. He'd had to find her, the mortal who would save them all from dying under the freezing anger of his mother. Now, he had to find a way to strengthen the court without pushing his queen further away, to make allies among faeries who had every reason to hate him, to find a way to love Donia without being with her, and once again try to do the impossible.

A second wave swept over them, and Innis' form surrounded him. He knew that he would not choose to die here, but knowing didn't negate the pain in his lungs. He didn't fight the waves. *It would be so much easier.* As the water filled his lungs, he wondered—not for the first time or even the fifty-first time—if they'd all be better off without him.

He kicked toward the surface.

It is a pleasure to drown you, my ally. Innis' voice filled the water around him. *Call and we will come to you.*

CHAPTER 3

Donia exhaled a gust of frigid air as she watched Aislinn approach. The Summer Queen's guards had stopped at a safe distance, and the queen herself came forward cautiously. She had her hands tucked into the pockets of a heavy woolen coat, and her almost-black hair was hidden under her hood.

"Shall we walk?" Donia asked.

Aislinn gestured to a path that led away from the same fountain where they'd once sat and talked. Back then, Aislinn was a mortal hiding her Sight. Back then, Donia was weaker. Those things had changed in such a short time. What hadn't changed was that the actions of one faery, Keenan, both drew them together and kept them at odds.

"I'd hoped he would . . ." Aislinn's words faded, but she glanced at Donia.

"No. He's not contacted me. Nor you, I see. If he were *gone*, you'd feel it, Ash." Donia kept the sting of envy from her voice with effort. "The rest of the court's strength would leave him if he . . . died."

"But if he were hurt—"

"He's not," Donia snapped. "He'd let us know. He's either sulking or staying where it's warmer or . . . who can know with him."

"*You* know. If you wanted to find him, I'm sure *you* could."

Donia chose not to address that particular truth. She *did* know him, and she'd heard rumors of his activities from those eager to curry her favor. That did not mean, however, that she'd go chasing after him like a lovesick girl. He'd walked away on his own, and he'd return on his own.

Or not.

For several moments, they said nothing more as they walked. Icicles formed on the trees they passed. The ground whitened with a thin sheen of frost. It wasn't anywhere near what the Winter Queen could do, but the earth had been frozen for too long during her predecessor's reign.

If we are to survive, we need balance.

Summer was to be happy, but neither the Summer King nor the Summer Queen was happy. It weakened their court. *Which should not bother me.* It did, though: Donia wanted a true balance. She wanted them to be strong enough to stand against Bananach and her growing cadre of troops. *To stand at my side.* She broke the silence: "I will allow spring early this year. My court is strong enough to do otherwise, but I see no need to press yours to submission."

"My court isn't what it ought to be," Aislinn admitted.

"I know." Donia sighed. A plume of freezing air rolled out from her lips. "I cannot weaken my court overmuch, but I can try for a truer balance."

The Summer Queen shivered. "And when he returns?"

"That changes nothing, Ash." Donia kept her face expressionless. "He made his choice."

"He loves you."

"Please. Don't." Donia turned her back to the faery Keenan had chosen over her.

Even standing on the still snow-covered ground, the Summer Queen had her court's impulsivity. She persisted, "He *loves* you. The only reason he wants me is because he was *cursed*. If not for that, he would've chosen you. You know that. We *all* do."

Donia paused, but didn't turn around.

"Donia?"

The Winter Queen glanced over her shoulder. "You make it difficult to hate you, Ash."

Aislinn smiled. "Good . . . but that's not why I said that. I mean it. He—"

"I know," Donia interrupted before the Summer Queen could begin another passionate outburst. "I need to travel tonight. The slight snow I scatter here will determine what happens elsewhere. If there is nothing else?"

"There is, actually," Aislinn started.

"No more talk of him."

"No, not him." Aislinn bit her lip, looking like the

nervous mortal she had once been.

Donia looked at her expectantly. "Well?"

"I don't know if your court has . . . lost anyone, but some of my faeries have *left*. Not many, but some." Aislinn's voice faltered a little. "I'm trying to do right, but I'm suddenly the only regent, and they've been weakened for nine centuries, so used to doing . . . *whatever they want*."

Despite everything she felt toward Aislinn over the situation they were in, Donia softened at the worry obvious in the Summer Queen's voice. She knew as well as Aislinn did that none of their issues were by their own choice. *Or Keenan's, truth be told*. Donia sighed. "My court has lost faeries too. It's not you, Ash."

"Good. Well, *not* good, but . . . I thought maybe it was me." The Summer Queen blushed. "I'm trying, but I'm not sure if I'm messing up sometimes. He promised to help me figure this out, but I don't know where he is, and I'm not even sure they're *mine* to lead."

"They are yours." Donia narrowed her gaze at the doubt in Aislinn's voice. "You are the Summer Queen—with or without a king, this is *your court*, Ash. They don't make as much sense to me as Winter or Dark . . . or even the High Court, but I do understand faeries. Don't let them see your doubts. Frighten them if you must. Wear whatever mask you need to convince them you are sure—even when you're not. . . . Actually, *especially* when you're not. Bananach is luring our fey to her, and we can't be weak."

As Donia spoke, slivers of ice extended into small daggers

in both of her hands. It was instinctual, but it proved her point all the more.

"Right." Aislinn's expression shifted into something more regal. "It gets easier sooner or later, doesn't it?"

Donia snorted. "Not yet, but it had better . . . or maybe we just get used to it."

"How did he do it without the strength we have?" Aislinn asked tentatively, bringing *him* back into the conversation.

And to that, the Winter Queen had no answer. She shook her head. It was a question she'd been asking for most of her life. She couldn't imagine dealing with her court with her powers bound. "Advisors. Friends. Stubbornness."

"People who believed in him," Aislinn added with a bold stare. "You believed in him enough to die for him, Donia. Don't think either of us will forget that. If not for you, I wouldn't be their queen, and he wouldn't be unbound."

At that, Donia paused and asked the question she'd wondered in silence: "Do you regret it?"

"Some days," Aislinn said. "When I think about fighting the embodiment of war? Yeah, I regret it a little. Life was a lot easier when I thought all faeries were 'evil.' Now I worry about keeping them from dying, ruling them, trying to be a queen, and dealing with the impulses that aren't *me* but Summer. Sometimes it's like being *me* and someone else all at once . . . if that makes any sense. I'm not impulsive, or, umm, so concerned with pleasure, but Summer is—and I'm Summer. It's like fitting parts of a season into *me*. You know?"

"I do." Donia nodded as the ice in her hands retracted. "I thought the ice was going to kill me when I was the Winter Girl, so becoming a queen was a *lot* easier. I like the calm, the sense of quiet. Before, it wasn't easy. I carried the pain of the cold without being at peace for decades, so being filled with winter and having the power to handle it . . . I don't regret that—or the choices I made. *Any* of them."

They stood silently for a moment, and then Aislinn nodded. "I can do this. *We* can . . . even with our mortal 'taint.'"

Donia smiled. "Indeed. I will talk to Niall and Sorcha. Niall has a bit of sympathy for mortals—and for your court, however much he may try to deny it—so he's been plagued by the same sort of unrest that Bananach has provoked in our courts. We can do this, Ash, without Keenan, without failing our courts or breaking under our natures."

And in that minute, Donia believed it.

CHAPTER 4

Aislinn walked toward the edge of the park where her guards waited. She'd considered keeping them nearer to her, but she'd wanted to show Donia that they were rebuilding trust. Aislinn was still wary of the Winter Queen—and didn't entirely understand why Donia had thought it was necessary to *stab* her last year—but she knew enough about the Winter Queen and Summer King's love that she had resolved the stabbing as an act of passion. Aislinn understood passion. There were a lot of things she still didn't grasp, but as the embodiment of the season of pleasure, she had no difficulty accepting that passion could make a faery impulsive, desperate, and sometimes utterly irrational.

She paused and looked at the trees that lined the sidewalk. They were still coated in snow, but spring was only a few weeks away, so she exhaled and melted the frozen branches. In these next two weeks, she'd continue to grow stronger, and as Donia wasn't going to try to prolong winter, there was no reason not to begin warming the earth now. Her skin tingled with the realization that summer was in reach.

There was a strength in that if it was harnessed; she understood this now. These past six months that Keenan had been away—and Seth had been refusing her best efforts to be together—she'd learned a lot about being the Summer Queen. Accepting her nature was coming easier, and accepting that other faeries' natures were foreign to her was becoming reflexive. In truth, she'd learned more in half a year without her king than she could've expected.

Unfortunately, she still didn't have the confidence that echoed in Donia's voice—yet. *I will. Be assertive. Believe.* She smiled to herself. Sometimes being a queen wasn't that different from being a Sighted mortal: rules, reminders, pretending to feel differently than she did on the inside. *And a horrible cost if I fail.*

She had just stepped onto the sidewalk, not yet beside her guards, when a faery she did not know appeared seemingly from nowhere.

He asked, "Are you in need of escort?"

At first glance, she thought he was one of Donia's fey, as he seemed as pale as the snow around them, but when she looked again, he seemed to be as dark as the sky at new moon. Light and dark shifted in and out of his skin, and his eyes flickered to the opposite of the hue his skin was in that instant. She furrowed her brow as she tried to study him.

Her gaze kept slipping to his garishly red shirt. It was

hard to miss. Along with being an assaultingly bright shade of red, it clung to his chest and arms so much that it would look foolish on most people. On him, it looked natural. Despite the chill, he wore no coat over the thin shirt. She tried to lift her gaze to his eyes, and again, she had to glance away.

"You'll get used to it in a moment," he said.

"To what?"

"The shifts. I'll settle into one or the other for our visit." He shrugged, and as he spoke the words, he did just that: his skin became the dark of all colors combined, and his eyes blanched to a complete absence of color.

"Oh." Somehow, she'd believed that she'd stopped being astounded by faeries, but she was at a loss. She tried to think of anything she knew that would explain him, but he was unlike any other faery she'd encountered—which wasn't at all comforting. She offered a false expression, a surety she wished she felt, the confidence the Summer Queen *should* feel.

"You are safe. I came to your"—he gestured expansively— "village for other reasons than finding you, but I am intrigued." The faery smiled at her then, as if she'd done something of which she should be proud. "I mean you no ill this day, Queen of Summer. If I had better manners, I would've said that first."

No ill this *day?*

This far outside of her park, when it was not yet spring and she was standing in the cold, Aislinn wasn't at her strongest, but she concentrated on summoning sunlight to her hand should she need to defend herself. "I'm afraid that you have me at a disadvantage. I'm not sure who you are or why you would be here."

"Do you ask, Aislinn?" The faery caught her gaze. "Not many ask questions of me."

"Is there a cost for asking?" Her nerves were increasingly unsettled. As a faery monarch, she was safe from most threats, but she'd been injured by two of the other regents—faeries she'd trusted—so she knew very well that she was not impervious to injury. Her first year of being a faery had made that truth very clear to her.

The second year isn't going very well either.

The strange faery in front of her extended a hand as if to touch her face. "I would accept permission to caress your cheek."

"For an answer?" Aislinn rolled her eyes. "I don't think so."

"The recently mortal are"—he shook his head—"so brash. Would you refuse my offer if you knew who I was?"

"No way of telling, is there?" Aislinn turned and resumed walking toward her guards. The skin at the back of her neck prickled, but she didn't feel like playing guessing games.

And I am afraid.

"If you allow me to cradle your face in my hands, it will not injure you, and I will allow two questions or one gift for the privilege," he called.

She stopped walking. One of the detriments of being so new to ruling was that she had no favors to call in, no years of bargains to rely on, and—of late—no king with such connections to help her. *If we are to fight Bananach, I have no secret arsenal.* She looked over her shoulder at him and asked, "Why?"

"Would that be one of your questions, Summer Queen?" His lips curved slightly so that he looked like he would begin laughing in another moment.

"No." She folded her arms over her chest. "You know, I've been fey for a while now, but faery word games still don't amuse me. Later, I suspect I'll understand this, but right now, I'm irritated."

"And curious," he added with a laugh. "I'll allow one free answer. Why? Because the recently mortal fascinate me. Your king assured I had no business with the other girls when they became fey. You are here; he is not . . . and I am curious."

"I'm not sure bargaining with you when you seem to *want* to so badly is wise." Aislinn stayed where she was, admitting in action if not in word that she was willing to consider negotiation.

Don't let this be a mistake. Please don't be a mistake.

The faery walked several steps closer to her. "One question now, and one held in reserve. What if I know things you'll want to know later? What if a question owed could be an asset to your court?"

"One question now, and one question *or* favor later, and"—she took one more step away—"your assurance that no harm will come to me by your touch . . . which can only last for less than a minute."

He stopped a few feet from her. "I'll allow the terms, *if* you allow me to escort you to your loft."

"To the door, but not inside, and we walk there directly with no detours, and my guards will join us."

"Done." He came forward.

"Done," she echoed.

Then he cradled her face in his hands, and the world became utterly silent around her. Neither sight nor sound remained. There was only darkness, complete and absolute. If she hadn't secured a promise that no injury would come to her, Aislinn would have been convinced that she'd left her body and fallen into a void.

What have I done?

To her mind, it seemed as if days passed as they stood together. Then he leaned toward her. In the void where she somehow now was, she felt his movements. Nothing existed before or after him. His voice was of corn husks whispering in barren expanses as he told her, "My name is Far Dorcha. The Dark Man."

Aislinn knew that it had been only a few moments that she'd been in the void, but when Far Dorcha pulled his hands away from her, she stumbled. The world was too harshly lit; the ice that hung from the trees in the distance glistened so brightly that she had to avert her gaze. Only he, the Dark Man, was painless to see.

"You're . . . death-fey." She'd met a couple of his kind, and while they weren't a proper court, they were under his dominion. Death faeries had no need for a court: they had no enemies. Immortal creatures weren't imprudent enough to tangle with those who could and would kill them with as much effort as they expended on breathing. Aislinn took several steps backward. She'd willingly consented to a caress from the faery equivalent of Death. *What was I thinking?* If not for the things Keenan and Niall had taught her about faery bargains, that could have gone very poorly.

It still might.

"They hadn't told me you could've been so near my reach. Almost dead. Almost mine." Far Dorcha frowned slightly as he peered into her face as if to read words written on her flesh. "Winter stabbed you."

At that, Aislinn's worries over the bargain were replaced. *Near death?* She had known she was injured, had felt doubt that she would survive, but she'd come to believe that it had simply hurt worse than it was. Before she could find words to reply, he exhaled his cloyingly sweet breath.

She stumbled as the pain and emotions of that injury came to her as clearly as they had been that day. The scent of funereal flowers made her body remember what her mind wished to deny. *Had Donia meant to wound me so badly?* It was a subject they hadn't discussed: the Winter Queen's ice could've easily been fatal. *If not for Keenan.* He'd saved her, and in doing so, he'd pushed her—and pushed Seth—into confronting the undeniable connection between the Summer King and Queen.

However, it wasn't the pleasure of her king healing her

that she felt now: it was the pain of ice coursing through her body that washed over her anew as she breathed in the death-fey's sugar-sweet breath. She put her hand on her stomach. "What . . . how . . ."

"You weren't completely in my reach before your king interfered," Far Dorcha said.

The Dark Man sighed again, and Aislinn felt memories tugging her back. She could feel slivers of winter buried inside her body; she could feel the horrible sense that *this* wound was the one to end her newfound immortality. *This injury will be fatal.* Aislinn felt her knees give out.

"Enough." She clutched the grass, seeking the buried fecundity of the earth to steady her. *This isn't an* injury; *it's a memory.*

The pain was still intense enough that she stayed on the ground for a moment longer, letting the warmth of summer life flow from under the ice through the soil and to her.

Then, her guards were there. A rowan had her arm, as if to steady her, but she shook him off and stood. She took a step toward Far Dorcha.

Be confident. Aislinn could almost laugh at taking advice from the faery whose injury to her she was now reliving. *I am the Summer Queen. I can do this.*

"You do not come here and attack a regent," she said.

"Attack?" The Dark Man laughed. "We had a bargain, little queen. It is not my fault that you are uncomfortable with the results."

With sunlight pulsing into her body as truly as if Keenan had stood beside her, sharing his light with her, she pushed her sunlight into Far Dorcha's chest, not as a strike but as a reminder of what—*who*—she was. "I don't know what you are doing, but that's *enough*."

None of the guards touched Far Dorcha, but one did step closer to her. "My Queen? Perhaps—"

Aislinn held up a hand. "I didn't agree to that . . . whatever it was."

"Remembering," Far Dorcha said. "I'm only remembering."

"It's not *your* memory." Aislinn motioned for the guards to stay where they were even as they tensed. A queen kept her court safe, and she was pretty certain that attacking the head of the death-fey wasn't likely to go well.

"It should've been my memory," he said. "If he hadn't found you when he did, you would've been dead not long after."

Far Dorcha exhaled again, sending that sugar-sweet breath toward her in a prolonged sigh.

Aislinn turned her head to avoid inhaling.

Expression pensive, Far Dorcha looked past her. Then he said, "Some wounds take longer to kill. I should've been summoned. Your king has questions to answer, Summer Queen."

"Well, I'll be sure to mention that to him." She motioned to the street. "I agreed to your escorting me to my door—"

"Another day," Far Dorcha said absently, and with as little sound as he'd made when he arrived, he left.

The temper she couldn't fully repress flared to life as Aislinn strode through the cluster of her guards, letting them scurry to reorganize themselves as they escorted her.

By the time she reached the loft that was now her home, her temper had faded and clarity struck her: there must be a reason the head of the death-fey was in Huntsdale—and she couldn't think of any reasons that didn't worry her.

Who has died? Will die? Her mind swirled with thoughts of Seth and Keenan, of her court, of faeries who weren't *hers* but whom she'd still mourn. *Seth and Keenan are away. It's not them. Right? Where* are *they?*

She raced up the stairs, shoved open the door, and called, "Tavish! I need advice. *Now.*"

Instead of her trusted advisor, Quinn came into the main room. "Tavish is with the Summer Girls, but I'm here."

The birds that used to be Keenan's swooped around manically as Aislinn's temper spiked again. "I need answers."

Quinn ducked as one of the cockatiels flew dangerously close to his ear. He was wise enough not to swipe at the bird, but the scowl he flashed it wasn't fleeting enough for her to miss. "Can I help?"

Aislinn extended her arm for the offending bird. It settled on her wrist and walked sideways up to her shoulder. She wasn't going to tell Quinn about her encounter with Death, but there were other subjects that he could address. *Be assertive.* She'd been patient for almost six months, waiting for the Summer King to return to his court. She'd waited for Seth while he was in Faerie. *Is Keenan hiding in Faerie now? Is that where Seth is again too?* Seth had disappeared several days ago, and given that he had been claimed as a child to the High Queen, Aislinn suspected his disappearance was tied to *her*. Keenan might not be close with Sorcha, but he'd had centuries of dealing with her. *Did he go to Faerie for something too?* The High Queen had answers, and had been at odds with her mad twin sister, Bananach, for centuries longer than Aislinn had lived, but she wasn't coming to offer aid to any who now dealt with the strengthened War—and Aislinn didn't expect her to do so. According to Keenan, the High Queen had kept herself withdrawn from the centuries of conflict between Winter and Summer. *And I cannot ask her for insight because I can't go to her. I can't even go find out if my king or my . . . Seth . . . is with her.*

"How is it that I'm not aware of how to enter Faerie?" Aislinn let her temper simmer in her voice and on her skin. "Where are the gates to Faerie?"

"My queen—"

"No," she interrupted before he could begin another litany of the dangers of entering Faerie without the High Queen's consent. "Everyone else seems to know how to enter Faerie. Seth knows. Niall knows. Keenan knows. Why do I not know?"

"If you'll forgive the impertinence, my queen, the others are not new to being fey, aside from Seth, who is the Unchanging Queen's. . . . She is fond of him."

At the flash of light that sizzled from the Summer Queen's skin, Quinn added hurriedly, "But in a different way than you are, my queen. She knows he is your . . ."

Quinn's words faded, and he ducked his head rather than try to finish *that* sentence.

What is Seth?

Once he'd been her friend; then, he'd been her everything. Then he'd become a faery, and she'd made some stupid mistakes. Now she wasn't sure what he was. *Which doesn't mean Seth should take off without telling me.* Aislinn scowled. *Neither should've Keenan.* Her king had walked out on her, left her in charge of a court with only half the strength of the regency, and she was trying her damnedest not to flounder too much.

Be assertive, she reminded herself. *Maybe I should do so with Keenan and Seth too.*

"Aislinn?" Quinn said her name cautiously.

"What?" She looked at him, only to realize that the room was filled with rainbows from the tiny rain shower and sunbursts that had begun while she was thinking. "Oh."

The plants and the birds and the various creatures that lived in the stream they'd put in the room all thrived under these conditions, but Quinn looked a bit perturbed by his sopping clothes.

There's a psycho faery who thrives on violence and has noticed Seth and who took him to Faerie once already. My king has bailed. Oh, and Death *is visiting.*

She shook her head. "Send Tavish to me."

Quinn tried to wipe the rain from his face surreptitiously. "For?"

The Summer Queen paused midway through turning

away from Quinn and glanced back at him. *"Excuse* me?"

"Is there a message?" Quinn's expression was the carefully bland one that she'd quickly learned to identify as a mask.

"The message, Quinn, is that his queen—*your* queen— has summoned him." She smiled, not kindly but with a cruelty that she'd had to learn when Keenan left her to rule the Summer Court on her own. With a deceptively soft voice, she asked, "Is there a reason you want to know what I say to another faery? A reason you question your queen?"

Quinn lowered his gaze to the muddy floor. "I hadn't intended to insult you."

For a breath, she considered pointing out that she noticed that he had avoided the question she'd asked. Misdirection, omission, and opinion were the faery standbys to work around the "no lying" limitation. Quinn, and a number of other faeries, seemed to think that her relatively recent mortality and her age made her easier to mislead. *And sometimes it* has *meant that. Not always, though.* She kept her own expression as mask-bland as his.

"Fetch Tavish. Find some answers on where in the hell Seth and Keenan are. I'm tired of excuses . . . and I want instruction on how to enter Faerie," she said.

Then, before her mask of confidence slipped, she turned away.

CHAPTER 5

"My staying here in Faerie is not an option," Seth repeated to his queen. "You know that as well as I do."

Sorcha turned her back to him, as if the movement would hide the silver tears that trailed down her cheeks, and walked away.

"Mother." He followed her into the garden that had replaced the wall of his room as she had approached it. "You needed me, and I came."

She nodded, but didn't face him. Tiny insects that were neither dragonflies nor butterflies darted toward her, fluttered briefly, and zipped away. The metallic glint of their wings made the air around her appear to glitter.

"I'm not going to respond well to being caged. You knew that when you chose to be my mother." He put a hand on her shoulder, and she turned toward him.

"I can't *see* you, and their world is . . . treacherous." She pursed her lips in a pout that made her seem childlike.

"If I were the sort to abandon those I love, I wouldn't have come home to you," Seth pointed out. For all of her centuries of living, parenthood was new to Sorcha. Emotion was unfamiliar to her. There was bound to be a bit of adjustment.

Her adjustment just about ended the world. He put his arm around her and led her to a stone bench. *If she were angry . . .* The thought of a furious almost-omnipotent queen made his skin grow cold. Devlin had done the right thing in closing the gate to the mortal world, trapping Sorcha here in Faerie.

Sorcha clutched his arm so tightly that he had to hide a wince of pain. "What if she kills you?"

"I don't think Bananach will." Seth pulled her to him, and she let her head rest on his shoulder.

"I can't go after her." Sorcha, the very embodiment of reason, sounded petulant. "I tried the gate."

"I'm sure you did." He bit back a smile, but she still lifted her head and looked at him.

"You sound amused, Seth."

"You've been all-powerful since you first existed, and now there are restrictions . . . and emotions . . . and"—he squeezed her briefly—"you wanted to change, but it's not as easy as you expected."

"True . . . but . . ." She frowned. "How is that humorous?"

He kissed her cheek. "Your worry and your desire to be near those you love are very human. For someone who isn't my birth mother, you have traits I share. I return to the mortal world to be with those *I* love."

She leaned her head against his shoulder again. "I would rather you stay here in Faerie, where I can keep you safe."

"But you understand why I'm not going to?" he prompted.

For several moments, she didn't answer. She stayed next to him, and together they were silent. Then she straightened and turned to face him. "I don't like it."

"But you understand?" He took both of her hands in his so that she couldn't walk away. "Mother?"

She sighed. "If you get killed, I will be vexed."

"And if I kill your sister?"

"I would be pleased." Sorcha's voice became softer.

"Was that your plan when you made me a faery?"

Sorcha didn't flinch from his gaze. "I needed you to be bound to my court even more than you were bound to the others. By giving you a part of me, I knew I would be no longer balanced by Bananach. I believe now—as I did then—that you are the key to her death." She looked away. "I thought you might die as a result, but not that your death would *matter* to me."

"We cannot see our own futures," he reminded her.

"I saw yours until you became *mine.* You would have died. If I hadn't remade you, you would be dead now. My sister would have tortured you, and your *Ash* would have led her court to a battle they could not win." Sorcha frowned. "I would not object to the Summer Queen's death, but I did

not want War to have what she sought. If I gave you this"—
Sorcha motioned around Faerie—"you would be mine to
use as I required."

Seth felt the flash of unease he'd felt when he first met
Sorcha, remembered how alien she was to him, but he
also remembered that mere days ago she had come near
to destroying Faerie because she missed him. He smiled
at his mother and assured her, "I don't *blame* you. You
gave me what I sought—even if it was for your own selfish
reasons."

"And for *your* selfish reasons, Seth." The High Queen
almost laughed then. "You are impertinent, but I am glad
that you are mine."

Seth felt his tension vanish. His queen, his mother, was
serene again, and she'd admitted that which she hadn't
wanted to tell him, that which he'd known already: she'd
intended to use and then discard him.

"Devlin's decision to close the gate to you was wise," he
said.

Sorcha leveled an unreadable gaze on him, but she said
nothing.

"I saw that," Seth said. "Not with future sight, but with
logic, and I can guarantee that if I don't survive, he will be
here for you. You may not call him your son"—he held up
a hand as she opened her mouth to object—"but he is. He
loves you, and he will be here if you need him. Faerie is in
good hands."

"You *are* impertinent," she repeated, but her tone was

undeniably affectionate.

"I love you too." He kissed her cheek.

"Far Dorcha walks in Huntsdale. He is, like all death-fey, able to bring about the end of life for any faery. Unlike most death-fey, he is the only being allowed to do so without consent or order." The High Queen paused. "When War strikes, he will be there, as will his sister, Ankou. You must not let them touch you."

"I will do what I must do. It's why you made me, Mother. Bananach won't *stop*," Seth reminded her. "Those within Faerie will be safe. *You* are safe. Sealing the gate has done that . . . and I will go to Huntsdale and do what you sought: I will try to kill her. I've been training with the Hounds for this reason. They will want her death now. Niall will. It's what we *all* want."

Sorcha turned away to watch the garden as it shifted around them, and Seth felt as much as saw the moods she was trying to keep in order. She was balanced now, but she was still unused to having emotions.

After several moments, she turned her attention back to him. "I do not like when the consequences of a choice are not what *I* wish them to be. I want you to . . . I want you to *not* go, but since you are going, I require a promise that you will not get injured as Irial did. He could have avoided it. If you can avoid injury, you *will* do so."

Wisely, Seth decided not to answer. Instead, he asked, "Did you know he would do that?"

Sorcha nodded. "And you?"

"I did," Seth admitted. "I looked at the other possibilities. They were worse."

"It would be better if Niall did not know of your foreseeing Irial's death." She frowned, and the garden became less orderly. "He cares a great deal for Irial's well-being. He's denied it for centuries, but his denial was transparent to many of us."

"And the new Shadow Court? How will that affect him?" Seth prompted.

"My court balanced the Dark for forever. Without the balance, Niall will be . . . unwell." The High Queen lifted one shoulder in a delicate shrug. "The gates are sealed to me, so that world is not my concern."

"You know he matters to me, Mother. He's my sworn *brother*. When I was vulnerable, surrounded by faeries, he protected me. He gave me family before I found you, and he's taken me into his." Seth frowned. "I want him to be well; I need that."

"I will be his balance again. . . . Simply convince the Shadow Court to disband; convince them to unlock the gates from Faerie to the mortal world," she suggested.

"No."

"Then there is nothing I can do. Niall will fall, or he won't. I am unable to assist in either path." Sorcha kissed both of Seth's cheeks. "No foolish sacrifices."

"I can't make that promise," he admitted. "There are three faeries I'd sacrifice myself for. Two of them are in the mortal world."

"In fairness, you should know that I would kill them to keep you from doing that." Sorcha began to walk toward his quarters, and he followed.

"Which is yet another benefit of the gates being barred to you," Seth said.

The High Queen stopped and turned around. The assessing gaze she leveled at him reminded Seth that this faery had existed since before he could fathom, before—by her admission—she could remember. He wasn't yet old enough to legally drink, and although he'd been on his own for a couple of years, he had lived only a moment compared to her.

"Do not vex me, Seth." Sorcha closed the distance between them and brushed his hair back. "I am well aware that you were influential in encouraging that *Hound* and Devlin to create a new court. I do not forget that you had a role in barring me from the mortal world."

"I want you to be safe," he reminded her.

"And unable to reach the mortal world." She kept her hand on his head. "You are *mine*. You matter to me as no one else ever has, but it would be wise of you to remember that I am *not* mortal. Don't forget that when you make such decisions in the future."

"I didn't forget *any* of it. I also won't forget that you love me enough to destroy your world." Seth put his hand over hers. "Don't threaten me, Mother. I'm bound by our agreement to come to Faerie every year for the rest of eternity, but I'm *not* bound to love you. I do love you, but you are not the only one in my heart."

They stood for several moments, and then the High Queen nodded. "Be careful of Niall's temper . . . *please?*"

"He is my brother. It will be fine," Seth promised, and then he left her and went in search of the Shadow King.

CHAPTER 6

"He will not wake," the new healer said.

Niall's abyss-guardians flashed into existence at the pronouncement.

"Get the next healer," the Dark King ordered.

A Hound whose name he couldn't recall nodded. With a quick look at the Dark King, she grabbed the offending faery's arm and hurriedly escorted him out of the room.

"Stab one or two healers, and everyone overreacts," Niall said.

No one answered. Irial had fallen into unconsciousness and was not rousing.

Yet.

Niall drew out the cloth from the basin on the bedside table. He leaned down and pressed his lips to Irial's forehead. "Your fever isn't any worse. It's not better yet, but it's not worse."

As he'd been doing most of the past day, he sat next to

the unconscious faery and dabbed the wet cloth on Irial's face and neck again.

"I can stay with him," Gabriel said from the doorway. "If he wakes, I can send someone for you."

"No." He didn't tell Gabriel about the peculiar dreams that he and Irial seemed to share now. It didn't make sense to think he was really in the same dream with Irial. *But it is real. It feels real.* Niall had lived a long time, wandered for years, spent time in three different courts. He'd never heard of being able to dream together as he and Irial seemed to be doing. *Is it madness?* In his dreams they'd talked about all of the things they hadn't spoken of in centuries; they'd been close as they hadn't been in far too long. *Am I imagining it?*

The Hound tried again: "You need to rest. Court's strength is from *you*. If you're sick—"

"Don't." Niall glared at him. "Leave us."

Gabriel ignored him. Instead of departing, he came farther into the room. He stood beside Irial's bed and lowered one hand onto Niall's shoulder in a gesture of support. "My pup is dead. Ani and Rabbit are over in Faerie. Irial's hurt. I *understand*."

The grief in the Hound's voice almost undid the scant self-control Niall was desperately clinging to. "I can't," he admitted. "I can't leave him. . . . Something's not right."

Gabriel snorted. "Lots of things aren't right. Probably easier to list the things that *are* right."

Silently, Niall dipped the cloth into the basin again. He

stared at the water, trying to make sense of the feelings that had come over him. His reaction to Irial's injury seemed too intense. Unpredictable thoughts clouded his mind; he couldn't follow them from moment to moment with much clarity. Urges to violence pressed against his better judgment. In the couple days since Bananach had stabbed Irial, Niall had gone from angry to positively unhinged. He *knew* it. He'd felt emotions overwhelm him, but there was something else.

Something is wrong.

"Niall?"

The Dark King shook his head. "I'm not sure what I'll do if I walk out of this room. I'm coming unraveled . . . without Irial. . . . I can't do this alone, Gabe. I can't. I'm not *right*."

"You're grieving. Normal reaction, Niall. You two have . . . *issues*, but you both knew what you were to each other."

"Are, not were," Niall corrected halfheartedly.

Gabriel took the cloth from Niall. "You're not alone, either. Most of the court is here. The Hunt stands with you. *I* stand with you."

When Niall looked up at the massive Hound, Gabriel extended his arms. "Give me a command, Niall. Your words, my orders. Tell me what you need."

Niall stood. "No one touches Irial without my consent. No one not of our court enters this house unless I summon them. No speaking of his injury to anyone outside the house. Increase the guards on Leslie."

The Dark King paused as the fear of the only other person he loved being injured by Bananach swelled inside him.

Gabriel nodded, and the Dark King's orders appeared in ink on Gabriel's flesh as the words were spoken. "Leslie will be safe," he promised. Then after a minute, he prompted, "And Bananach? And the ones leaving the court to stand with her?"

The Dark King blinked at Gabriel. "She cannot enter our home, but Irial said we could not kill her without killing Sorcha and, thus, all the rest of us. I will not send forces after her. . . . The others . . . I don't care what you do to them once we get through this. Not right now. Right now, Irial is what matters."

A brief frown flashed across Gabriel's face, but he nodded.

Niall walked over and dimmed the light. "Wake me when the next healer arrives."

And then he lay down on the floor beside Irial's bed and closed his eyes.

CHAPTER 7

As Seth approached the gate, Devlin had one hand raised as if to touch the fabric that divided the two worlds, the veil that now separated the twins.

Seth had spent the past hour thinking while he sought Devlin. He would've liked to ponder longer, but time didn't allow for it. He'd been in Faerie less than a day, but every four hours in Faerie was a full day in the mortal world. That meant he'd been gone two days, and he had no idea what had been happening in the mortal world during that time. Irial had been stabbed, and the Hounds were fighting with Bananach's allies when he had come to Faerie with Ani, Devlin, and Rabbit. *Did they all survive? Is Niall okay? Is Ash safe?* Until he went back, he had no answers.

"Have you thought about the consequences?" Seth asked. He felt a loyalty to Faerie, but he was of both worlds. Devlin, however, was not.

He turned to face Seth, but did not speak. The new

Shadow King was the oldest male faery, the first, the one
Sorcha and Bananach had created. In sealing Faerie, he'd
assured that neither of his sister-mothers could kill the
other. Asking him to consider the consequences beyond
that appeared to perplex him.

"For *them*"—Seth gestured to the other side of the
gate—"now that Faerie is closed?"

It was clear to everyone in Faerie that *they* were safe now.
For that, Seth was grateful. However, he didn't live solely
in Faerie, nor did he intend to do so. If Sorcha could forbid
him from leaving Faerie, she would, but he wasn't going to
give up on Aislinn—or abandon his friends.

"They are not my concern." Devlin let his hand drop
toward the *sgian dubh* he carried. "The good of Faerie is my
concern."

"I'm not here to fight you, Brother." Seth held his hands
up disarmingly. "I will fight Bananach, though."

Devlin's frustration was an interesting thing to see. After
an eternity of repressing emotions, the new Shadow King
was now letting emotions influence him. That, too, was
good for Faerie.

"And if Bananach's death still kills your *mother*?" Devlin
asked. "Why should I let you cross over there, knowing that
it could bring disaster on us?"

Seth smiled at his brother. "*You* cannot keep me here.
The terms of her remaking me were that I can return to the
mortal world. Even you cannot negate her vow."

"If they came home, if the other courts returned here . . ."

Faeries giving up power? The arrogance of every faery monarch Seth had met made the idea especially illogical. Seth laughed at the thought of proposing such a thing to any of them. "Do you think that Keenan would give up the Summer Court? That Donia would give up her court? That Niall would become a subject to you or to our mother? Pipe dreams, man."

"They would be safe here now that Bananach cannot enter." Devlin didn't see that he had already become like them, thinking that his idea, his rule, held the answers for the others. The sense of clarity, of surety, was an essential trait in a faery monarch, but his suggestion wasn't feasible.

Seth shrugged. "Some things are worth more than safety."

"I cannot speak of what would happen to our . . . to *your* queen if you died." Devlin stared through the veil. "I would come with you, but protecting Faerie comes first. I cannot risk Faerie for the mortal world."

"And I can't abandon Ash or Niall."

Devlin paused. "Tell me what you see."

"Nothing. Over here, I'm mortal. I see nothing until I go back. . . ." Seth bit his lip ring, rolling the ball of it into his mouth as he weighed his thoughts. "I don't *see* anything, but I'm worried. . . . Ash is dealing with her court alone. Sorcha was to balance Niall, but now *you* balance her. What will that mean for him? Irial was stabbed. Gabe was outnumbered. Bananach is murderous and only getting stronger. . . . Nothing there makes me think everything is going to be all right."

For a few moments, they stood silently at the veil, and then Devlin said, "When you are ready . . ."

Seth stared at him for a moment. He hated the necessity of the words he needed to say—that Devlin needed to hear—but that didn't change reality. "If . . . you know . . . I *die*, she'll need you. She doesn't like admitting it, but she will."

Silently, Devlin put his hand on the veil. He didn't answer the question implicit in Seth's words, but Seth knew that Devlin had chosen the path he'd taken in order to protect not just Faerie, but also his sisters. Devlin had acted out of love for his family, for his beloved, and for Faerie.

As I do.

Seth put his hand to the veil.

Together, they pushed their fingers through the fabric and parted it. Then Devlin put a hand on Seth's forearm. "It will not open for you to return unless you call to me to be here also."

"I know." Seth stepped into the mortal world, leaving Faerie, leaving his mortality, and becoming once-more-fey. The return of his altered senses made him pause. He didn't stumble. *Much.* He took several breaths and then he started through the graveyard.

Behind him, he heard Devlin's words: "Try not to die, Brother."

Seth didn't look back, didn't falter. The logic that he possessed in Sorcha's realm was tempered in the mortal world.

Here, he felt the fear that he could ignore in Faerie; here, he knew that he was running from safety and headed toward danger. He might die. *So be it.* Fear didn't outweigh love.

Try not to die.

Seth smiled and said, "That's the goal, Brother."

And then he went to find Aislinn.

CHAPTER 8

Aislinn paced in the study. Once, she'd felt uncomfortable in the room, and then it became a place to relax with her king, and now . . . it was *hers*. Somehow, Keenan's absence had made her feel proprietary of a lot of things that were his first. *And a lot of people.* She had already felt connected to her court, but his choices had made her feel a protectiveness that bordered on maternal.

She looked up as the door to the study opened, and one of the few faeries she now trusted without hesitation stood there. Tavish was an excellent advisor. Where Quinn was intrusive and bordering on belligerent, Tavish was steady. He'd been the voice helping her see what traits were best employed as queen. He'd reminded her that Summer was both playful and cruel, that her new volatility was a tool to harness, that her maudlin worries were best surrendered to passions. If she thought on it, his skill in advising her was unsurprising: he had been the guiding force as Keenan grew into being the Summer King. Along with Niall, he had taught one Summer regent how to rule—and done so when that regent was her age—so teaching a second Summer regent was well within Tavish's abilities.

Tavish came into the room and held out a glass of what he habitually claimed was a "healthy vitamin drink" but she was pretty sure was vegetables and moss or something else equally unpleasant. "Drink."

She waved the glass away. "I'm good."

"My Queen?"

"I'm not thir—" The lie she started was unutterable. She sighed and muttered, "Those are disgusting."

"Keenan always thought so too." Tavish continued to hold the glass out to her.

"Fine." She accepted it and took a gulp. After forcing it down, she set the glass on the coffee table. "Some things aren't meant to be in liquids, Tavish."

"Winter isn't kind to Summer regents. Neither"—he picked the glass up—"is the stress you are trying to hide. Drink it."

She drank the rest of the noxious stuff. "Promise me that if you ever poison me, it will at least taste better than this."

"I will never poison you, my Queen." In a move too graceful for even most faeries, Tavish dropped to his knees. He stared up at her as he knelt in front of her, and despite the peculiarity of the setting, Aislinn suddenly felt as formal as if she were on a dais in front of her court.

For a moment, Aislinn simply stared at him. "I wasn't being literal."

"You are my queen. I've spent nine centuries seeking the mortal who would free this court, who would save my best friend's son, who would save the lives of the rest of the girls who were not you. I'd die before I'd allow harm to you." He bowed his head.

"I didn't think . . . I *know* you're trying to look out for me, Tavish." She reached out and touched his shoulder. "I trust you. You know that, right? I mean, I'm not great at all this stuff, but you *know* I trust you, right?"

"I do." He lifted his gaze. "The words are true all the same. You are our queen, Aislinn. You're a *good* queen, and gods know, that isn't an easy thing to be when you are tossed into the fray with no warning—and with the bias you had against faeries. You've done it, though. You put your heart into your court, stood up to Bananach when she first came to you, faced down the Winter and Dark Courts. You've weathered the king's manipulations and his absence. You are exactly what we need, and I am here to do whatever *you* need. At times, I'll argue with you because that's how I can help you, but I'd willingly kill or die for you. It would be an honor to do so."

"Right. The problem there is that I don't want you to *need* to kill or die."

"Nor do I, but we must face the situation," Tavish said, sounding characteristically imperturbable.

She flopped down on the sofa and patted the cushion. "Sit with me?"

With a small frown, Tavish sat in a chair across from her. Aislinn grinned at him. "You know, for a Summer faery, you are awfully proper."

"Indeed," Tavish said. "Is that on the agenda for our meeting? My propriety? Shall I add 'frolic more' to the tasks for my week?"

"No. . . . I met Far Dorcha. I'm sure the guards already told you." She paused, and Tavish nodded. "Right," she continued. "I need the girls to stay in the loft. Whichever fey have . . . defected are on their own. Those who are *mine* stay here."

"That is wise."

Aislinn took a steadying breath. "I need to find out where Keenan is. If he's not home, I'm going into war without him . . . which is not ideal. *Someone* knows where he is."

"I do not, my Queen. I give you my word that I will find out, though." Tavish's restrained facade slipped, and she saw the faery-cruel expression as he asked, "Are there limits to the methods?"

At that, she faltered. "Don't ask me to be a monster."

Affectionately, he reached out and squeezed her forearm. "You are a faery regent, Aislinn, and we are fast approaching war. Monstrosity will be called for. How far will you go to protect your court?"

Aislinn winced—as much because of the truth as because she had to admit it aloud. "As far as I must. The longer I am *this*"—she gestured at herself—"the harder it is to remember how much I loathed what he did to me. He took away my mortality, Tavish. I *hated* him. I hated all of you. . . ."

"And now?"

"I hate any who threatens my court." She sighed. It seemed foolish, but her first lesson in being a faery regent had been to trust her instincts. She hoped that she was not erring as she said, "Speaking of, I don't like Quinn's arrogance. He questions me, not to help, but . . . I don't know his game. He *has* one, though."

"He is not who I would've picked to replace my former co-advisor." Tavish's expression was unreadable.

Pretending a self-assurance that she rarely felt for more than a heartbeat, Aislinn said, "When Keenan returns, I want to fire Quinn."

At that, Tavish's lips quirked in a small smile. "For arrogance?"

"No." Aislinn pulled her feet up and tucked them under her so that she was sitting cross-legged. "I'd have to cast out everyone if that were the charge."

Tavish's slight smile blossomed. "Present company excluded, I'm sure."

For a moment, Aislinn peered at him. "I think you just made a *joke*."

"I am not as solemn as you'd think, my Queen." Tavish smoothed a hand over one of his already impeccable sleeves. "I am merely as solemn as I need to be to protect my regent."

With a comfort she didn't think she'd ever felt before, she told him, "I don't think you're truly solemn, Tavish. If you were, you'd be in a different court. You belong to Summer. I'm sure of that. I can feel how strongly tied you are to my court, to me. You're mine, Tavish. I have no doubt with you."

Her advisor rewarded her with a joyous look, and in the moment, she knew this was the side of him the Summer Girls saw. He was captivating in that faery way that made her think of the old stories where mortals believed them gods. He had uncharacteristically dark eyes, and his hair was silver—not silvered as mortals' hair turns with age, but true silver. It was, like Keenan's copper-colored hair, a metallic hue that made clear that he was very much not mortal. She'd never seen his hair unbound; it was kept in a braid of sorts that stretched down his back. The braid bared part of a small black sun tattoo on the side of his throat. That tattoo stood out in a mostly undecorated court. Of course, so, too, did his High Court reserve and his Dark Court eyes. Those eyes were watching her, so she said what she'd wanted to: "I don't trust Quinn."

"I spoke against his selection." Tavish's gaze was focused on her, but it was—as it had been increasingly in the past few months—an approving look he gave her. "My king made the choice."

"Well, your king isn't here. Until I decide otherwise, watch Quinn. No . . . extreme measures yet, but keep a close eye on him. Who he talks to. When. Everything." Aislinn knew worry was in her voice, but unlike with the rest of the court, she didn't need to hide that from Tavish. With her advisor, she could be unguarded. It was a welcome honesty. She twisted her hands together. "Both Seth and Keenan could be . . . in who knows what sort of danger, and neither of them have the sense to tell me where they are."

Tavish moved to sit beside her. "They will both return, Aislinn."

"What if Ba—"

"She would've told us had she killed them." Tavish reached out and smoothed back her hair in an oddly paternal gesture. "Their deaths would be of more use to her if you knew of them. They are alive. Bananach attacked Dark Court fey. Seth was there, and he left with the High Queen's brother."

Aislinn considered rebuking Tavish for not telling her that news the moment he came into the study, but it was of little use to do so: he would only remind her that court matters were her first priority. His withholding that information for the few moments they'd discussed Quinn was negligible. It *had* to be this way.

Court before everything. Before everyone. Before myself.

"You learned this when?"

"That Seth was safe? Today." Tavish paused to let her know he was weighing the degree of truth he would offer. "That there was conflict? Two days ago."

Before she could speak, he continued, "You are my queen, and my job is to advise and protect you. If anything could have been served by telling you sooner, I would've done so. I know he was in the conflict with Bananach, and that there were injuries and deaths."

Aislinn's heartbeat faltered. "Who?"

"A halfling the Dark Court protected, the Hound-tattooist's sister, was killed."

She thought about the girls, their seemingly endless energy, and felt grief wash over her at the thought of either of them being gone. "Was it Ani or Tish?"

"Tish," he said.

"Poor Rabbit!" Even as she spoke, Aislinn's thoughts flew to her own family. If Grams were injured in the impending violence, Aislinn wasn't sure how she'd function at all. "Send Grams away. With guards."

Tavish nodded. "A wise decision."

"I need to know she's safe and out of Bananach's reach." Aislinn crossed her arms, hugging herself to keep from trembling. "Send her on a cruise, so she's moving around. Somewhere as warm as possible."

Tavish nodded. "There is talk of another death . . . not quite complete. My sources in the Dark Court are not as forthcoming as I'd like, but it is my understanding that Irial has been injured."

"Irial?"

Tavish nodded once. "The details beyond that are not available. Yet. It does not bode well. If Irial is . . . gone, Niall will not cope well."

"I don't understand." Aislinn disliked admitting ignorance, but there were times that doing so was essential. Tavish was her advisor, and he'd lived longer than she could yet fathom. His ability to explain the long histories of the faeries she had only just met was one of his many valuable skills.

Expression inscrutable, Tavish began, "You know that Niall and Irial have a history?"

He paused, and she nodded.

Tavish continued, "Niall has held on to his anger at Irial's deceits and betrayals for centuries—and rightly so—but becoming a regent makes one see the challenges that might motivate choices that otherwise appear cruel." Her advisor paused again and gave her a pointed look.

"Some faeries," he continued, "don't realize the complexities of ruling as quickly as you have, my Queen. Niall is stubborn, not nearly as willing to listen to advice as a regent needs to be . . . unless he hears it from Irial. The arrangement they've settled on has made the former Dark King the advisor to the new king; it is unprecedented."

Aislinn was trying to make sense of the nuances Tavish wasn't explaining. "So Irial advises Niall, and they're . . . what?"

"Irial has moved back into his home . . . with the new Dark King," Tavish said.

"Right," she drawled. "You live here. So?"

Her advisor lowered his gaze. "With all due respect, my Queen, I have no amorous intentions toward you. I am advisor to the Summer Court. I advised Keenan's father, Miach; Keenan; and before them, I guarded Miach's father."

She smothered a laugh at Tavish's pursed lips.

"After a millennium of discord, Niall and Irial have

found a sort of peace together," Tavish added.

"And now Irial's injured. Dying, perhaps." She took a deep breath and let it out in a slow sigh.

"Aside from advising Niall, Irial has been tending to some of the less palatable Dark Court businesses as well. Niall, for all of his recent changes, is not as cruel as the Dark King sometimes must be. Irial has fewer . . . restrictions," Tavish said in a very quiet voice.

"This just gets better and better, doesn't it?"

"Precisely," Tavish agreed. "And I have no doubt that Bananach struck Irial for these reasons. She is striking at the courts, looking for weakness, and whichever court is not strong enough will be destroyed if she has her way."

"Our court is *not* strong enough to stand against any of the others." Aislinn looked up and saw the somber expression on her advisor's face before he spoke. She knew where his words would lead, had known for months that the Summer Court was not getting strong enough. "Tavish . . ."

"There is a way to change that, my Queen."

"He's not even here, and he doesn't . . . Keenan and I don't . . ." Her words faded.

"I suspect the news would reach him if we were to let word be known that you were still willing to consider being his queen in all ways—"

"If that's what it takes to get him back here, do it." She did not avert her gaze. "Perhaps it's time I was the one *doing* the manipulating."

"As you will," Tavish said.

Aislinn hated the fact that she wasn't sure whether she was more relieved at the possibility of her king's return or terrified that Donia would see her actions as a threat. *Donia is smarter than that.* Of course, the Winter Queen already believed that the Summer King and Queen would inevitably become a couple, and sometimes, Aislinn thought that Seth's refusal to be fully in her life was because he felt the same way.

If it's between giving in to that fate or sacrificing our court's safety, I'm not sure what choice we have.

CHAPTER 9

Far Dorcha stood outside the Dark King's home, waiting. Inside the house, the nearly dead king's shade lingered. Unfortunately, the complications that Irial had created in his last days made the situation unprecedented.

Clever maneuvering.

It was enough to make Far Dorcha smile. The Dark Court could be counted on for the unexpected.

"The door isn't open." Ankou suddenly stood beside him. Her winding-sheet dress hung from her gaunt body, but he wasn't sure if she'd grown thinner or if he misremembered how delicate she appeared. "The body is in there, but the door—"

"Sister." He brushed a lock of white hair back and tucked it behind her ear. "I wondered when you'd arrive."

Ankou frowned. "The door should be open."

"The old king's shade is still anchored in the world," Far Dorcha said. He didn't remind her that no one could deny him entrance, that no one could fight him if he chose to stop them, that his very presence could impose mortality on a faery if he willed it. Resorting to such measures was crass.

"Perhaps you ought to knock," Far Dorcha suggested.

His sister closed her eyes and drew in the air around them. He felt the stillness grow heavier and, as always, chose not to question how the air could take on weight. Something about the change in it felt like pressure in his lungs, as if soil filled them. Ankou blinked and approached the door. This was why he was at the last Dark King's house with her—not to protect her, but to keep her from disturbing an already untenable situation.

Bananach's machinations had drawn faeries from all of the courts, as well as from among the solitaries. She'd poisoned the former Dark King, and in doing so set herself against the court to which she'd always been allied. *A declaration of war must be spoken by at least one regent before Bananach can have the fight she seeks.* And none of the courts were declaring war.

"Open." Ankou hammered her fist on the door. "I am Ankou. *Open.*"

A gargoyle that clung to the door opened its mouth, but predictably, it didn't speak. The invitation to shed blood for entry was clever. *What else for a king clever enough to dodge death?*

"Sister?" he prompted. "It seeks a taste."

She narrowed her gaze.

"If you place your hand here"—he gestured at the open

maw—"the creature can find you acceptable or not."

"I am Ankou," she repeated. "I am always acceptable. We are *Death*. How could that be unacceptable?"

Far Dorcha took her hand in his. "May I?"

She nodded, so he extended her skeletal hand to the creature. It sank fangs into her flesh, and she stared at it dispassionately. Once, Far Dorcha had let another beast remove every drop of his sister's blood. It was an experiment born of curiosity, nothing more, but it was as meaning-less to her as other seemingly cruel experiments he'd tried. Ankou watched; she waited. When she was called upon, she collected the corpses where they fell. All of her tenderness was reserved for fallen faeries. Even he was only important to her because of his connection to the dead.

He tugged her hand free and suggested, "Tell it again."

"I am Ankou." She leaned closer to it. "You must open."

The gargoyle blinked at them, and for a moment, Far Dorcha wondered if the new Dark King could prohibit their entry. *Is he as unexpected as the nearly dead king?* Then, the gargoyle yawned, and the door cracked open.

Before they could cross the threshold, several Hounds stepped forward. They were battle-bloodied, but they were no less daunting for their injuries.

"I am Ankou," she announced. "I have work here."

A growl behind the Hounds caused them step to either side. There stood the Gabriel, the Hound who led the Hunt. He looked haggard. His eyes were darkened, and his skin seemed sallow.

"The king won't let you take him," Gabriel said in a low rumble. "Can't reason with him just now."

"The body is about to be empty." Ankou stepped toward the Hound.

Gabriel nodded. "I know."

"I should be able to take it."

"Him," Gabriel corrected. "Irial. The last king. He is not an *it*."

"The body is," Ankou said.

On both sides of Gabriel, the Hounds surged forward, and Far Dorcha reminded himself that his sister needed guidance. "She could free him from his—"

"No." Gabriel held out his tattooed forearms. On them, the Dark King's commands spiraled out, etched there in flesh for any and all to read. The Hound, and thus his whole Hunt, had orders to protect the last Dark King.

Ankou reached out with her bone-thin hand as if to grip the flesh where the orders were written. "So be it."

Far Dorcha caught her hand in his. He entwined those fatal fingers with his own, lacing their hands together, and told Gabriel, "You cannot stop Death. If we choose to enter, you will all die."

"I know." Gabriel shrugged. "I obey the Dark King, though. Not everyone's pleased with his choices, but the Hunt stands with him."

"At what cost?" Ankou prompted.

"My pup died. More will fall. I *know* mortality, and it's good that Iri rates your attention. Didn't see the ones who took Tish's shell away." The Hound's expression grew tenser still, but he shook his head. "Can't take Iri yet, though. King says. I obey the Dark King . . . regardless of the cost."

Far Dorcha nodded. "I will speak with your king soon." Then he turned to his sister. "Come, Sister, there is time yet."

When Ankou nodded, Far Dorcha released her hand— and she extended it faery-fast to cup Gabriel's cheek.

"You should not interfere with my work," she told the Hound. "I could have offered mercy."

Then, Ankou leaned up and brushed her lips over his cheek, marking him for a fate that only she could see.

"Come, Sister," Far Dorcha repeated, and then he led Ankou away from the Dark King's house.

Chapter 10

Gabriel slammed the door behind the departing death-fey. "No one is to open the door. Was I not clear?"

The Hunt scattered as he turned around and snarled at them.

"The king . . . both of them . . . need to be guarded, and letting *them* in will not help anyone." He looked from Hound to Hound. "Niall needs a little time to—" The door chime sounded as the gargoyle on the outside of the door bit someone.

Gabriel spun around and yanked the door open again. "What?"

But it was not the death-fey; instead, one of the Winter Queen's Scrimshaw Sisters stood on the step. She curtsied. "The Winter Queen—"

"King's not receiving visitors," Gabriel cut her off. He shoved the door, but the implacable faery put a hand out and stopped it from closing.

"*The Winter Queen,*" she repeated, "seeks audience with one of the Hunt."

Then the faery turned and walked away as if staring into the face of the Hunt had not been terrifying at all. Gabriel grinned for a moment as he closed the door, but as he walked through the darkened house and into the room where the Dark King paced restlessly beside Irial's death-bed, his grin vanished.

"Niall?"

The Dark King looked at him, and for a moment, there was no recognition in Niall's eyes. He stared at Gabriel, but did not speak or indicate awareness in any way. Then, the shadows in the king's eyes flickered, and Niall said, "I am awake now, right?"

"You are."

"I don't want to be," Niall rasped.

"I know." Gabriel had thought about his options: he couldn't bring Sorcha here; Keenan was still away from Huntsdale; that left Aislinn and Donia. The Summer Queen wasn't as powerful as the Winter Queen, and Niall had unpredictable reactions to her. Donia, on the other hand, wanted to talk to a Hound and was friend to the Dark King. Hoping his emotions were hidden, Gabriel told Niall, "My Hounds are here. I've called in others we trust, Niall. We've hired solitaries whose loyalty can be bought."

"Good." Niall wasn't looking at Gabriel now; his attention was once more on Irial. "That's good."

"I can get more aid." Gabriel stepped over to stand beside the king he'd served for centuries and the grieving king he'd sworn to protect at cost of his own life. "I can bring help."

Niall glanced at Gabriel. "Aid? Healers?"

Gabriel weighed the words he needed; as the head of the Hunt, he was not used to needing to twist truth. The faery he sought was not a healer, but a regent who could hopefully help his king. Gabriel looked at Niall and said, "I think I can get aid for my king."

Niall nodded. "Yes. The other healers were wrong. They had to be." The Dark King motioned to the far corner, where a faery was sprawled motionless. "That one said Irial was past saving."

"Chela will keep you safe while I go," Gabriel assured Niall, but the Dark King had already turned away.

Silently, Gabriel gathered the healer, gave orders to his second-in-command, and went to see the Winter Queen.

CHAPTER 11

"Where the hell is Keenan?" Aislinn grumbled. "I'm not ready for a war. I'm not ready for a grief-mad Dark King, either. . . . I don't know how to do this on my o—"

A knock at the study door interrupted her, and barely a blink had passed before Tavish was in front of her. Even here in the loft, he kept himself between her and the door. A sword hung at his side, and she knew that another weapon, a sliver-thin steel blade, was strapped to his ankle. The very fact that he could wear cold steel spoke of how strong—*and old*—he was.

The door opened, and Seth walked into the room. "Ash?"

Her first instinct was to run to him, to throw herself into his arms and cling to him, but that wasn't where they were—not anymore, perhaps never again. She brushed her hands over her skirt, smoothing it down, and smiled at him. "Seth."

"I will find you answers, my Queen. Summer is to be

happy if we are to be as strong as we need, my Queen. Indulge in your happiness, if not for you, then for your court." Tavish gave her a pointed look and then turned to Seth. "I am glad you were not killed in the fight with Bananach."

Seth quirked a brow. "Me too."

"Indeed." Tavish nodded and left.

For a moment after the door to the study was closed, Aislinn simply stared at Seth. He looked tired. Dark circles were under his eyes, and his shoulders were drooping slightly. His left cheek was discolored, and his bottom lip had a cut. There were no other visible marks, but she couldn't see through the shirt and jeans he wore. The shirt, however, *did* confirm that he'd been to Faerie. Instead of one of his usual T-shirts, he wore a silky shirt that fit him as if it had been tailored especially for him.

And probably was.

"I . . . I know it sounds repetitive, but I wouldn't have vanished without telling you if there was a choice," he said. "There was a fight with Bananach and her Ly Ergs."

"I know. Tavish told me . . . and about Tish." She couldn't look away from Seth. "You're okay?"

"Mostly. Bruised up, but"—he shrugged, though his eyes gleamed with pride—"after all the training with Gabriel's Hounds, I held my own."

The thought of it, of Seth fighting War and her minions, overruled the fear of rejection, overruled the fear of what could come. *If not for me, for my court*, she told herself. *Happiness is a choice.* She wanted to choose Seth; if it were that simple, she would've already done so. *If it's between love and duty . . .* She still wanted love.

She crossed the room and wrapped her arms around Seth. The rightness of being in his arms hadn't ever stopped. For a moment, she rested her cheek against his chest; then she looked up at him.

Before he could speak, she pulled his mouth to hers. Now that he was fey—and seemingly stronger than he realized—she didn't worry about injuring him with her affection. Before, she had to be careful not to break him. Now, the risks of a faery loving a mortal were erased. Barring fatal injury, he'd live for centuries. She leaned into him, gave herself over to the thrill of his kiss. It wasn't a trick or faery enchantment. It wasn't for power. It was just them.

And I don't want it to ever end.

When he started to pull away, she tangled her fingers in his hair. "Don't stop. Please?"

"Ash? Hey? It's okay," he whispered in the fraction of space between them.

She felt his words against her lips.

He repeated, "I'm okay. I'm *here.*"

She didn't step away. "I don't know what I'd do without you."

"I'm here." He smiled. "Right here *with you.*"

"You'll leave again, though." Aislinn tightened her arms around him. "War is fighting with Niall's fey. Your . . . mother would come unglued if . . ." Her words dwindled at the look on his face. "What?"

"She had a bit of a, umm, *grief* thing over my absence."
Uncharacteristically, he blushed. "She's new to the whole
emotion thing . . . and . . ."

"And?"

"She almost destroyed Faerie." He bit his lip ring as he
watched her face for a reaction.

Without meaning to, Aislinn laughed. In light of all the
threats looming outside the door, of all that they stood to
lose, the sheepish look on Seth's face was too much.

"She almost destroyed Faerie because she *missed* you?"
Aislinn asked. When he nodded, she added, "Bit different
than Linda, huh?"

"Just a bit. I'm still not sure where Mom is, but"—he
shrugged—"they're just different."

"Oldest faery and mortal mother with wanderlust?"
Aislinn giggled.

Seth tried to look serious for a second, and then he
laughed too. They stood there for a moment, and the laughter fled.

He kissed her softly and then said, "I never imagined
how much life would change or how quickly."

She held his gaze. "Do you ever wish . . . I mean, if
you and I hadn't . . . If I hadn't told you about faeries that
day . . ."

"I love you." He looked directly at her. "You are the
single most amazing person, faery, *woman* in this world
or the other. Because of you, I am a part of this strange
new world, have a second mother, and . . . eternity. I have

almost everything I could want."

"*Almost* everything," she repeated.

"Ash? That wasn't pressure. You know what I want from you. Until he's back and you're sure you're able to refuse him, I'm not going to cross that line. He's your king, and you can't promise either of us that the temptation to strengthen your court by being . . . *with* him is over." A look of regret crossed Seth's face, and then he added, "He'll be back, Ash. Equinox is coming, and there is no way that the Summer King won't be here for the start of *his* season."

"I thought he'd be back at Solstice for Donia," Aislinn said, and then, before Seth could reply, she added, "I don't want to talk about him. Actually, I don't want to talk at all."

"Ash," Seth started.

"Just for a minute, can we leave all the things out there"—she looked toward the door he'd entered only moments before—"alone? Can we be just *us*?"

A look of hesitation crossed his face, but he didn't push her away.

"Just kiss me, Seth. Please?" she urged. "Later. Tomorrow. We can tell each other all of the things that are going to cause stress. Can't we just let it alone and . . . *be*? I need you."

He swept her legs from under her and lifted her into his arms. She wound her arms around his neck. Silently, he walked over to the sofa behind her and sat. She was sideways on his lap now; her arms were still looped around his neck.

"You could stay here in my arms," she invited.

Seth kissed her softly and then pulled away. "No, I can't."

"Did I mention"—she let her sunlight fall around them—"that I want to be *with* you?"

As she knew they would, his eyes widened at the touch of sunlight on his skin; his whole body tensed as the pleasure of the sunlight slid over him. Still, he forced out a sentence: "That's not fair."

"Maybe I don't want to play fair, Seth." She breathed the words and was rewarded by his arms tightening around her. "Faeries have been seducing mortals—"

"Not mortal right now, Ash."

"Mortals *and* each other," she continued, "for centuries. You're asking me to pretend I'm content with a few kisses?" Aislinn didn't blush as she said it: there was no reason to hide what she wanted. "I *love* you, and I *want* you."

He groaned. "Ash—"

She brushed her lips over his in an invitation. Thankfully, he didn't resist, so she kissed him for real.

After only a moment, he pulled away again. "You're killing me here, Ash."

"Good," she said. She'd bend a few rules, but they both knew she wasn't going to push him beyond where he chose to go. Love wasn't to be based on trickery.

But reminding him what he's refusing isn't *trickery.*

With sunlight pulsing in her skin, she trailed her fingertips over his chest and stomach. As she did so, she held his gaze.

His hands went to her hair, tangled there, and held her.

"As much as I wish I could stay . . . even if we just do this . . . I need to go."

She frowned, but she moved to sit beside him. "Why?"

"I'll tell you after. Promise." Seth played with a strand of her hair. "Trust me?"

"I do, but—"

"Please?" Seth interrupted. "I'll explain, but I need to go now."

"Okay." Aislinn turned her face to kiss his palm. "Maybe afterward, I can convince you to let me lock you away for a few days. I want to. . . ."

"You're the Summer Queen," he said, as if that was all there was to it.

"Summer or not, there's no one else in my bed. No one else has ever been there," she reminded him.

A look of sorrow crossed his face almost too quick to see, but he didn't point out that the only reason that was true was because Keenan hadn't accepted her invitation. Instead, Seth only said, "I hope that's always true."

Me too.

CHAPTER 12

The Winter Queen had curled into a snowbank in her garden for a moment's rest and found herself in one of the dreams that inevitably meant she would wake with tears on her cheeks, but someone was repeating a phrase yet again and the words were out of context: "I am sorry to wake you, but your guests are here, my Queen."

In her dream, Donia had been walking toward the boardwalk where she'd met Keenan. Sand caked her feet. A gull cried out behind her. Donia woke. She stared up at the face of the person speaking to her. *Evan.* His leafy hair was brittle at the tips, frozen by the snow that fell as she'd slept. He wasn't the one in her dreams.

"Gabriel and some of his lot are here. Not one Hound, but several." Evan's disdain for the Hounds was obvious in both his tone and expression. "I do not like their presence."

Donia smiled at his protective streak. She knew as well as he did that creating allies was essential, but he still held old angers at the Hunt. She rubbed her hands over her face, letting the chill in her palms seep out to sooth her skin. Then she looked up at him as the clarity began to settle over her. "And you've no information yet."

Frost clung to his skin, sparkling on him as it did on true trees. A roar from the gate drew his gaze, and when he looked back, he said only, "I do not want to invite your guests in."

"They will not harm me," she said evenly, as she willed the snow around her to form a throne.

"With all due respect, they are the *Hunt*, my Queen." Evan scowled at the increased growls outside the garden. "They are not the sort of fey we—"

"I am the Winter Queen."

"As you wish." He gestured to one of the Hawthorn Girls at the door to the garden.

In a fraction of a moment, Gabriel stood before her.

To greet him without aggression would be an affront, so she fixed the leader of the Hounds with a stare that would make most fey tremble. "I would not summon the Gabriel himself to ask what I would know. I asked only to summon a Hound."

"The girl said you wanted a Hound. I am the Gabriel." Gabriel bowed his head.

The other Hounds bowed in turn. They dressed differently from one another—running the gamut from biker to businessman—but the expression of each was the same predatory one. Sometimes it was a posture, a tilt of the head, a wide-legged stance. Sometimes it was a look, fathomless eyes, bared teeth. No matter the garb or the face, the Hounds always evoked terror in a way that defied categorization.

And Donia knew instinctively that being as direct as she could was the right tactic. She started, "Word has come to me that Bananach took one of your number. That there was a fight with her. . . ."

"My own flesh," Gabriel snarled. "My daughter."

Donia stilled. "*Your* daughter?"

The Hounds as one let out such a howl that even she wanted to run in terror.

"The Winter Court . . . *I* offer our sympathy." She caught his gaze. "How is the king—"

"I cannot speak of the king's . . . state," Gabriel interrupted.

She held Gabriel's gaze, ignoring the feel of her fey sidling into the garden. They weren't a noisy lot, but they murmured among themselves as they came. Their soft voices and crackling footfalls tumbled together in the silence of the garden.

A thick snow began to fall as she sent her assurances to her faeries. Several rebellious lupine snapped their teeth audibly. They weren't aware that the Hunt had been invited, and even if they had known, they'd spare little love for the insult of the Hounds standing in their territory.

Donia looked around, taking the opportunity to assess where her Hawthorn Girls were, noticing the lupine fey and one of the glaistigs who'd joined them. Each of her fey stood facing one of the bulky Hounds. The glaistig faced Gabriel with a look that announced to all and each that she'd claimed him if violence were allowed.

The Hunt's baying made enough noise that Donia suspected her words would be unheard. Still, she lowered her voice. "Has Bananach injured the king?"

"I cannot answer that." For a moment, Gabriel stared at Donia as if willing her to understand the things he could not speak. Finally, he said, "The Dark Court has exiled her."

"Exiled War? For her action against your daughter?" Donia's incredulity was great enough that she wasn't sure how to process that detail. Bananach had been among the Dark Court from almost the beginning. Sure, she'd pursued her own goals, but for nearly all of forever, the raven-faery had been tied to the Dark Court just as her twin, Sorcha, was a part of the High Court. They were of a pair, balancing their urges to chaos and order in two courts that stood in opposition.

"No." Gabriel flexed his hands, fisting and unfisting them as the glaistig, Lia, eased closer still. "Not just that. Things . . ." He broke off and held out his forearms.

"I can't read them. I'm sorry," she said. The language used for his orders wasn't one she knew.

He growled in frustration. "Can't speak things I would say. Told my king I sought aid. I do seek aid for—" He stopped, growled again. "Can't say."

Startled, Donia stood.

Behind her, Evan waited. At some small gesture of his, two of the Hawthorn Girls floated nearer and stood on either side of Donia.

She stepped forward, but Gabriel did not move, so she was all but touching him. Quietly, she said, "I will learn what I need to know."

Gabriel's words were a rough whisper: "I would owe you a great debt. The Hunt would owe much."

His voice seemed to tremble in a most un-Houndlike way, adding to Donia's increasing sense of alarm. *Something is very wrong in the Dark Court.* She briefly put her hand on the massive Hound's upper arm. "I've been thinking of calling on the Dark Court."

Relief flooded Gabriel's expression. "The Hunt defends the Dark Court. I can no longer stand near the *last* king, but I will stand with the Dark King. . . . I would protect him from further . . . I would make him well."

Make him well? The possibility of Bananach having struck Niall hadn't occurred to Donia. As a member of the Dark Court, Bananach shouldn't be able to injure Niall. No one else was truly safe from her, but faeries could not kill their regents. *Does exile nullify that rule? Who else would be strong enough to injure Niall? Had Bananach found a strong solitary to do the deed for her?*

"Niall lives?"

Gabriel gave a terse nod.

"Is he injured?"

At that, Gabriel paused. "*Niall* is not fatally injured."

But someone is, Donia finished silently. "Is Ir—"

"Can't," he interrupted.

And the Winter Queen felt a burst of panic threaten her

calm. She nodded and suggested, "Perhaps I should seek out your king to tell him I will stand with him against Bananach."

The Hound cleared his throat and asked, "Soon?"

"At first light," she promised.

Gabriel bowed, and Donia walked toward the door to the house. Behind her, she heard snarls and growls, but she resisted looking back until she reached the doorstep. Donia glanced past the Hawthorn Girls and said, "I am sorry for your loss. If a tussle would soothe you, my fey seem amenable to it."

The Hound's expression flickered from sorrow, to rage, to confusion, and then finally to hope. "Can't bargain anything on my king's behalf, but—"

"Gabriel?" Donia interrupted. "The Hunt is not only the concern of the Dark Court. You align yourself with his court, but it has not always been so. I would have you and yours not in sorrow."

The massive Hound flashed her a grateful smile. Then he looked back at Lia, and the glaistig launched herself at him.

The Winter Queen lifted a hand to her fey and exhaled, setting a blizzard shrieking through the garden, darkening the sky, and sending hailstones to clatter all around the grinning faeries.

Then she closed the door against the screams and howls that rent the air.

CHAPTER 13

Evening had fallen as Keenan stood at the same door where he'd once been afraid to knock, where the last Winter Queen had lived. Beira was dead, by his hand, but the lingering fear of icicles ripping into his skin was well earned. For years, she'd shredded his skin—and his dignity.

The impotent Summer King.

Times had changed.

Because of Aislinn.

Now that he'd come back to Huntsdale, he should be with his queen, with his court, but he'd been gone long enough that a little longer wouldn't matter. He wanted to be the king that the Summer Court deserved; he wanted to love his queen as she deserved; but the moment he'd returned to Huntsdale, he went to the Winter Queen. For decades, Donia had been his haven. She saw him for who he was, not *what* he was. Even when they stood in opposition time and again during his attempts to convince mortal girls to take the test, she was his first and last comfort.

Why couldn't it have been her?

He'd pondered a lot the past several months, but he hadn't arrived at many answers. Instead, he had to face the unpleasant possibility that he brought only pain to those in his life. His steadfast desire to strengthen his court had been necessary, but it had also led him to hurt those he cared for: the faeries he owed the most were also the ones he had failed the most.

And I don't know how to change that.

"Are you going to knock or stand there?" Donia's voice was as cold as he'd ever heard it, but the Winter Queen wasn't much for warmth.

He turned away from the door to look at her. She stood in the snow-covered yard behind him. It took his breath away to see her. Her skin was icy perfection, and her eyes glittered with a crystalline sheen. Her long, pale blond hair was unbound, and her feet were bare on the snow. Touching that frozen surface would pain him. Merely *being* here made him ache. He shouldn't be out this time of year, especially in her domain. She parted her hawthorn-berry-red lips, but didn't speak. For a breath, he couldn't speak either: his memories never did her justice.

Neither do I.

"Would the door open if I knocked?"

"Hard to say." Donia flicked her wrist absently, and the snow swirled up to form a divan. Without looking, she sat and curled her legs up on the snowy sofa. She didn't invite him to join her—which was wise. Despite efforts to keep himself in check, he'd melt the divan if he touched it.

He did take several steps toward her. "I've missed you."

Wispy tendrils of frosty air slipped from her lips as she laughed. "There were days when I'd have done anything to hear those words . . . but you know that. You've always known."

He stood an arm's length away from her and wished he could close the distance, but the whole of his strength was necessary to be this near her. Every drop of sunlight had become essential to face her. If he could, though, he'd leave it at the edge of her domain, so he could reach out to her. "Don, I'm sorry."

She motioned for him to continue. "Go ahead, Keenan. Tell me the next line. You started this. We might as well go through the whole drama."

"I know I don't deserve—"

"Oh, you deserve all sorts of things." Her voice was as sharp as the remembered tortures that he still dreamt of. "You deserve things that I'm too kind—even now—to give you."

"I love you," he said.

Icicles formed on his skin as she stared at him for several heartbeats. "Do you suppose that changes anything?"

"I want it to." He knelt at her feet, but didn't even dare touch her hand. "Don, I want it to mean everything. It *should*."

"I've wanted that for decades," she admitted. "I wanted to believe that love can conquer all, that somewhere along the line, in the middle of the ridiculous game of finding your missing queen, that *I* would be loved by you just once the way I've always loved you."

"Don—"

"No." She narrowed her gaze and stood. The divan drifted away as if it had never been. The ground was a perfect, unmarred surface. "Not *'Don'* in that I'm-sorry-and-now-you'll-forgive-me-like-you-always-do way. Not this time, Keenan."

"I made mistakes."

"Dozens of them. Hundreds of them," she agreed. "Winter Girls and Summer Girls, a Winter Queen and a Summer Queen: you want the world. You expect everyone to bow to your wishes. You collect our hearts like trinkets. No more."

Reminding her that he'd done so because of being *cursed* wouldn't change the way it had made her feel. He hated Beira and Irial a little bit more just then; the curse hadn't hurt only *him*. Dozens of faeries suffered because of the curse, including the two he most wished he could have protected from *any* pain. The faery he loved and the faery who shared his throne had suffered more than most.

Or maybe I just know how much they hurt.

Still on his knees, he stared up at Donia. "Tell me how to make things right. Please?"

"I don't think you can," she said. "We had our chance. You gave up on us."

I didn't. He couldn't say it, though. It wasn't a lie, but it wasn't a full truth either. He'd stepped away to try to win his queen, to heal his court.

What else was I to do?

Donia waited; she *knew*. In truth, she knew everything he would say, could say, and she understood it. She was a regent too. The problem, of course, was that he didn't know how to give her up.

Even now.

"Tell me there's a way to be—"

"Keenan," she interrupted. "We've done this already. You failed."

He looked up at her, holding her gaze, hoping for something that he didn't see there anymore. "And now?"

"I have no idea." There were no tears in her eyes, no softness in her voice. "I suppose you return to your court and try to make amends with Ash or you keep running. It's not my concern anymore. It can't be. *You* can't be. The cost to both of our courts is too high. I'm done with you."

In the months he'd been away, he'd imagined this moment so many different ways. Her absolute dismissal still hurt more than most every pain he'd known these last nine centuries.

"I've never loved anyone the way I love you," he whispered.

"Lucky them."

Donia made it as far as the foyer before the tears she'd held in check since he'd left started to flood her cheeks. *He gave up on us.* She hadn't wept then. When he left, she'd accepted the news with no reaction. *He didn't want me when Ash was free.* She turned her face to the wall and wept the tears she hadn't shed in all this time.

"Tell me what you need."

She didn't have to look up to know that Evan was there, that he'd heard every word spoken outside her door, that he'd waited here in the house to console her and to protect her if she called for him. She reached out for his hand, and he pulled her to him.

"No one will judge you for your choices," Evan said quietly.

She didn't hide her tears from him. He was her friend. He'd known her when she was the Winter Girl, angry and bitter and lashing out at every one of Keenan's guards she could.

"My Queen? What do you need?" he asked again.

"To not love the one faery I can't be with?" She pulled away from Evan and wiped her cheeks with the back of her hand.

For a moment, Evan was silent. His bark-covered skin made it difficult to read his expressions under the best of conditions, and in that moment, he was trying very hard to be unreadable.

"He still loves you," Evan reminded her. "He cannot help but be who he is. When you weren't his queen . . . that was the only time I'd seen him so broken by the test."

"Yet the results are what they are. I am *not* his queen."

Evan's posture was as still as the trees he and his family resembled. "You cannot let your anger at him sway you from working with the Summer Court."

Mutely, she laid a hand at the fold of his arm and let him lead her back to the now somewhat trampled garden. He remained silent as they crossed through her house and into the wintery paradise enclosed behind the building. A massive snow bear came over and sniffed her. Here, the creatures of her domain coexisted in peace because she willed it. As the bear lumbered off, apparently satisfied that all was well enough, Donia leaned against Evan. What they shared was not romantic, but he was her closest friend.

Resigned, Donia nodded. "I will work with his court because I do not want to see my court injured . . . or his." She sat on one of the ice-carved benches. "I can see the value of allies, even though we *are* still the strongest of the courts."

"Which means Bananach will strike us hardest or she will eliminate the others first. When we do not ally with her, she will see us as the threat we are." Evan's warm, woodsy scent comforted her as much as the cadence of his words did. Unfortunately, the import of the words was not soothing.

"You're right." Donia drew in the cold air. "While I see Niall, you will go to the veil and request an audience with the High Queen. It is her twin we must deal with; perhaps she has wisdom to aid us." Donia held out a hand, palm up, to an arctic fox that eased toward her. "I am afraid that it is Irial whom Bananach has injured. Gabriel's words . . . and silences . . ."

"That is what I inferred as well."

The fox came to her hand, and she brought it to her lap as she thought on Niall. They hadn't been friends, not truly, as he'd had opposing interests for most of the time that they'd known each other. His former position as Keenan's advisor had put them at odds. *Not always.* Even then, he'd assured her safety as best he could; he'd arranged "accidental" meetings with Keenan in hopes of fostering a friendship between them. *Always a romantic.* Absently, she stroked the white fox nestled into her lap. *Why didn't I fall for someone like him?*

Donia wondered briefly if Niall knew she'd visited Leslie, the mortal girl he loved, if he knew she'd offered her friendship to the girl. *No doubt Irial does.* Whether or not Irial had told Niall remained to be seen.

Donia paused in petting the sleepy fox and frowned at Evan. "I am worried."

"You are the Winter Queen. You are wise and able. Trust yourself," Evan advised. "Unlike Dark and Summer, you have control of your emotions. Unlike the last Winter Queen, you are pure in intention. I serve the *only* regent who can lead us to peace."

"You make me sound far more capable than I feel." Rather than look at her advisor and friend, she resumed the comforting motions as the little fox fidgeted in her lap.

Evan touched her shoulder, and she looked at him then.

"I've been watching over you too long to be purely objective," he said, "but I'm old enough—and now Winter enough—to know what's truth. You helped give the Summer King the strength to rule his court. You stepped away from him for the good of *our* court. You are even now trying to figure out how to reach Niall. Your fey know what sort of ruler you are. That's why so few winter fey have joined Bananach."

Donia leaned her head on his shoulder. "Why are the ones who *do* leave the ones I can't stop thinking about?"

"Because you are a good queen." Evan wrapped an arm around her. "Even good rulers lose followers, though. I left Summer for Winter because of what I needed. Perhaps some of Bananach's followers are seeking something they don't find in their courts."

"If that meant peace, I wouldn't mind as much. I don't want any of you to die." She closed her eyes. "Be ready to go to Faerie at first light."

CHAPTER 14

Niall found himself back in a dream again. Since Irial had been injured, the only time Niall felt anywhere near *right* was in his dreams.

With Irial.

"You need to let me go," Irial muttered as Niall approached him. "This is no good for anyone."

"Since when did 'good for anyone' matter to the Dark Court?" Niall scowled. "You're not healing. I don't know what to do."

"I'm not *going* to heal."

Niall looked away from the weakened appearance of the last Dark King and remade the room. An immense fireplace with a roaring fire appeared, chasing the cold away, as if it would chase the threat of death away. "I sent for another healer. The last one must have missed something."

"She didn't."

"She could have," Niall insisted.

"But she *didn't*. Neither did the fifteen before her."

Niall dropped to the floor beside Irial's sofa. "I'll keep looking. I'll find the right healer, and until then, I'll visit you here and—"

"No. My body cannot recover from this. Even *you* can't stop it," Irial said. "If it were possible to stop time, I'd believe it of you. It's not."

As he had the past two days, Niall ignored the topic. "Pick a book."

For a moment, the only sound in the dream room was the crackle and hiss of the fire. Niall didn't see the benefit of arguing, not over this. He wouldn't give up on finding an answer, and he knew well enough that Irial wouldn't give up if possible.

"Do you think you could still surprise me?" Irial's voice was steady, but it was far from strong.

Niall reached out to collect the book he'd just imagined and began to read: "'The Demon is always moving about at my side; he floats about me like an impalpable air.'"

Irial laughed. "Baudelaire. Nicely chosen."

"I'm not giving up. Not now." Niall laid the book down. "Stay with our court, Irial. With me. I'm getting used to having a demon by my side again."

"Demon?" Irial chided. "I'm no more evil than you are . . . and you're far from evil."

"I'm not so sure about me right now," Niall admitted. "I want to kill Bananach. I want to test the truth of the whole 'Bananach's death kills Sorcha and thus all of us' theory. I feel wrong when I'm awake."

"You will take care of our court and yourself, but right now . . . if you're not going to read"—Irial remade the dream then, replacing the sofa on which he'd been reclining with a massive bed heaped high with pillows—"rest with me. You can't lead our court if you are too exhausted to think or react. Everything will be fine. You'll figure out what to do with Bananach, keep our court strong, and find what you need."

"I need *you*." Niall stood, but remained beside the bed.

Irial held out a hand. "I'm right here, Niall. Let us both rest."

There was something peculiar about sleeping in a dream—*and about Irial wanting to sleep*—but the edges of the world were blurring.

Why?

"Join me, Niall," Irial invited.

Niall climbed onto the bed. "Just for a minute."

"Relax, Gancanagh," Irial implored.

A few hours later, Niall woke with a startle in the real world. He looked around the room. *His room.* The light outside the window revealed that evening had fallen while he slept. He reached a hand out to touch Irial's forehead, to see if the fever had abated.

Niall stared at Irial and roared, *"No!"*

"My King?" Gabriel suddenly stood in the doorway. "Niall? You . . . yelled."

Niall shook his head. "He *knew*. He knew that. Even

at the end, he tried to protect me. He never chang—" The word broke as the reality of it settled on Niall. Irial *had* changed: he was dead.

And Bananach is responsible.

CHAPTER 15

Invisible to mortal sight, Keenan walked through the streets of Huntsdale. It took effort to not fade in the cold. He'd considered waiting, but he needed to return to his court.

He hadn't expected Donia to welcome him back easily, but in all the years they'd loved and drifted, he'd always been sure of her. *Only her.* Truths he wasn't able to admit to anyone else in this world—or in Faerie—he could share with her. He didn't know what he would do without her. *Did I really just lose her?* If nothing else, he'd figured that they'd be friends. She knew him better than anyone. She understood how he'd struggled when Beira had struck him down year after decade after century. *She has given up on me, on us.*

Keenan paused outside Bishop O'Connell, the school where he'd briefly been a student. With Donia at his side, he'd stood in this street more than a year ago watching then-mortal Aislinn; he'd thought all of the Summer Court's problems would be resolved if he won her. Everything he believed he'd understood about the future was wrong. He shivered and folded his arms over his chest.

I shouldn't be out here.

As if in answer to his thoughts, he heard the beat of wings, and in the following instant, Bananach descended from the sky to stand in front of him. Like him, she was invisible to anyone other than the fey or the Sighted.

But not weakened by the weather . . . or much else from the looks of it.

The raven-faery was smiling; her previously shadowed wings were solid. They unfolded to full width, casting the street into near-total darkness, and then refolded to lie still against her back. Her arms were bare despite the chill, but she was dressed in pseudomilitary attire: very snug urban camouflage trousers tucked into tall black boots. No human soldier would wear such a fit for their work garb, nor would a faery feel inclined toward false camouflage. Bananach was a singular entity, though. Her sense of humor and her sense of the practical rarely meshed with anyone else's—faery or mortal.

"Little king," Bananach greeted him. "You've been missed."

"Not by you, I'd gather." He forced sunlight to the surface of his skin, hating that he was faced with conflict when he shouldn't be out in the cold at all, but strangely excited by the possibility of fighting. The Summer Court did not typically thrive on violence, but they were a court of passions, and in that instant, directing his hurt into anger was decidedly appealing.

Keenan reached inside a false pocket in his trousers and unfastened the strap that wrapped around the hilt of the short bone blade that had once been his father's. Along one side of the blade, fused there with the Summer King's sunlight, shards of obsidian gave it a serrated edge. He withdrew the weapon.

"You would fight me?" Bananach tilted her head at an inhuman angle. "Have I done you ill?"

"Today? I'm not aware of any, but I am feeling cautious." Keenan kept the blade tip pointed at the sidewalk for now.

From across the street, three faeries approached. They were solitaries he didn't know, but they were walking toward Bananach. *A trap.* He glanced at them only briefly. "Do you intend to strike me down, Bananach? There are those who would respond poorly to that."

"And there are those who would not." She widened her eyes. "I debated the matter. I ran the possibilities. In the current schedule, I would find you more useful injured than dead, but if you aren't cooperative . . ." She shrugged.

One of the faeries broke off from the other two and crossed the street so that her approach would be from behind Keenan. The other two spread out and continued to close in from the street side. That left Bananach in front of him, and the glass front of a shoe store to his side. *I hate plucking glass from my skin.* He tightened his grip on the blade's hilt. Sunlight thrummed under his skin; every strand of muscle was a live wire filled with energy. He could turn that sunlight into a blade for his other hand and drive it into Bananach's flesh.

It wasn't Bananach who launched herself at him. War watched as all three of her faeries attacked as one. He pushed the bone-and-obsidian blade over a faery's throat. The faery fell backward, but the other two pressed on him—one behind and one to the side. Keenan angled, trying to fend off the two assaults.

And Bananach stepped forward. He saw the movement out of the corner of his eye, but he couldn't react in time. She swiped her talons over his right side, gouging furrows through the cloth and into his skin.

Keenan reacted by pulling back his left hand, the one holding the sunlit blade, and trying to force it into the avian faery's throat.

She moved too quickly, and it cut her across the shoulder. Instead of responding with anger, she smiled at him.

He felt, rather than saw, her talons sink into his right bicep. The numbness started to creep across his side and radiate through his arm. He turned to look and saw one of the remaining two faeries swing a blade toward his left knee, but before the blow could connect, someone shoved it away.

Bananach backed away temporarily. "You meddle where you are not wanted."

With confusion, Keenan looked at the faery suddenly beside him. *"Seth?"*

"Trust me, you're not my first choice to fight next to, Sunshine, but as much as it would simplify things, I wouldn't be able to live with myself if I left you to her tender mercies." Seth didn't spare him more than a glance; instead the pierced newly fey boy looked to the street with unexpectedly military attention.

"Auntie B," Seth greeted her. "You need to reel it in."

Bananach snapped her beak at him. "Order should've kept you in Faerie. You won't survive here."

"I will, but if you continue, you will die," Seth told her as he put himself in front of Keenan. "Your brother heals."

Bananach grinned—a peculiar sight with her beak-mouth. "The *other* doesn't. He won't."

The Hounds arrived then like an angry swarm, and before they finished their approach, Bananach and two of her faeries were gone. The third lay lifeless on the sidewalk.

"You do that?" Seth asked.

"I did." Keenan didn't look at the dead faery. He had no desire to gloat over the loss of life. He couldn't say that he was happy the slain faery was fallen, only that he was glad he was not fallen.

I think.

He didn't cringe, not in front of Seth or the Hunt, but the gouges from Bananach's talons stung more by the moment.

The Hounds enclosed them in a protective circle. Around them, mortals continued to pass, unaware of the invisible conflict in their midst. They were, however, all easing farther away from the sidewalk where the Hunt waited.

As when Bananach approached, the mortals felt an aversion
to the faeries. With War, it was the feeling of a discordant
presence, but with the Hunt it was the urge to run.

No one spoke for a moment. Neither Gabriel nor Chela
was there, but rather than look to another Hound for direction, the Hunt seemed to be awaiting Seth's command.

"Go see her," Seth said without looking at him. "They
will escort you."

Keenan stilled. "Her?"

This time Seth did look at him. "Ash. It's inevitable. No
matter which way the threads twist, that's the next step."

"The threads . . ." Keenan gaped at him.

"Yeah, the *threads.*" Seth bit the ring that decorated his
lip and looked at the air as if there were answers hovering
in it. Then he looked directly at Keenan again and said, "I
can't see everything, or see most things clearly enough, but
you . . . *you* I see."

"My future?" Keenan felt a fool as he stared down the
faery that stood between him and his queen.

He's a seer.

"Don't ask," Seth snarled. "Go to the loft. I just left her
to be *here*, to stop your death, so we're even now."

"Even?" Keenan echoed. There were many words the
Summer King could choose to describe their standings, but
even wasn't one of them. Seth was a child, a recent mortal,
an obstacle to be overcome; Keenan, on the other hand, had
spent centuries being near powerless, but still protecting his
court—the court that Seth's very existence endangered.

The Summer King let the heat of his anger slip into his voice and said, "We'll never be *even*, Seth."

"You told me once that you didn't order my death because it would upset Ash. I came here to keep you from death. That makes us *even*." Seth spoke the words in a low voice, but the faeries near them were Hounds. Their hearing was better than most, and at this distance, it was no challenge to listen.

Consequently, Keenan didn't try to lower his voice. "Killing you wasn't the right course of action then. If you had died, she would mourn—which she did anyhow when you were in Faerie." Keenan stepped closer to Seth. Anger that he'd not been able to completely purge filled him. "You left. By choice. She mourned your absence for *months*. She was in pain, and I was her friend. I waited. I was *only* her friend for months."

"During which you knew I was in Faerie."

Keenan shrugged and immediately decided not to do *that* again. Carefully keeping the pain from his voice, he said, "If killing you would've resolved the situation, I'd have done it. If you stayed in Faerie or got yourself killed, it would've been *your* choice. Why would I cross Sorcha for a mortal I'd rather see out of my way?"

"I get that, but I'm *not* a mortal now." Seth bared his teeth in a decidedly not-mortal expression.

"But you're still in my way."

"Right back at you," Seth muttered.

They stood silently for several moments; then Seth shook

his head. "You need to go to Ash now, and I need to go to Niall. . . . I am Sorcha's heir, and"—he looked embarrassed for a moment—"that means that I'm not free to do only what I want."

"None of us are," the Summer King said. Then he turned away, moving at a speed that made the mortals he passed clutch their coats and brush hair from their eyes. Some looked around curiously, seeking the source of the gusts of wind that sent dust swirling into the air.

CHAPTER 16

Whatever slight tether Niall had had to stability had vanished. Time slipped in and out of order. He walked into a rarely used room. Faeries crawled through debris. A fire burned, consuming what appeared to be a sofa or perhaps a small bed. It was hard to tell with the smoke. Obviously there had been a fight of some sort.

Were we attacked?

"Bar the doors." He drew a knife from a sheath on his ankle and looked around the shambles of the room. "Set guards at every window."

"We did," a trembling thistle-fey said. Something had happened to the faery: his arm was bent the wrong way.

"She's not in the house? Bananach?"

"No, my King," another faery assured him. "She isn't here."

"I won't let her hurt you." Niall looked around at the battered faeries in the room. "None of you will leave."

"Yes, my King," they said.

He could feel their fear, their worry, and their desperation. It filled the room as thickly as the smoke from the
smoldering furniture. The Dark King drew in their emotions, trying to fill whatever void had opened up inside of
him. He considered asking them when the court had been
attacked, but revealing his missing memories wouldn't help
his court.

Protect them, a voice urged.

Niall nodded. He wasn't sure if he could, but he knew
better than to show doubts. He blinked, and when he looked,
he was in another room. A new group of battered faeries
stood waiting. Two Hounds were in front of the faeries.

"Niall?" Gabriel came into the room. "Should I go get
her?"

"Her?"

"Leslie has a right to know. He'd *want* her to know, but
I can't do everything." Gabriel held out his forearms. They
were covered in so much ink that they were unreadable.
Words layered atop words; oghams blurred and moved.

Niall didn't remember issuing so many orders.

"You can't do everything," Niall repeated. "Things . . .
other things . . . There are other things."

"Yes. Wise call, my King. I'll send another Hound."
Gabriel's relief washed over Niall. "And I can stay here for
you and Iri."

"Irial . . . He's here?" Niall looked around. Something
about that was wrong; something was wrong with Irial.

Gabriel stepped into Niall's line of vision again, blocking out the sight of the faeries, who cringed when Niall's gaze fell on them. "Probably need to send a few faeries to keep Leslie safe."

Niall's gaze snapped to Gabriel's face. "Leslie . . . yes. We need to protect Leslie. There's danger. Bananach . . . she . . . Bananach . . ."

Images collided in Niall's mind. Bananach had a sword-knife-talons-beak-knife. The Dark King blinked and repeated, "Leslie needs protection."

But Gabriel wasn't there. No one was there. He was in a room of shadows and smoke. Walls of darkness encircled him, and the Dark King couldn't remember why. He walked through them, crossing the barrier of darkness and wandering through the house.

A sharp pain made him look down, and he realized that he'd lost something. It was in the house, but as Niall walked he couldn't remember what it was or why he needed it. The house was in a state of destruction. *How will I find anything?* He looked around and saw a faery who appeared to be clinging to the wall.

"Did you bar the doors?"

"Yes, my King." The faery swallowed audibly. "And the windows."

"Good." Niall nodded. "She won't get in. You will tell the others to stay inside. I can't protect you if you . . . Someone should tell Leslie. Where is Gabriel? My orders . . . I have orders for Gabriel."

CHAPTER 17

Keenan opened the door and stared at her and *only* her. His queen looked as regal as any ruler he'd known. Her chin lifted. Her gaze was on him—not welcoming, but judging. Her once blue-black hair had sun streaks as if she'd lived at the beach, and within her eyes he could see a hurricane in motion. She still wore common clothes—jeans and a simple shirt—as she had when she was a mortal, but her bearing made them the clothes of royalty. Sun sparks of emotion danced over her skin. The tiny bursts of light made her seem to flicker like the sun itself.

She didn't rise to greet him. Instead, she sat in judgment within the study that had been his retreat. It, like most everything else, was hers now; his court, his advisors, the struggle of correcting the court's weaknesses, the challenge of finding balance—they all belonged to the Summer Queen as much as to him.

In the hallway beyond him, several of the Summer

Girls sighed, and others started dancing. Keenan smiled at them briefly before returning his attention to the Summer Queen. Unlike his dancing Summer Girls, the queen was not smiling.

At all.

"Nice of you to remember where we live," she said.

"I needed a little time. . . ."

"Almost *six months?*"

"Yes," he said.

As he approached his queen, sunlight flared from his skin. It wasn't by choice; the sunlight inside of him burned brighter because of her. The king and the queen were drawn together. *Attraction without love.* It was the final piece of Beira's curse. Keenan hadn't realized how much he wanted an all-consuming love until the past year. He'd spent so long looking for her that he'd assumed they'd be perfect together. She was his missing partner; how could it be otherwise?

"Did you get my message that quickly? If I had known that's all it took, I'd have sent word of the court's predicament sooner." Aislinn didn't look away from him as she asked, and Keenan saw in her the queen he'd sought for so many centuries. She was bold where she had once been tentative, aggressive with him in defense of their court as she'd once been for her then-mortal beloved.

"I received no message," he admitted. "I came back because it was time."

The gleam in her eyes flashed brightly. "At least there's that."

"I . . ." he started, but he had no words, not when she looked at him with a tangle of hope and anger. He wasn't sure if he should ask what message she'd sent or not, but as sunlight shimmered around her in a light show to rival the aurora borealis, he decided the question could wait.

She folded her arms across her chest. "You *left* me . . . our *court*. Do you have any idea what's been going on?"

"I do. I had reports, and I knew"—he sat on the sofa beside her—"I was able to stay away because the court was safe in your hands."

"You abandoned your court to do who knows w—" She turned to face him and gasped.

She reached out with one hand. She slid her thumb across his cheek. "You're injured."

Keenan pulled her hand away from his face.

"It'll wait. Come with me," he said softly, not a command—*because she is the queen*—but something more than a request.

He stood, but she remained where she was.

"Please?" he urged.

After a glance at the faeries who waited outside the room, Aislinn stood. Keenan put his arm around her waist, and happy murmurs filtered through the loft. With Aislinn at his side, Keenan walked down the hallway to his rooms.

At the door, a faery bowed.

Keenan nodded and led Aislinn across the threshold.

Once the door had closed behind them, she pulled away. "That wasn't fair."

He winced as she elbowed him in his injured side.

"Holding you, or letting them believe I intend to return to where we were when I left?"

"Either."

"Aislinn?" He walked toward her. "I need you."

He stripped off his shirt.

She stared at him, and he felt the temperature in the room spike.

"Keenan? What are you . . . I can't . . ."

"I need your help." He tossed the shirt against the wall and lifted his arm. By peeling the shirt off, he'd reopened the gashes from Bananach's talons. Blood trickled over his side.

"Why didn't you tell me you were this badly injured?" Aislinn was beside him in an instant. Without thinking of the consequences, she laid one hand on his stomach and her other on his arm. "Who did this?"

"Bananach." He let her push his arm out of the way so that she could see the ugly wounds. "She and three others cornered me."

He silently apologized to Donia for what he was about to do, but the Summer Court would never be strong enough to survive the coming war if he didn't force a change. *I need my queen. My court needs this.* For a faery king, he'd been patient since Aislinn had become queen. *No more.*

He looked at his queen. "Help me?"

She hadn't moved away yet, but she had pulled her hands from him. "What do you need?"

He twisted to look at the injury and held his arm out

from his body. "It needs to be cleaned, and—never mind."
He stepped away. "I can do it myself."

"Don't be ridiculous." Aislinn scowled.

He hid his smile. "If you're sure . . ."

"What do I clean it with?"

Keenan pointed toward a cabinet and winced. "There's
cleaning supplies on the top shelf."

His queen opened the cabinet and stretched up, balancing on her toes.

"Can you reach them?" Keenan followed and used the
excuse to put his hands on her waist. The pain of the toxins in his body was starting to make him feel weak, but he
wasn't yet at the point of exhaustion.

"Got it." She pulled down the box of medicinal supplies
and spun around so that she was facing him. "Why do you
have these in here?"

"My mother used to take pleasure in injuring me every
time I told her about the girl I thought could be my"—he
touched her face with his hand, trapping her between him
and the wall—"who could be *you*. I didn't like the court to
see my injuries."

"Oh." She took a steadying breath and then exhaled—
against his bare skin.

He shivered at the feel of her breath, letting her see his
reaction, showing her that he was far from immune to her,
and then before she could ask him to move, he turned and
walked away. *Tease and retreat.* He'd done this so many
times that it was frightfully easy to slip into the role. *I hate*

it. He pushed the distaste away. *The court comes first.* An unhappy regent was a weak regent; a weak regent created a weak court. *We cannot be weak.*

He glanced over his shoulder at her. "Is it easier if I stand or sit?"

"Your back is bruised too." She walked up behind him and laid her hand flat between his shoulder blades. "Do we need a healer?"

"You can heal me," he reminded her. He turned so they were face-to-face again. "After you clean the wounds, if you choose to, you could erase these injuries."

"It's not that easy." She started to back away.

He caught her hand and held it against his skin. As his sunlight pulsed and drew out her light, he slid her hand toward his injured side. "All you need to do is touch me and let your sunlight make me stronger. I need you, Aislinn."

"When I do . . . I would if it were life threatening, but . . ." She blushed and tugged her hand free of his. "You're not being fair. You *know* what it feels like."

"I do. It feels right."

She opened the medical box and pulled out an antiseptic wipe. "Sit."

He did so, and she leaned down and wiped the blood from his skin. She was careful as she cleaned the four gouges in his side. When she was done, she asked, "They look worse than they feel, right?"

"No," he admitted. He put his right arm behind him to brace himself. "She's War. Her touch is always worse than most faeries, and right now, she's strong."

Aislinn's attempt at self-control faltered. Wind snapped through the room as her instinctual protectiveness flared to life.

"But you seemed fine in the study and"—she shook her head—"you were ignoring that, despite being in real pain, to explain to me. I thought we came in here because you were being . . ."

"Assertive?" he offered. "I was, but I didn't want them to see me weakened, Aislinn. You know that they are already tentative. I'll not show them anything that gives them doubts. My duty is to them. It has been so since I was born."

Silently, she sat beside him and splayed one hand over the still-bleeding cuts. Pulses of sunlight slipped into his torn skin, burning the darkness of War's poison from his body. He closed his eyes against both the pain and the pleasure. He wasn't sure at first if Aislinn realized there were toxins inside him that she was destroying, but when he opened his eyes, she was staring at him. She'd felt the poisons, knew what he'd hidden: if she'd not helped him in time, he could've died.

"No different than the ice Donia poisoned you with, Aislinn." He smiled at her. "Telling you wouldn't have changed anything. You felt it. You're fixing it."

"Idiot." Then, she put her other hand on his injured ribs and forced the sunlight into his skin. The feel was of honey just this side of too hot, soaking through his skin, seeping into the now-healing cuts. As they healed, he pushed back, letting sunlight loop toward her. He might be injured, but he'd been playing with Summer's elements for centuries. Then, he was a bound king; now, he was freed. *Because of you.* He could feel the almost tangible edge of how strong they could be.

He returned the sunlight she was pushing into his body, and her fingers curled until her fingernails were scratching his skin. She didn't push him away. *Or pull me closer.* His queen wasn't sure what she wanted, and he wasn't going to walk away until they both knew.

All or nothing.

Aislinn couldn't keep her eyes open. She might not love Keenan, but there was no denying the way her body responded to him. She slid her hand from his side onto his bare stomach and felt the muscles under his skin tense.

He had his arm around her lower back and started to pull her onto his lap.

With more effort than she wished it took, she stopped him. "Keenan."

His eyes opened, but instead of answering, he wrapped both arms around her, and fell backward onto his bed, pulling her with him. Her hands were flat on his bare chest, and her hips were against his. The shock of being in that position made her still for a moment.

"You're not going to seduce me." Aislinn pushed away and stared down at the Summer King, who was shirtless and prone on his bed underneath her.

Summer is the court of impulsivity. Keenan was offering her what Seth was refusing her. *His kisses make me forget the world. His touch would be . . .*

She sighed. "I'm tempted. You know that."

"That was a no," Keenan said.

"It was." She sat beside him.

He didn't sit up. Instead he rolled onto his side and looked at her. "Because of Seth."

Aislinn nodded.

"So are you . . . completely together then?" Keenan stretched one arm over his head.

Despite her best intentions, her gaze traveled over him. Several thin scars marred the expanse of tanned skin, but they didn't detract from his appeal. He was toned without being bulky, and his well-defined abs made her briefly think he shouldn't ever wear shirts. *Except no one would get much done if that were the case.* Even when they'd been growing closer, she hadn't seen him like this. He'd been careful around her then.

"You're doing this on purpose," she said in a voice far too breathy for her comfort.

He didn't pretend to misunderstand. "I am."

"Why?" She forced herself to look only at his face.

"Answer my question, Aislinn."

"No, not totally. We aren't . . ." She blushed. "Not by my choice."

"Did he tell you what he sees?" Keenan asked in a voice too benign to be truly innocent.

She made sure her gaze didn't waver from his face—much—and asked, "Sees?"

"In the future."

"I don't . . ." She frowned. "What do you mean?"

"Seth sees the future," Keenan told her. "If he was certain you weren't going to be in my arms, he wouldn't refuse you. He knows you aren't certain."

"He wouldn't hide that. . . ." Aislinn felt tears well up in her eyes, though.

"But he did. Seers are able to see possibilities. Not their own futures, but he can see *your* possible futures. No matter what you've said, he can see that you aren't certain yet. We have not reached the point where you can say that you truly won't be with me. You know—as well as I do, and as well as he does—that you don't want to sacrifice your court for love. You're their queen. Will you tell them that their deaths, their fragility, their court mean so little?"

"No."

"Can you say you don't want me?" he challenged.

Aislinn looked away, but Keenan laid his hand on her cheek and made her face him. "I am your king, Aislinn. Seth sees futures where you make the choice to be mine."

"How do you know?"

"Because Seth is the one who helped me fight Bananach today."

When several moments passed and she didn't reply, Keenan asked, "What was the message you sent?"

"Keenan . . ."

"What message would you send to bring me home so quickly, Aislinn?"

In a steady voice, the Summer Queen said, "I told Tavish to send a message to bring you home, not that it was truth . . . but a misdirection, a faery manipulation."

"Aislinn, what was the message?"

"That I was ready to let you convince me," she confessed.

"Then, convince you I shall." In one of those faery-fast movements that used to unsettle her, Keenan sat up so he was knee-to-knee with her. "I'll be yours, and only yours, for all of eternity. We will move the court away from here."

"But, I didn't mean it. . . ."

"One week," he said. "We will be together, or I will leave. I will do what I must from a distance. It is not how a court should be ruled, but we can make it so if necessary. I will not stay here and watch my queen choose to be with another. I *will not*. I will not stay here and fight against our natures. We will be together, or we will not see each other at all."

"You're not being fair, Keenan."

"None of this is *fair*, Aislinn." He slid his fingers through her hair, and flower petals showered them. "The indecision is keeping us from being happy, and that weakens the court. I could make you happy."

Then he pulled his hands away, but as he did so, sunlight rained down over them. Vines twined up the bed and burst into bloom. Somewhere in the distance, she heard an ocean crash onto the shore, and she slid backward.

With effort, she kept her eyes open. "I just wanted you to come back."

"And I'm here." Keenan knelt beside her in the midst of a riot of summer blossoms. "We've tried approaching this as a job; we tried being coregents, but not truly together. It didn't work."

"Maybe—"

"No. The court needs to be strong, and having its rulers in stasis isn't going to make our fey strong . . . or safe from Bananach. You can stop this at any point by telling me we will rule the court apart from a distance, but until you do so"—he let liquid sunlight drip onto her skin—"I'm playing for keeps. I'm not a mortal, Aislinn. I'm the Summer King, and I'm done pretending to be anything other than that."

He leaned down and said, "We could be amazing together."

Then he was gone.

CHAPTER 18

Seth thought he was prepared; he thought that he understood Niall. As he walked into the Dark King's house, he realized just how wrong he was. The floor was covered with the evidence of the Dark King's fury: broken furniture and glass, bits of paper, a half-charred log from the fireplace that looked like it had still been burning when it was thrown. The debris was ankle deep in places.

A thistle-fey huddled against the wall with a strange expression on his face. As the faery turned, Seth realized that a fireplace poker had been driven through the faery's thigh and pinned him to the wall. It hadn't been obvious at first because it was so deeply embedded in the wall that only the handle was visible.

"The king is in mourning," the faery said.

"I know." Seth gestured at the handle of the poker. "May I help?"

The faery shook his head. "The king shouldn't suffer

alone. It is an honor to be in pain with him."

"You did this?"

"No. My king did." The thistle-faery leaned his head back. "I didn't understand how I should feel at the loss of our last king. I understand more now."

"Let me help y—"

"No," the faery interrupted. "It is brass, not iron."

For a moment, Seth felt a flicker of fear. *Would Niall strike me?* He looked at the destruction. *Only one way to find out.*

As he walked through the house, more than a few faeries lay bleeding. One Ly Erg dangled half on, half off a chandelier. The Ly Erg's eyes were closed, but it appeared to be breathing.

Several Hounds walked up behind Seth. One, Elaina, asked quietly, "You sure you want to go in alone?"

"No," Seth admitted, "but I'm going to."

"The king is distraught. We could go in first so he can have someone to strike," the female Hound suggested.

Seth shook his head. "I think I'd better go alone from here."

The expression on Elaina's face made quite clear that she thought he was being a fool.

She may be right.

"It'll be fine," he assured her. "He is my brother."

She scowled, but she held up both hands in defeat.

No one in the house appeared to be moving. The faeries that Seth passed were either injured, unconscious, or staying still to avoid attention. Many were half buried under the apparent destruction of everything in the house.

Following the sounds of crashing glass, Seth made his way through rooms he'd never seen, down more hallways than seemed possible to fit into the dimensions of the building. *Like Sorcha's palace in Faerie.* At the end of a hall was a room, and in the room was a very battered, bleeding Dark King. All around him, shadow figures—the same seemingly insubstantial amorphous bodies Seth had seen when they stood at Ani's house—reassembled what remained of the contents of the room, handed them to Niall, and watched as he broke them again.

"Niall," Seth said softly.

For a moment, Niall paused. He looked at Seth without recognition, and then he glanced at the green cut-glass decanter in his hand.

"Niall," Seth repeated a little louder. "I'm here. I've come to help you."

"He's dead. Irial. Is. *Dead.*" Niall dropped the decanter and walked away.

After a few steps, Niall slammed his fist into the wall.

Seth grabbed him and pulled him backward. "Stop."

Niall looked at Seth. "She killed him."

"I know." Seth held on to his friend's arm. "I was there when she stabbed him. Remember?"

The Dark King nodded. "I tried to stop it. Healers . . . I tried. . . . I failed. . . . I thought I wanted him dead once.

I thought that . . ." Niall's words trailed off as he looked past
Seth to the destruction in the hall. "I did that?"

"I think so."

"I don't remember. . . ." Niall reached up to rub his face,
but he stopped mid-motion. "I didn't remember things, but
now . . . *You* make me remember. He died. I remember that.
Irial is dead."

"There are other things you need to remember. You can
do this, Brother." Seth waited. He couldn't tell Niall what he
saw. That was the limitation of being a seer. *One of them at
least.* He couldn't try to manipulate the future he wanted by
telling Niall what could come to pass; Sorcha had explained
that at length. As it was, he was playing with the rules more
than he probably should.

"I've been trying; since you left, I tried. . . ." Niall shook
his head.

Seth led him away from the now blood-spattered wall.
"You would cope a lot better if you slept."

Niall pulled away. "I *can't.*"

"You can. You *need* to." Seth used a foot to push a bunch
of glass to the side. It crunched under his boot.

Niall looked down at his own bare feet. "I'm bleeding."

"Yeah. I know," Seth said.

"I wouldn't hurt you."

"What?"

Niall made a vague gesture. "You're afraid. I wouldn't
hurt *you.*"

"I didn't—"

"I can taste it," Niall interrupted.

Seth quirked a brow.

"Dark King thing," Niall muttered. Then he swayed. He leaned against the wall. "I'm tired, Seth." He pushed off the wall immediately. "No. I'm not. Find me something—"

"No."

Niall turned then, and the abyss-guardians snapped to life around them. "I am the Dark King. If I say—"

"Niall. Seriously. Chill the fuck out." Seth grabbed him by both shoulders. "You need to sleep. Trust me."

"I can't. No sleep since he's been gone . . . He haunts my dreams." Niall leaned his head on Seth's shoulder. "I'm afraid . . . and I cannot do this on my own, Brother."

"Where's Gabe?"

"With Iri." Niall glanced toward a closed door. "I ordered him to stay with Irial. I needed to leave the room, but I didn't . . . I can't . . . This is our home."

"Do you trust me?"

"I do."

"I want you to remember that, Niall," Seth said, and then he called, "Elaina!"

The blur of Hounds raced toward them. Niall stared at them as they encircled him.

"Your king needs to find rest," Seth told the female Hound.

Then Seth looked at Niall. "Give me permission."

"For?"

"Trust me," Seth pleaded. "What I do is necessary."

Niall stared at him—and hesitated. "You have permission for the acts of the next minute."

"That'll do it." Reluctantly, Seth gave the order he knew his friend needed: "Knock him out. He needs sleep."

CHAPTER 19

Early the following morning, Donia stood at the veil to Faerie. Her requests for an audience with the Dark King were refused, so she decided to try the next regent on her list. She put her hand out into the air, grasping at nothingness again. The fabric should twist around her skin; it should writhe like a living thing. It did neither.

"It's not here."

Beside her, Evan nodded. "That's what I was trying to explain."

"It can't not *be* here." Her hand sliced through the empty air. "Do they move? I mean, I haven't been a faery for *that* long. In the past, did they move?"

"No."

"That doesn't work, Evan." She turned to face him, and as she did so, she absently reached out to touch Sasha. The wolf had been growling as Donia grew increasingly agitated. He kept a watchful gaze around the cemetery as if seeking out whatever threat had unsettled his mistress.

"If I had an answer, I'd offer it to you." Evan's tone was uncommonly sharp.

Donia drew a calming breath and then exhaled a plume of frigid air. "I'm sorry. I know that."

Her advisor nodded. His berry-red eyes were still widened, and his posture was as tense as she felt. For a winter faery—or for a rowan—it was akin to hand-wringing. Evan started walking, and as they began pacing through the cemetery, more of her faeries joined them. The lupine loped at the edges of the cemetery in a loose formation. Several Scrimshaw Sisters drifted alongside the lupine. Others of her court fanned out in scouting patterns, and still more faeries assumed the position of guards.

"What does it mean? Is Faerie gone?"

"We would know." Evan stared at the air, as if to find a trail, a hint of something that made sense of the vanishing of the gate to Faerie. "We would. We'd have to know."

"Do you think she . . . they . . . oh gods, Evan, if it vanished . . . the people and the faeries there. The deaths." Donia lowered her voice until it was little more than a whisper. "It's just the gate that's gone. It has to be."

"The Summer Queen's beloved goes to Faerie. He would know something." Evan motioned to the faeries who were looking, unsuccessfully, for some other gate to have appeared to replace the one that had vanished. "It is necessary to call on the Summer Court or try the Dark Court again. The boy will be with one of them."

"And War? Could she have done this?" As her faeries moved closer, Donia spotted a stranger among them. A tall, pale faery walked through the cemetery toward her. "Evan? Who is that?"

Evan stepped in front of her so suddenly that she had to put a hand on his back to steady herself. "Stay behind me."

Scrimshaw Sisters fluttered toward Donia and encircled her. In barely more than a breath, the lupine were gathered around them. One particularly anxious Hawthorn hovered, her eyes flashing angry red.

"A wall of faeries between us, Donia?" The faery shook his head. "Surely, this is not how one greets old friends."

"We've never met," Donia said.

"Forgive me." He bowed his head briefly. "I saw you in a memory. Icicles like knives tipped those dainty hands." He lifted his gaze to hers. "You skewered the Summer Queen quite neatly."

A wave of something like regret filled Donia at the thought of that day. "She healed."

"Curiously, she healed better than one would expect." The faery straightened to full height then. "I am Far Dorcha."

Donia hoped her expression didn't betray the terror she was attempting to resist. *I am Winter. I am at my strength.* Unfortunately, every assurance she could think of was quashed when she realized that the faery before her was the Dark Man, wielder of true death. He mightn't be a king, but the death-fey obeyed him without hesitation—in part, perhaps, because his touch could end their lives as well. Only Far Dorcha could kill any of the death-fey. It made for a degree of instant obedience that other regents couldn't demand.

"You've not been fey but a blink." He took another step toward her.

Evan extended a hand, but didn't actually touch the Dark Man. "Keep your distance."

"Evan." Far Dorcha shook his head. "You've switched courts again, I see."

Again?

"I serve the Winter Queen," Evan said in a perfectly level voice. "I organize her guard, and I would lay down every life here for hers."

Far Dorcha laughed, a horrible sound of claws scrabbling over metal floors. "And when they were all gone, I would still reach her . . . *if* that was my desire."

The Dark Man wasn't threatening her, not overtly, but the reminder carried the force of a threat. Her fey tensed further. She laid the palm of her hand against Evan's back and stepped to the side so that she was able to look up at Far Dorcha. In doing so, Donia drew his attention back to her.

"Do you come for me?" she asked.

"No. I was *here*"—he motioned around the cemetery—"because of the gate. I was in Huntsdale for other business matters."

Evan tensed. "Who?"

Keenan? Aislinn? Niall? Irial? The head of the death-fey

wouldn't come for just any death. *Who will die?*

Donia asked, "Why are you here?"

"Ah-ah-ah." Far Dorcha shook his finger. "Not telling you. The surprise is part of the fun."

The Dark Man sighed, and Evan bodily blocked that exhalation from touching her. Her guard had his head turned to the side as he did so, yet as she watched, he swallowed with some difficulty. His hands fisted.

"Evan?"

"Please, my Queen, not now." His voice was ragged, but he didn't move.

"Curious. Despite her temper then, you chose to be hers." Far Dorcha's gaze lifted from Evan to fix her in a stare. "Did you mean to kill them? Petulant behavior, striking out at the Summer King's guards. You've taken lives for no reason."

The calm of Winter filled Donia. "You are not a judge. I am not your subject, nor was I then."

"I am Death. Killing is *always* mine to judge." Far Dorcha didn't blink. The lack of any semblance of humanity made his scrutiny more uncomfortable. Most of the human-looking fey had adopted various human behaviors. He hadn't.

She stepped around Evan. "I was almost killed by the last Winter Queen, and if I or those I protect are threatened, I will kill again. I am not a mortal, Far Dorcha. You might be Death, but unless you are here to kill me, do not try to intimidate me." The snow that she'd relied upon to hold her temper at bay was no longer enough. Ice rose up, and she felt a rime of it coat her skin. "Unless you have reason to touch them, you will leave my fey alone."

Far Dorcha laughed, and visions of scurrying things in the dark washed over her. *Wet soil and absolute silence.* If there was humor in those tones, it was beyond her comprehension.

"The young king has chosen well," he pronounced.

"What?" Donia's temper slipped a little further, and a snowstorm flared to life.

"Two queens." Far Dorcha stood untouched by the battering winds. In the whiteout, the black of his eyes and red of his lips were impossible to look away from. The stark white of his skin blended so that he was barely there. "He found two queens. I doubt that your predecessor expected that."

"There is only *one* Summer Queen." Donia's words were clear despite the shrieks of wind that came rushing from her lips.

"And you are very obviously not her," he murmured.

Her faeries were all around her, and the weight of winter spread out from the spot where she stood. Grave markers dotted a whitened ground. Ice shimmered over branches. The world was hers.

But Keenan is not.

Far Dorcha reached out, but instead of touching her, he caught a silver veil that she hadn't seen. "The gate has been locked against those on this side. Faerie is not open."

Donia gaped at him. "How did—"

He let the cloth in his hands slip free, and as soon as he wasn't touching it, it vanished. "No one closes a door I cannot open if I choose to do so."

"Who did that?" She pointed at the once-more-missing gate. "Why? Do they live?"

"They live." Ignoring the rest of her questions, Far Dorcha glanced around the cemetery. His gaze lingered on the deep snowfall, and the jagged spears of ice that had formed between him and her faeries. "I am pleased."

"Can you tell me *anything*?" she asked with the calm she felt now that the earth was cloaked in snow as it should be.

"There are rules." Far Dorcha tilted his face to the sky and let snow fall on his cheeks. "None that would stop me from speaking, but"—he looked at her with snow clinging to his skin—"I don't feel inclined to speak yet."

She raised her hand, and with the gesture, bars of ice encircled him. Outside them, spears of ice were aimed toward him. "Perhaps—"

"Go see other kings, Donia. I am not the one who will speak." Then he turned and walked through the barriers she'd built.

She saw the ice pierce him, watched red fall to the white ground like raindrops, but he did not pause.

CHAPTER 20

Seth heard the roar that heralded the Dark King's waking only a moment before he found himself lifted from the sofa where he'd slept and thrown across the debris-scattered library. Without faery speed and faery strength, Seth would be dead.

"You!" Niall strode across the room.

As Seth came to his feet, he held out both hands toward Niall. "I am not your enemy, Niall."

"You had *no* right. I am the Dark King, and you are . . . *nothing* to this court."

"I am your brother, Niall. You are coming apart. You needed sleep." Seth eased to the side, moving so that the expanse of the room was behind him. "Grief and exhaustion and the imbalance—"

"No." Niall lashed out. He didn't land the first punch, but his fist grazed Seth's jaw. "You set my Hounds against me, struck me, left the court without leadership."

"You're leaving the court without leadership. Look around you." Seth dodged another blow. "*I'm* trying to help you."

"Bullshit." Niall narrowed his gaze. "Fight back, Seth."

"I don't want to fight you; I want to help you." Seth stared at his friend. "You needed sleep. You needed your dreams."

"Do *not* speak of my dreams." Niall closed the distance between them and grabbed Seth by the throat. He didn't squeeze. *Much*. Niall was far more coherent than he had been when Seth arrived, but he was still filled with rage.

"I fought alongside you; I want Bananach dead. We are on the same side, Brother," Seth started. Speaking with Niall's grip on his throat hurt. "Niall—"

Niall gripped harder. "Irial is dead."

"And we can avenge him," Seth promised.

"She cannot be killed. Devlin said—"

"Things have changed." Seth reached up and grabbed Niall's wrist. He didn't try to force the Dark King to release him; instead, he squeezed Niall's wrist in affection. "Listen to me. Please?"

"Why?" Niall pulled his hand away, both releasing Seth's throat and refusing his comfort.

"Because I know what Devlin did not." Seth stepped backward. "I am certain of this: Bananach *can* die."

"Without killing Sorcha and the rest of us?" Niall shook his head. "Irial trusted me with the court. I won't fail them or him by risking their deaths on your belief."

Seth didn't point out that Niall *was* failing them already. "It's not just belief. I can see future threads."

The friendliness that had crept back into the Dark King's voice vanished. "For how long?"

"Since I became a faery."

The emotions that flickered over Niall's face were devastating to see, but Seth didn't look away. Shock faded under outrage. Then the hurt filled Niall's eyes as he said, "You could have saved Irial."

"No, I couldn't." Seth reached out, but Niall flinched away. "Niall . . ."

"You saw . . . you *knew* he would die, that Bananach would kill Tish and stab Irial." Flickers of shadows darted around the already trashed room as Niall's emotions shifted to anger. "You saw that she would *poison* Irial. You said nothing, but you *knew*."

"I did," Seth admitted. "I couldn't interfere. Irial's death led to the creation of the Shadow Court—which balances the High Court so that Faerie could be sealed."

"Faerie is closed?" Niall frowned. "Since when?"

"Three days ago." Seth shook his head. "Devlin and Ani and Rae—she's this—"

"I met her," Niall interrupted. "They visited in a dream and . . ." His words faded, and a pensive look came over his face.

"Niall?"

The Dark King blinked. He stepped back and withdrew a cigarette case and lighter from his pocket. Silently, he packed a cigarette, lit it, and exhaled. "So . . . *Seth* . . . Faerie is sealed? And you foresaw deaths you didn't reveal? You put your own wishes above my—*this* court?"

Seth nodded.

"Well, you are filled with surprises; aren't you, boy?" Niall smiled, a very peculiar expression given the circumstances.

"Only the one," Seth said.

The Dark King looked at him then, not as a grieving faery or as a friend, but as a calculating faery king. "Tell me, seer, do you see my future? Can you tell me what I will do next?"

"No, not entirely."

Shadowy abyss figures took shape on either side of Seth, and he hoped that he wasn't about to die. There was no one else on this side of the veil who could balance the Dark King, and if this was what he was like *with* a High Court presence near him, Seth couldn't fathom what the Dark King had been like in those couple of days between the gate being sealed and now.

I'm not sure how I am to balance him—or if I can.

"You withheld what you saw because it brought a chance to kill Bananach." The Dark King took a long drag of the cigarette.

Seth chose the words carefully: "I am sorry that you're mourning, but Irial made a choice. That choice set events into motion that protect Faerie. If Bananach had gone there, in time she would have killed Sorcha. If Sorcha came here . . . that would be dangerous."

The Dark King stared at him. "So Bananach's death is important enough to you that you hid the truth from all of us?"

"It is," Seth admitted.

The Dark King formed bars of shadows around Seth, imprisoning him in a cage that was solid to the touch despite the seemingly ethereal nature of its origins. He stepped closer. "Who all would you sacrifice? Your friends? Your lover? Yourself?"

"You and Ash are the *only* faeries I wouldn't sacrifice to protect Sorcha." Seth had a flicker of irritation that the three faeries he loved were so difficult, but even so, he suspected that their passions were part of why he *did* feel more for them than for anyone else. "In either world, no one means more to me than the three of you."

"So I am to believe you'd choose the Dark King over her royal tediousness?"

"No. Not the Dark King. *You*, Niall." Seth shook his head. "It's not about courts or regents. It's about the people— the *faeries* who matter to me. You matter."

"So much that you sentenced Irial to death." The Dark King wrapped one hand around the shadow-wrought bars of the cage. "Well, I feel so . . . cherished."

Seth didn't move away from the bars. "I did what I had to."

"Once, I might've killed you for what you've hidden. I fear that I've grown"—the Dark King exhaled a plume of disgusting cigarette smoke into Seth's face—"*merciful* over the last year."

Seth blinked, but after a childhood in dive bars and pubs, a bit of posturing wasn't particularly intimidating. *Maybe a little.* He had faced the two oldest faeries—and their son. He'd been nearly gutted by the last Winter Queen. He'd trained with the Hunt. *And Niall is my friend.* Seth stepped forward so that he was as close to the bars as he could be. "I am not afraid of you."

"Then you are a fool," the Dark King said. "In case you missed it when you came into my house, I have been a bit out of sorts . . . because of the actions you allowed to happen. Tell me why I shouldn't kill you right now."

At Seth's feet the shadows solidified into a floor; above him, a shadowed ceiling formed. "Because you need me," Seth said softly.

"Perhaps." The Dark King reached into the cage and slammed Seth's face into the bars. "The court that has possession of a seer would have an advantage, but don't think that means I need you uninjured." He shook his head, and for several moments, he simply stared at the cage.

"Niall?" Seth prompted.

Niall blinked, and in a blur he grabbed Seth's shirt and slammed him into the bars again. "You betrayed me, and Irial is dead because of it. . . . You took him from me, Seth. You *took* him." Niall's voice broke. Then he released Seth as suddenly as he'd grabbed him, and turned away.

After a few moments, the shadow-formed cage lifted and

floated behind Niall. In the foyer, thistle-fey and Hounds silently watched their king walk toward them with Seth imprisoned in a cage of shadows.

"I'm sure Irial had cells of some sort hidden away in the house. See that he is put into one until I prepare more fitting accommodations for him." Niall glanced at Seth then as he added, "*And* the Hound who helped him. Fetch her."

"Don't do something you'll regret," Seth urged. "You're angry and—"

"Shut up, Seth," Niall interrupted. He raised his voice. "This faery accepted brotherhood with us, and as such, he is mine to sentence for his transgressions."

As Niall spoke, faeries came into the room. Many of them were bloodied from their king's rage. One hopped forward, dragging a badly misshapen leg behind him.

The shadowed cell rose into the air, so they could all see Seth inside the cage. Then, Niall spoke: "Seth Morgan, for the crime of allowing the death of a king, I sentence you to imprisonment in the Dark Court until such time as I find myself appeased."

Softly, Seth reminded him, "Irial wasn't a king when he died."

Niall's eyes filled with black flames. "Silence!"

But Seth continued, "Irial sacrificed himself. He made that choice."

"No. *You* made a choice to hide what you knew, and in doing so injured what is mine. For your crimes, you will remain here at my disposal." Niall's expression fluctuated between pain and fury. "Your actions have weakened the Dark Court, and you will make amends."

"I would stay without being imprisoned," Seth offered. "I won't tell you things that aren't yours to know, but I will tell you what you need to avenge him. We want *the same thing*. She can die, Bro—"

The cage vanished, and Seth plummeted to the floor.

Niall grabbed Seth and jerked him to his feet. "Don't try me right now, Seth."

Then he threw Seth at the wall and walked away, saying as he went, "A cell. Preferably one of the least pleasant ones we have."

CHAPTER 21

It was mid-morning as Aislinn sat in the wide-open front room of the loft with a cup of tea. The Summer Girls and guards had become accustomed to her taking a few moments to herself at the start of her day.

The Summer King, however, had been away for almost six months, so he was unaware of her morning routine. She opened her mouth to tell him she wasn't ready to deal with anything just yet, and he leaned down and captured her lips in a searing kiss.

He caught her hands in his and pulled her to her feet. Their sunlight met and mingled in an electrifying current as he parted his lips and invited her in.

Instead, she pulled back and asked, "What are you doing?"

"Winning, I hope." Keenan turned his back on her, walked to the doorway, and grabbed Eliza.

As he pulled the Summer Girl into the room, more of

their court followed her. In a blink, the room was filled with smiling faeries.

Keenan waltzed the giggling Summer Girl across the room, and sent her spinning into another Summer Girl's arms. As the two danced away, he caught the hand of another Summer Girl and pulled her into an embrace and dipped her. The vines that slithered over her body were vibrant. Their leaves stretched toward the Summer King even as he stood and kissed the girl's cheek.

As Aislinn watched, he continued throughout the loft, dancing and smiling at the Summer Girls. The room was bright with sunlight that radiated from his skin. *And mine.* This was what the Summer Court was meant to be like. *Which is the point of this dance.* To his court, it looked like joyous frivolity, and to some degree, it was. Another, more serious part of this whole giggling chaos was that this was his job: summer was to be pleasurable.

Keenan caught her watching him, and the intensity of his gaze almost frightened her. If she'd been most anyone else, she would think having that sort of passion directed at her was thrilling. *It is, but I want it from Seth.* If Seth were truly gone, she could've found happiness with Keenan, but it wouldn't ever equal what she felt for Seth.

But the Summer Queen could do as the Summer King had done all of these centuries: she could put the rest of her worries aside and be their queen. She had been doing so the past several months on her own. She would continue to do so. Aislinn smiled and took the hands of the Summer Girl who had just gone spinning by. "Dance with me, Siobhan."

Siobhan smiled approvingly and called out, "Why is there no music?"

And from somewhere in the loft, music began to play. At first Aislinn thought it was the stereo, but then she realized that some of the guards were singing. As they walked into the room, several of them began drumming on the wall and on a table they upended. Overhead, the cockatiels joined in, and Aislinn laughed in sheer joy.

This is as it must be. My court must be happy.

When Siobhan spun her toward Keenan's outstretched hand, Aislinn smiled at him.

He pulled her with him up on top of the coffee table. "They've been fine under your watch. Despite your worries, you've kept them strong."

"I am their queen," she said.

He released her and stepped backward from the table onto the floor. For a moment, he paused and looked up at her. All around them, their court danced. Some of their furniture was breaking from faery exuberance, but music and laughter filled the room. Sunlight radiated from both the king and queen.

Then, he reached out and lifted her to the floor. When her feet touched the carpet, he released his grip on her— and she missed his touch. Without thinking, she stepped toward him.

"Being apart is unnatural, Aislinn. Tell me you don't feel it." He smiled at her, and she thought back to the first time he'd kissed her. Then, she was a mortal, and she didn't understand how anyone could refuse him. Then, she'd thought it was simply faery allure, and she didn't think it would stay so difficult when she became a faery. Now, she understood. *I wanted him then because I* am *the Summer Queen, not because he's a faery.* As long as they were sharing the court, this feeling wouldn't end when they were near each other. When he was gone, she was fine. She'd missed him as a friend, but that wasn't what he deserved.

"I don't love you the way you need to be loved," she said.

"I know." His smile was sad for a fleeting moment. "Summer isn't renowned for soul-searing love, Aislinn. *Passion* is the domain of Summer."

"We both feel that sort of love, though," she reminded him.

"Because you weren't always Summer, you are different." He gave her a sad smile.

"And you? Why are you different?" she asked.

He said nothing, but he pulled her back into his arms.

Aislinn swayed to the music. Summer Girls and guards danced slower, tangled together in embraces, and in some cases danced and kissed. She understood. The Summer Queen and King both felt the longing for what their faeries had: touch and passion.

He followed her gaze. "We could have that too. Pretend it was the night you asked me to seduce you, start from that moment again. I can make you happy."

At that simple statement, Aislinn's sunlight flared

brighter. She had no doubt that he could make her happy—maybe not for all of eternity, but there was little doubt that she could know passion in his arms. "In moments I shouldn't admit to you, not here, not ever perhaps, I've wondered what it would've been like."

"Say the word, my queen, and we can answer that question right now. We are Summer. Ours is the court of forget-your-name pleasures. I promise you that it will be good . . . and good for our court." Keenan's sunlight had brought her own light to the surface, and between them, the plants in the loft were growing visibly. Summer Girls laughed, and the room was filled with song. Keenan didn't look away from her, however. He stared directly into her eyes. "Let us answer your question, Aislinn. Be my Summer Queen. Take the pleasure that is your *right*."

Even though she was breathless with the things she wanted—*things Seth refuses me*—Aislinn had the sense to say, "Maybe some questions aren't meant to be answered."

Keenan leaned close enough that his words were whispers on her lips and asked, "Are you sure this is one of them?"

A rowan cleared his throat. "My Queen?" he said, and then added hurriedly, "and King?"

Aislinn stepped away from Keenan. "Yes?"

"The Winter Queen is here."

CHAPTER 22

Keenan stood in the study and watched Donia walk into the room with a mixture of joy and fear. Neither was evident in his expression, but the combination of the two made him momentarily speechless.

"Donia," Aislinn greeted the Winter Queen from the sofa where she sat.

The Winter Queen pursed her lips as she looked at the two of them. "If I had any other regent to visit, I would."

"Has something happened to Niall?" Keenan asked.

"Yes. Maybe. . . . I'm not sure." Donia folded her arms. "Gabriel visited me. He wasn't able to tell me anything overt, and my requests for an audience with Niall were denied. The guards turned me away at the door." A troubled look came over her face. "So I went to the gate to Faerie, but *that* was inaccessible as well. The gate to Faerie is *closed*. Now I am here."

With a self-confidence that befit her position, Aislinn

gestured at the sofa across from her. "Please, sit."

"The gate is closed?" Keenan echoed.

"I couldn't even *find* it." Donia looked directly at him as she added, "And Niall is locked away in his house."

Despite the worry writ plain on her face, Donia was regal as she walked over to the sofa. The Winter Queen sat opposite the Summer Queen. Whether it was intentional or not, the two queens had made it so that he had to sit next to the faery who shared his court or the faery who owned his heart. *What I want and what I can have in life are not ever the same.* Keenan took his position next to his queen. *Duty first.*

"Tavish has had reports that Irial was injured in the fight with Bananach," Aislinn said.

The surge of shock he felt wasn't masked quickly enough. Donia's gaze narrowed as she realized that he had been unaware of this news until that instant.

My queen has become used to ruling without me. He gave Donia a wry smile, but neither of them commented. *That's what I get for leaving.*

"I have reason to believe that Irial's injury is a fatal one," Donia added. "Perhaps Niall is mourning."

"Maybe . . . Seth went straight from the fight with Bananach to Faerie. He returned here yesterday, to see me." Aislinn tensed slightly, but did not look at Keenan as she added, "He had to leave suddenly, but he didn't mention anything about Irial's injury when he was here . . . or about Faerie being closed."

"And where is Seth *now?*" Donia prompted. "Did he return to Faerie?"

"He didn't say where he went, just that it was something he had to do immediately," Aislinn told them.

Keenan did look at Aislinn as he said, "When I left him, he said he was going to see Niall."

His queen scowled at him, but said nothing.

"And neither of you thought to tell the other one these details?" Donia asked incredulously. "What were you *doing?*"

"The day had just begun, and we were dancing," Aislinn said.

"Dancing?" Donia looked at the Summer Queen with the same disdain Keenan had once seen on her face when she looked at the Summer Girls. "Of *course* you were. Bananach is attacking faeries, stealing from our courts. Irial is injured. Faerie is closed. Yes, *dancing* is precisely what will help."

Before Keenan could speak, Aislinn said, "Your court is not ours. Snowy calm may be what *you* need, but summer is joyous. They require rejoicing to stay strong. Maybe you should try it."

"Not all of us have reasons to rejoice," Donia bit off.

Aislinn's skin sizzled. "Then maybe you ought to *find* one."

"Perhaps I should." Donia smiled a sad smile, and then took a deep breath. "When I went to the veil to enter Faerie, it was gone. While we searched, Far Dorcha approached me."

"I met him as well . . . after I left you." Aislinn walked to the counter and grabbed her cell phone.

Keenan looked from one queen to the other. "You *both* met the head of the death-fey?"

"It *had* to have been there yesterday. Faerie, I mean," Aislinn said absently as she dialed and raised the phone to her ear.

While she waited for Seth to answer, Keenan told Donia, "Seth stood beside me yesterday when Bananach attacked me."

"After he left here." Aislinn clutched the phone, but she spoke to them: "He came from Faerie to the loft, and then left here to . . . help Keenan."

The question in Donia's eyes wasn't one Keenan was sure he should answer. He had spent decades keeping secrets from her because of the search for the missing queen.

I don't want secrets between us anymore . . . but she is not a part of my court.

They sat silently, looking at each other while Aislinn texted Seth.

"I'll go see if Tavish has any new information." Aislinn glanced at the phone again, and then she looked from Keenan to Donia—and left.

Once the Summer Queen was gone, Donia stood and walked to the window. Her arms were folded tightly over her chest, and her gaze was fixedly not on him.

"Don?"

She glanced at him and then quickly looked back at the window. "Please, Keenan, not right now."

"Can I do anything?" He didn't move from his spot on the sofa. "Would you rather I left the room? Maybe you and Aislinn can talk and I could . . . wait somewhere?"

She turned to face him and smiled wanly. "I am worried for Niall. I am worried for *all* of us. I haven't lost many of mine to Bananach, but almost a dozen of my fey are missing. I suspect they are with her . . . or dead . . . or running away."

"Ours as well," Keenan said. "Tavish mentioned that a full score of ours have vanished. I have no idea what has happened in the Dark Court."

The Winter Queen relaxed a little, so that her hands were not clutching her arms so tightly. "He loves Niall, you know. Irial."

"He *hurt* Niall. I've seen Niall fall apart time after time when Irial was in town. It destroyed him. The scars on his back and chest . . ." Keenan remembered the first time he'd seen the webs of scars that covered much of Niall's torso. He'd been young, too foolish to know not to ask, but he'd regretted it the moment after he'd spoken the question. The look of pain on Niall's face was one he'd not forgotten nine centuries later.

"Irial has been living there. If he dies, Niall won't deal well. You *know* him." Donia shivered. "He doesn't forgive easily."

"I am well aware of that, Don," Keenan muttered.

Donia relaxed enough to sit on the arm of the chair farthest away from him. It wasn't unusual for her to be so

far away. They'd had more time of tentative distance than
trust, but the memory of holding her in his arms made the
renewed distance hurt like it had when she'd failed the test.

*I want to tell you I can change. I want to tell you we can run
away and abandon everything.* He watched her in silence for
several moments. Every promise he should be able to make
was forbidden to them. No gift, no word, nothing would
undo all of his failures. *I want to be the faery you saw when
you met me. I want you to see me that way again.* Even if they
couldn't be together as he had dreamed, he wanted her to
look at him like she had so many times, to see him instead
of the Summer King.

"I could talk to him, to Niall," Keenan blurted. "If you
think it would help, I can try."

She startled. "The last time you saw him, he knocked
you unconscious."

"That wasn't the *last* time." Keenan flushed. "He was
trained in the Dark Court. It's not like it was just anyone
who punched me."

"I wasn't judging. Merely reminding."

"Perhaps rejoicing a little that I was knocked down?" he
asked.

"No," she sighed. "Even when you infuriate me or break
my heart, I don't rejoice in your pain. Would you relish my
pain?"

"Never," he swore.

Aislinn came back into the room. She stayed in the
opposite doorway, placing herself at the far end of the room

from Donia. "Tavish has heard nothing about Faerie. He has our people looking into it, and he'd"—she gave them a small smile—"'very much appreciate it if the regents had the sense to stay here until such time as we have more data,' as he says."

"You don't need to stay that far away, Ash. I won't injure you just because he's back."

The Summer Queen grinned. "Nor I you, Donia."

The two queens smiled at each other, and Keenan couldn't help but think—*again*—that they'd both be happier if he was gone. Awkwardly, he looked from one to the other. "I need to talk to the rowan. Make sure that everyone is safe and accounted for." He stood and glanced at Donia. "If you leave before I'm back, I would ask that you summon your guard or take some of ours to see you home."

The Winter Queen smiled, not cruelly, but with an unpleasantly familiar reserve. "I am not your concern, Keenan."

"You will always be my concern, Donia." Keenan bowed to her before he could see her reaction to his words and walked away.

At the doorway, Aislinn squeezed his hand briefly, but said nothing.

CHAPTER 23

Seth stretched his legs out as much as he was able to within the confines of the cell into which he'd been cast. It wasn't as horrible as he'd expected, but the size was more fit for a small animal than a six-foot faery. The space was barren: no cot, no blanket. The cell was nothing more than a scarred and pitted floor and a dirty open grate in the back corner. Dark stains on the floor reminded Seth that he was lucky he'd only been bruised. *So far, at least.* The cell across from him had no visible floor. All Seth could see were broken metal spikes jutting up from somewhere beneath the empty cell. It made him extremely glad that he hadn't actually been given the worst cell in the dungeon—neither had Elaina.

"You okay, pup?" she called from somewhere off to his right. He couldn't see her, but he had heard no screams when she was brought down to the cells.

"Great. You?"

She snorted. "Been better."

He stood, crouching slightly as he did so. Neither sitting nor standing allowed him to be remotely comfortable. "Been worse?"

Elaina's low laugh carried through the distance. "A few times, yeah."

"That's something." He paced to the front of the small cell.

The Hound was quiet. "Is it true that you are the High Queen's heir now?"

"It is." Seth closed his eyes, imagining the fury that would have been unleashed in the mortal world if Devlin hadn't closed the gates to Faerie. *Faery regents in mourning really shouldn't be allowed loose.* He sighed. It wasn't his mother who was running amok this time, though. Instead, it was the grieving, infuriated, sleep-deprived, volatile, no-longer-balanced Dark King.

Seth weighed the benefits of telling Niall that the closing of Faerie had unbalanced him. He had seen the madness lurking in Niall's eyes; he had watched dark fey cringe as they approached their king with battered bodies. Now that the Shadow Court balanced the High Court, Niall was left untethered. *Unless I can figure out a way to help him.* Unlike with Sorcha's recent spate of instability, Seth couldn't see a solution to Niall's.

"You still there?" Elaina called.

"I am." Seth squatted in front of the door, examining the bars that kept him caged. They were woven of something no other faery could weaken. If it had been sunlight, Donia could negate it; if it were ice, Aislinn or Keenan could remove it. If Seth were in Faerie, Sorcha could undo it with a thought. He was in the mortal world, though, and trapped by bands of darkness that were the material of a regent without an opposing court in this world.

And Faerie is sealed.

The same fact that comforted Seth also removed hope of any rescue.

This is on me to sort out.

There was only one faery of the High Court in the mortal world, and the High Queen had only one heir. Of course, that didn't provide any grand insight on how one became the balance to a grief-mad, tether-free king.

Maybe there is a strong solitary who can balance him.

Once they got past the grief of losing Irial, Niall and the other regents could talk about it. Seth might not know who could balance the Dark King, but assuming Niall released him, Seth would try to find that answer—even if it meant going to Keenan for help.

For now, Seth tried to sift through the ever-changing threads of possible futures, hoping for some clue that would help him reach Niall. Not all of those threads revealed things Seth wanted to see; some made his chest constrict in fear; and none of them offered any more clarity into the immediate future.

He wasn't sure how many hours had passed as he sorted through future possibilities, but eventually a thistle-faery approached the cell.

"Come." The faery opened the door to the cell and grabbed Seth's arm. The thistles that covered her skin pierced him.

"You don't need to hold on to me: I'm not going to run," Seth said. "You have my word. I will walk beside or in front of or behind you to where your king wants you to take me."

The faery reached out with her other thistle-covered hand and grabbed his shoulder. "I follow my king's *precise* orders."

"Right," Seth said.

As he was escorted from the cell and through the hall, Seth tried to ignore the stinging of the thistles. Body piercing was perfectly fine—and sometimes pleasurable—but the sensation of dozens of tiny cuts was far from appealing. Later, if there was a *later*, he and Niall would have work to do in order for their friendship to stand a chance of recovering from the injuries they'd both inflicted.

Before Seth had become a faery, he hadn't truly understood the weight of the decisions the fey made. Now, he was facing the possibility of an eternity of seeing the threads of those around him. Interfering with the future could change the future. *At what point is that my right? At what point is it wrong to act? To not-act?* He didn't know if he'd have been able to make the same decisions if the faery who had fallen to Bananach's poison that day had been someone else. If it had been Niall, could Seth have let him die to save Faerie? *What if it had been Aislinn?* Those were choices he was glad he hadn't had to make.

"Up." The thistle-faery released Seth's arm, but immediately pressed the flat of her hand to his back and shoved him forward.

She took every opportunity to inflict stinging pain on Seth as she conducted him from Niall's house, through the streets, and into the warehouse where the Dark King currently held his court.

The same Dark Court faeries who'd trained him to fight now watched Seth as he was shoved into what looked like an enormous metal birdcage. It was tall enough that he could stand and wide enough to walk several paces. Many faeries in the court could reach through the bars to injure him if they so desired, but it provided just enough room for him to try to dodge them. *Got to make it sporting.* In the moment, Seth clearly saw the side of the Dark Court that Niall had once said he wanted to keep hidden from Seth. *And here I am.*

Niall sat on his throne, silently watching as the cage—with Seth in it—was raised to the ceiling. He remained still and silent until the denizens of the Dark Court began to shift nervously. All the while he stared at Seth.

Seth sat in the middle of the cage and stared back at the Dark King.

As if he were a bird, he'd been provided with a bowl of water, a bowl of dry cereal, and a pile of newspapers in the corner. The only concession to civility was the bucket beside the newspapers. Seth couldn't decide if the cleaner but very public cage was better or worse than the too-small cell. All he did know was that both were preferable to the cell with the metal spikes in place of a floor.

When their king finally looked away from Seth, he seemed surprised by his faeries' presence. He frowned and said, "Depart. All of you."

Niall watched as all too eagerly they fled. His rage and grief had made him capable of cruelty they hadn't expected. What he hoped to do now was a step beyond grief. He was willing to bargain for things that he shouldn't, but he felt as if his mind was only barely in order. Even before Irial died, Niall had stopped feeling anywhere near sane. He'd heard of humans "snapping," and that was as close to an explanation as he could get. In one sudden moment, he'd felt like the parts of himself that weren't already grieving, worrying, or raging were all swept away. Something inside of him tore.

If I had been clearheaded, could I have found a way to save Irial?

The Dark King shook his head. He wasn't clearheaded. Great chunks of time had vanished, and he had no idea what had happened in them. Yesterday, he came to himself with Seth caged, and he wasn't sure how long they had conversed or what had been said.

"What are you going to do?" Seth asked.

"You see the future. You *know* what I'm about to do." Niall glanced at the warehouse door. "Will it work?"

"Niall—"

"*Tell me.* He'll be here any minute. How do I make him

give me what I want?" Niall's abyss-guardians flashed into their semisolid state and patted his arms consolingly.

Mutely, Seth shook his head.

And then the Dark Man walked into the warehouse.

Death had entered the Dark Court's center, and Niall bowed low to him as if a supplicant before a deity. "I ask a boon."

"No."

"You haven't even heard what I seek." Niall's voice was barely more than a snarl, but it wasn't offensive.

Yet.

Far Dorcha sighed. "You seek what they all seek when grief becomes madness."

Undeterred, Niall offered, "I would trade my life for Irial's. Another's life. Anyone."

"Listen to yourself," Seth hissed. "This is *not* how you make a faery bargain, Brother."

Neither of the faeries present looked at Seth.

Far Dorcha prompted, *"Anyone?"*

"Anyone." Niall leaned forward in his throne. "There are those I'd gladly give you, but there are others I would mourn. . . . Tell me which faeries you would accept. We can make an exchange."

Far Dorcha waved his hand, and a table and chairs of carved bone formed. One of the chairs slid out as the Dark Man approached it. The bone legs scraped across the cement floor.

"What about the girl? Leslie."

"Leslie's not of your domain. She's *mortal*," Niall protested. "You cannot . . . *no*."

"Irial lent her his strength, let her leach bits of his immortality, bound her to the Dark Court with tears and blood. His essence is in her flesh." Far Dorcha sat in the chair at the head of his bone-made table. He rested his elbows on the table and clasped his hands together in front of him. "These things are so, yet you say she is not mine? If I ask for her, would you bargain?"

Niall came to stand beside the other chair. It slid out for him, but he did not touch it.

"If I said I would trade her still-briefer-than-fey life for his, what would you say?" Far Dorcha watched Niall with cavernous eyes. "Would you sacrifice one love for another?"

"No, but you can have *my* life," Niall proposed. "I would offer myself at the table."

Far Dorcha stood, but his hand remained on the chair. "Are you sure? She *has* some of his immortality."

"Not Leslie . . ." Niall's words faded as the table vanished.

"Then we are done," Far Dorcha said. "She would've done it if you asked, and the only trade I will take is one who is willing and one you will mourn."

"There are numerous faeries in my court who would—"

"Not by choice." Far Dorcha's gaze darted to Seth, acknowledging him for the first time. "Would you offer him? Sorcha's child."

Niall scoffed. "He wouldn't offer himself willingly."

"And if he would? Would you mourn him?"

"You're trying to distract me." Niall's mind grew clouded. "Tell me how to get Irial back. The court needs him."

"No," Far Dorcha said.

In the next heartbeat, Niall stood looking down at his own hand—and the knife in it. Between the words he'd heard and the moment he was now in, he'd shoved his knife hilt-deep into Far Dorcha's stomach. He didn't realize that he'd even moved. The memory of doing so was absent, but the knife and the hand were his own.

"I wish you wouldn't do that. It has never helped." Far Dorcha reached down and covered Niall's hand with his own. He squeezed so that he held Niall's hand to the hilt and then tugged both the hand and the knife away from his body.

"What . . ." Niall looked at the knife in his hand; he let go, and it fell to the floor with a clatter.

"You ruined a perfectly fine shirt." Far Dorcha motioned with his fingers in a come-here gesture. "Give over."

"Give what over?" Niall blinked and realized he was now squeezing Far Dorcha's throat. He looked at his hand and then back at Far Dorcha. Carefully, he released his grasp. "What . . . what happened?"

"Give me your shirt." Far Dorcha peeled off his ripped shirt. "You ruined this one."

Niall shook his head. "You're a madman."

Far Dorcha snorted. "You stabbed *Death,* child, so I wouldn't be throwing around any slurs just now." He tossed his shirt at Niall, who caught it reflexively. "It's cold."

Niall shucked off his coat. Then, he yanked his shirt over his head and threw it onto the ground at Far Dorcha's feet. "Fine."

Far Dorcha looked down at the shirt and then back up at Niall. "Are you trying to piss me off?"

"I'm the Dark King." Niall's voice was steady. Despite the oddity of the time gaps, he was not going to show his fear.

Especially because of it.

"And?"

"And I'm asking you to help me."

"The dead queen"—Far Dorcha frowned—"the last dead one. Beira. She asked too."

Seth started, "Niall—"

"No!" Far Dorcha interrupted. "*You* will stay silent unless you want to cross me. I've met your beloved. I doubt you'd like me to visit *her* house or your mother's." Then he told Niall, "The dead Winter Queen asked for un-dying. She wanted me to return the Summer King she'd killed. I tell you what I told her: I cannot."

"There has to be a way," Niall pleaded. "I feel a . . . madness threatening. My mind . . . Please?"

Far Dorcha lifted Niall's shirt from the ground and shook it. "There are rules, even for fey. The dead king is not within my reach."

The Dark King grabbed Far Dorcha's throat. "You're Death. You can . . . help."

"I will not." Far Dorcha shoved the Dark King. "Accosting me again would be unwise. You know the rules. The dead cannot reveal themselves to the living, and the living cannot compel the dead—including death-fey—to obey them."

Then, the Dark Man narrowed his gaze. "And no matter what foolish games you play here, you cannot break the rules unless you want the one you protect to die. You got into this situation; you will have to deal with it."

"What?" Niall blinked. "What situation?"

Instead of answering, Far Dorcha pulled on Niall's shirt and smoothed a hand over the fabric. "Very nice."

Then he turned and sauntered away.

CHAPTER 24

Donia stepped into the street outside the Summer regents' building and paused. *I can do this. I can lead my court,* and *I can be an ally to Keenan's court.* The alternatives all seemed to lead to violence. *We can work together.* The world they knew was unstable, but they were not their predecessors. Going into the Summer Court and not reacting with anger proved that. *That doesn't mean I will stay there a moment longer than I must.* Standing in the home he shared with Aislinn and trying not to think about them together was more than she was ready to handle. She didn't wait for guards to arrive, but Sasha had already appeared and now loped alongside Donia. Most of the time, the wolf didn't follow anyone's whim but his own, and if he thought she should be accompanied, she would be.

As Donia walked, she thought about the past, the moments she and Keenan were at odds, and the times they were close. He'd never wanted to hurt her, had never wanted to hurt any of the girls who'd tried to love him. Instead, he'd assigned guards, and of course, given Sasha to the first Winter Girl. Once, a long time ago, Donia had thought the unnaturally large wolf was a part of the Summer Court. He'd been there when she lifted the Winter Queen's staff, had helped her when she stumbled that first day.

"Even now, I want to protect him," she told Sasha. "It's never going to change, is it? I wish I could stop loving him, but . . . you should've seen him. He hates Irial—for good reason—and has had conflict with Niall, but if I asked him to go to the Dark Court, he would. He's *good*, even if he's not good for me."

The wolf paused and stared at her. He didn't, of course, answer, but she was certain that he understood her. Sasha wasn't an ordinary wolf. *Wolves don't live for centuries.* What he was, she didn't know. Keenan hadn't known either: a "creature of Faerie" was all he'd said.

Sasha nudged her with his massive head, and Donia resumed walking.

She trailed a thin line of frost in her wake. It wasn't enough to destroy all of the new buds that were starting to force themselves through the earth, but she wasn't trying to destroy them. A flux between seasons was natural and right. It wasn't yet time for true spring. *Soon.* This year, when spring came, she thought she might retreat to the far north. *If I survive the coming fight.*

After walking several blocks, Donia realized she was being watched. On the roofs nearby, crows lined up. One after the next, they came.

"You could go," she told Sasha. "Run."

The wolf glared at her and then continued to pad silently at her side.

The crows did nothing, but more and more of them swooped in and settled on every visible ledge. Mortals started pointing at the birds. *Just what we need.* Bananach was flaunting the rules. She was stronger than she'd ever been in Donia's life, and in her strength, she was brazen.

With a rush of wings, the embodiment of discord and violence dropped to the ground in the middle of the street. Cars honked, and drivers yelled. Bananach didn't deign to look at them. Her attention was fixed on Donia.

Her feathered wings were fully visible—even to mortals, whose hurled insults made clear that they thought she was "some freak." She was smiling, a terrible expression of contentment that unnerved Donia. The raven-faery had her hair bound into a long braid that she'd looped up on the back of her head. Some of her black feathers jutted out at odd angles.

"Snow! How lovely to see you," Bananach called out as if she were speaking to a friend she'd encountered by accident.

"I can't say the same." Donia rested a hand on Sasha's back, as much to steady herself as for the comfort of touching the wolf.

Bananach narrowed her eyes. "Well, *that's* not very sociable."

A car careened to the side, darting into oncoming traffic

to avoid hitting the raven-faery. She glared at the mortal driver, and then smiled as a bevy of crows dived down from the awning of a nearby building and effectively blinded him with their number. The car slammed into another— parked—car, and alarms sounded.

"I've come to discuss the future." Bananach swiveled her head back to stare at Donia. "You want a future, don't you, Snow?"

"I do, and I *have* a future." Donia felt the approach of her guards. The tendrils that tied her to her court tightened inside of her. They were here, and she was alternately relieved and terrified. Bananach was behaving so far outside the normal faery-mortal interactions that Donia didn't know what to expect of her.

"I need you to declare war," Bananach urged. "Pick a court. We will decimate them."

"No."

"Do not test me." Bananach shook her head. "I've no time for this. Not now. Tell me: do we strike the Dark? Eliminate the Sunlight? Both?"

Donia shook her head. "I have no quarrel with them. I've made peace with Summer."

The caw that came from the raven-faery's mouth was a hideous sound, more so as it echoed through the street from scores of crows' beaks. "No. You will not ruin my plans. You are strong, and you can bring me the war I seek." Bananach nodded. "Then, the Darkness. We can start with that."

"No. Winter stands as ally to the Dark Court. I've made

that clear to the king's Gabriel and, previously, to the present and former kings." Donia let her ice extend into a long sword. She'd not spent nearly enough years training to fight, but she wasn't going to stand idly by while Bananach killed her. "We shall have peace between the courts."

"Do you know what would enrage the Summer King? *I* know," Bananach singsonged.

Winter Court faeries—invisible to mortal eyes—came up behind their queen.

Scrimshaw Sisters drifted to stand on either side of Donia, and the lupine prowled the street. As minutes passed, the traffic decreased. Mortals mightn't see the fey other than Bananach, but they felt the tension in the air. They detoured away from the street, away from War and her violence, farther from the spot where destruction gathered like the storm clouds in the sky.

"I will allow your court the choice to be *with* me or under my foot." Bananach tilted her head and stared at Donia. "What will you choose for your faeries? Shall I kill them, or will they serve me? Give them into my keeping, and I will spare you."

"They are *mine*." Donia exhaled the words with a scream of wind. "My court will not serve you."

The crows all took to the air as one, and as they did so, Evan stepped in front of Donia.

"So be it," Bananach said.

Donia couldn't properly defeat War, but she could slow her. Donia did what she'd not thought she could do when she'd first faced the raven-faery: she stood against her with every intention of fighting. She exhaled all of winter that she could summon in that instant; ice covered the street, clung to the cars and storefronts. It was the perfect environment for her fey, but War hadn't ever waited quietly when the climate was cruel: Bananach merely smiled.

Donia began, "Ev—"

"Go." Evan didn't glance her way. As he advanced on Bananach, the sky turned black with the crush of crows descending.

And, in the midst of the feathered darkness, an unknown faery arrived and stood staring at them with cavernous eyes. Her body was partially wrapped in a torn gray winding sheet that trailed behind her like the train of a gown. Vivid spots of red stood out on the cloth, like scarlet poppies in a field of ashes.

The faery made no gesture toward them, no act of aggression, so the Winter Queen forced her attention to stay focused on the more obvious problems rather than the potential ones. Mortals were under attack; her faeries were in danger; and she herself was far from safe.

"Tend the mortals," Donia called to her fey, but before her guards could do so, the remaining mortals began to shift anxiously and leave on their own.

Fear comes tearing toward us.

Donia looked up as the Hunt arrived. They were invisible to mortal eyes, but the presence of the Hunt unsettled even the most obtuse mortals. Gabriel's steed was in the center of what, to their limited sight, appeared to be a sudden storm.

None of steeds were in car form. Instead, they looked like a deadly menagerie: an oversized lion snarled next to a lizardlike beast; something that resembled a dragon paced next to a chimera; and scattered among them all were skeletal horses and emaciated red dogs. Atop the steeds were battle-ready Hounds.

"If we might offer aid to Winter?" Gabriel growled. His steed was a giant black horse with a reptilian head. It opened its maw in a snarl that revealed pit-viper fangs.

"Your aid is quite welcome," Donia told the Hound.

Bananach raised an arm, so that she was pointing at the sky. As she lowered her arm, faeries who allied with War swarmed from the alleys and side streets.

Cath Paluc stepped forward into the fracas. The great feline faery tore through the Hounds and their steeds. The Winter Guard and the Hunt fought together against Bananach's faeries as one force, and Donia was grateful for the sudden allies.

What she wasn't grateful for was the appearance of Far Dorcha. At the edge of the fight, he waited on a macabre throne of his own making; the seat of his throne looked like nothing more than the spine and rib cage of some creature she couldn't identify. Far Dorcha himself sat within the splayed-open ribs as if he'd been swallowed by some great skeletal beast.

The faery in her winding-cloth dress walked toward

him, and for a moment Death smiled at her. The fleeting expression was the first proof of any emotion that Donia had seen. In a blink it was over, and he raised his gaze to stare at Donia. He nodded, and then looked over his shoulder to the unfamiliar faery, who now stood with her hand on the edge of his bone-wrought throne. Then, together, Death and his companion watched her faeries fall.

The Winter Queen turned her back to them and pushed farther into the fighting, bloodying her ice-made sword because it was either that or be bloodied.

Senseless death.

War was not to fight in this way. She was to incite discord, but she was not to simply attack regents or their faeries.

"I come to you not in full numbers, but in warning." Bananach's tone was conversational, despite the growing chaos in the street. "If you do not give me my declaration of war, you will die, Snow."

"You cannot simply go around killing our kind. There was no declaration of war, nor will there be." Donia said the words as much as a question to Bananach as a statement of Donia's hopes.

Bananach's faeries continued to flood the street, and the Hounds and Winter Guard continued to engage them in battle. Unlike the scuffle at Donia's garden, this was a fight with intent to kill. *My faeries.* Donia raised her sword as a faery launched himself at her. While she was defending herself, Bananach strode through the fight toward her.

Despite the nature of the faery who approached, Evan

and several others of her guard stayed in front of Donia. As she watched, the raven-faery lifted a hand, and Donia saw the inevitable about to happen. The movement was too fast for Evan to react.

"One by one"—Bananach sliced her hand across Evan's throat, dragging her talon-tipped fingers over his neck— "they will fall."

Despite the distance between them, Donia heard the words as clearly as if they were face-to-face. They weren't. They were far enough apart that Donia couldn't reach Evan before he dropped to the ground. In the space between one heartbeat and the next, he had been taken from her. There was no pause: he was simply made dead.

And Donia felt it. He was *hers*, and as his queen, she felt their connection vanish as his life was extinguished.

The desire to gather the slain rowan to her vied with barely bound rage. Rage won. She knocked several faeries aside as she pursued Bananach, but before she could reach the murderous faery, Donia was caught around the waist and dragged onto a steed.

She shoved her elbow backward to no avail. "Let me go!"

"No," the Hound holding her said. "The Gabriel pursues her. If anyone can catch her, it's him."

Donia glanced at Gabriel's mate, Chela. "You have no right—"

"Gabriel ordered you kept safe," Chela snarled back. "*He* rules the Hunt."

Beyond them, Far Dorcha stood and held out a hand to

the shade of Evan. Other shades walked with Donia's fallen guardsman. Their forms were almost as visible as when they were still alive. Far Dorcha looked past the dead to lock gazes with Donia.

"We could go with Gabriel," Donia suggested to Chela.

"I'd like to, but no. He's bright enough not to give me many orders, but when he does, I am still bound to obey. In battle, he is my Gabriel first, my lover second." Chela scowled a little. "If it weren't mutiny, I'd follow, but as his second, I stay here and mind our pack."

The faery who had stood with Far Dorcha now strode through the combined Winter Court and Dark Court forces that fought Bananach's faeries. Far Dorcha did not follow her, but he watched her with a studious gaze. She stopped at Evan's bleeding body.

Chela's arm tightened around Donia's waist, forcing the Winter Queen to stay on the steed.

"You must not let her touch you," Chela implored in a low voice. "Death-fey are not to be trifled with, Winter Queen." The Hound raised her voice: "Ankou."

Ankou glanced at Chela, but her attention quickly shifted to the fallen rowan. "I will take this."

"No." Donia exhaled a plume of frost with the words. She could not reach the faery to strike her, but she wasn't limited to what she could reach. The wintery air she exhaled encased Evan in a thick, icy shell.

Ankou frowned. "He is dead."

"And?" Donia tensed.

The faery shrugged. "What is dead in battle is mine to

take. The body will be trampled here. The fallen dead are mine."

"No," Donia corrected. "*He* is still mine."

"The rest?"

"Please, do not challenge her," Chela urged Donia. "There are fights you cannot win. Do not make this one of them."

"You are not welcome in Huntsdale. I know what you *both*"—Donia lifted her gaze to Far Dorcha—"are, but I will not allow you to take him. You do not *need* to. I will give him burial."

Ankou frowned. Her paper-thin skin seemed likely to tear at the slightest wrong movement. "I collect the battle-slain. It is why I come here. More will fall. He"— she gestured behind her—"will take the other part when they are not-living."

At Ankou's vague hand wave toward him, Far Dorcha crossed the street. "Sister, she wants to keep this one."

"And she will treasure the body?" Ankou asked.

"Yes. I do treasure him." Donia's voice wavered, but she did not hide her grief, not here, not from Death.

Ankou nodded and stepped past the Dark Man as a cart rolled up. To any watching mortal, it would appear to be a white paneled van. Ankou opened the back doors and began filling it with the bodies of the fallen.

Far Dorcha turned his back on the corpse collector's work. Around him, the shades of the dead waited—including Evan.

Her slain friend looked up at Donia. He touched two

fingers to his lips and then lowered them as if directing a kiss toward her.

"He does not regret his choice," Far Dorcha said softly. "He would rather you do not either."

Donia watched her friend, guard, and advisor stride away and vanish. Once Evan was gone from her sight, she angled her body toward Far Dorcha and said, "She killed him for no reason."

Behind Donia, Chela tensed, but the Hound remained silent this time.

"She cannot keep killing our own," Donia announced.

"While I am here in your village, she can be ended more easily." Far Dorcha looked only at Donia. "If Disorder ends, one will need to take her place. She . . . cannot be negated."

"What does . . ." Donia started, but her words dried up as the Dark Man sauntered away.

He did not pause beside Ankou or at the throne—which vanished after he passed it.

"What the hell does that even mean?" Chela muttered.

Silently, the Winter Queen shook her head. Killing Bananach was necessary, but there were consequences she didn't understand. The alternative, however, seemed to be that the raven-faery would kill them all.

CHAPTER 25

Gabriel alone pursued Bananach. His pack fell away, unable to keep up with him. On some level he knew that he should fall back, wait for them to catch up. Once, he would've gone to his king for orders; once, he would've lost himself in comforts that were the domain of the Dark Court or taken solace with his family. Now, his king was unwell; his last king was dead. The Dark Court was a mess, and two of his children were locked away in Faerie—and a third was dead.

All because of Bananach.

The Hunt served vengeance. It was who they were. They would pursue, and they would mete out justice. He *was* the Hunt.

She has earned my *justice.*

Something outside logic compelled him.

I can't kill her. Irial, Niall, and Devlin had explained that. *Bananach killed my king. Killed my daughter. Killed Evan.* If they didn't stop her, she would keep killing. *Till none of* us *are left alive.*

She was just out of reach, ahead of him, but not so far that he lost sight of her completely.

It's a trap.

Gabriel knew better than to stand against her when she was this strong. He had held his own, but only barely, when they'd fought. In his children's home only a few days ago, he'd felt Bananach's talons dig into his skin.

And watched her kill Irial.

The black feathers were in front of him, a blur as she turned another corner. Her mutinous faeries were gone. He dismounted and followed on foot. It was just the two of them now. As he entered the litter-strewn parking lot, he knew that he was making a mistake.

No help on either side.

Gabriel slid off his steed.

"Your child did not shriek overmuch when I gutted her," Bananach said. "For a mortal, it was strange."

The words were worse than a fist to Gabriel.

"Tish wasn't mortal," he forced out.

"No matter." Bananach circled him, and as she did so, Gabriel turned so he could keep her in his line of sight.

"I would rather not kill you," she added. "You fight well."

"I *want* to kill you," Gabriel assured her.

As Bananach laughed, her avian features repulsed him. Laughter from the raven's beak seemed worse than when it was through her lips. She narrowed her gaze. "I *want* to kill you, too, but you could serve my purposes alive."

"I serve the Dark King," Gabriel growled.

"And if I were queen?"

"You won't be." He swung, relished the feel of his fist connecting with her face.

She retaliated. Her answering punch fractured ribs, caused him to muffle a gasp as the broken bones pierced something inside him.

"Where are your minions?" he asked.

"Elsewhere." She dodged his next punch.

Fear filled him at the thought of the raven-faery's troops going to the Dark King's home while the Hunt was out.

Go back to the house, he told the Hunt. *Protect the Dark King.*

He'd never found her easy to fight, but never had her punches and kicks caused him to stagger as they did now. He'd understood that she was growing increasingly power-ful, but as she struck him now, he realized that War had become even stronger than she had been when she'd stabbed Irial mere days ago.

I'm sorry, Che. He sent his message through the Hunt. Privacy wasn't a big concern among them. *Protect the Winter Queen. Protect Niall.*

Then, he focused all of his attention on the fight he was not winning. He deflected as many blows as connected, but Bananach's punches were fierce. More bones shattered inside his body.

His own strikes against her were less sure, in part because he still carried bruises from their last encounter, while she seemed untouched by that fight.

He thought they might reach an impasse as they had so many times before—but then Bananach's talons drove into his chest and ravaged the flesh there. The wet of the injury soaked his shirt. In some distant part of his mind, it occurred to him that this was the sort of injury that could result in *bad* things.

He stumbled backward.

"The Hunt must be led by a strong Hound," Bananach crooned.

"*I* lead." He forced the words out without allowing a growl of pain to escape as well.

Bananach gouged his stomach, tore it open so that he instinctively covered the wound with one hand. "You did lead, Gabriel-no-more."

"Che . . . next . . ."

"Fine," Bananach said. "I'll kill her next."

"Not what . . ." Gabriel shook his head to clear away the darkness that threatened. "Not mean . . . *that*. Chela leads Hunt if I fall."

Bananach watched as he dropped to his knees. He didn't collapse completely to the ground. With one hand, he drew a knife from his boot. The other hand covered his bleeding stomach.

He slashed the knife toward her, but she stayed out of reach.

"You used to be a worthy opponent." She turned her back and walked away, leaving him on the ground, not bothering to give him the dignity of a killing blow. Instead, she turned her back as if he were already dead.

Still on his knees, Gabriel moved toward her, pursuing her as best he could. She didn't pause.

Hate doing this.

Gabriel let himself slip into that other form, becoming an animal as he so rarely did, sacrificing the part of himself that thought. His body shifted into something that resembled the monstrous offspring of a saber-toothed tiger and an oversized dire wolf. As he did so, he could no longer remember who the bird was, why she mattered, but as he moved he felt his wounds and knew she had made them.

The Gabriel launched himself at her, tasted feather-hair-flesh in his mouth. His claws sank into her shoulder and shredded one of her wings.

The raven-faery screamed.

And the Gabriel pushed her body to the ground. She rolled so that she could strike at him with both beak and talons.

With one paw, he slammed her face to the side, but the necks of bird-things didn't snap easily that way.

She slashed blindly at his throat with her talons and at the same time drove her other hand into his chest.

The Hound's eyes closed as he roared, and they did not open again.

CHAPTER 26

On the other side of Huntsdale, the Dark King looked up as Keenan walked into the warehouse. The Dark King appeared haggard and, for some reason, was wearing only a pair of tattered jeans. His shirt and boots were missing. Cuts and bruises covered his body. Despite his state of dishevelment, he sat quietly smoking a cigarette and staring up at a metal cage.

"I expected the other one," he said.

Keenan tried not to glance at the cage above the Dark King. "The other one?"

"The queen . . . no matter." Niall waved his hand dismissively. "I assume you're here about my pet."

"Your . . . *pet?*"

The Dark King pointed at the cage. "He's a troublesome thing, but you can't have him. He *owes* me, and I'm not going to dismiss his debt."

"I see. Who's in the cage?" Keenan couldn't see inside it.

This *was* the Dark Court, and neither prisoners nor cages were unheard of within their court.

Niall scowled. "I didn't expect it, but some animals are unpredictable."

"Who's in the cage, Niall?" Keenan repeated.

"Seth."

"You know you can't keep him there. I don't like him, but"—Keenan shrugged—"I do not rule my court alone. My queen will not accept this."

For several moments, Niall remained near motionless. If not for the regular inhalation and exhalation of his disgusting cigarette smoke, he would have seemed immobile. Then, Niall nodded. "I have a proposition. I'd thought to make it to her since I didn't figure you'd come here."

"Oh."

"My pet sees things. Did you know that?" Niall stood abruptly and walked over to a lever on the floor. The broken glass that clung to the dried blood on his feet was pushed farther into his skin with each step, but he didn't seem to notice.

"Your feet—"

"Did you know?" Niall roared.

"I did," Keenan admitted.

"So he's betrayed me there as well." Niall's expression grew dark, and he stayed silent for a moment.

"What has he told you?" Niall shoved the lever, and the cage plummeted to the floor. Once it slammed to the ground, he stepped up to it and stood with his hands gripping the bars of Seth's cage.

"Nothing about your court," Keenan said.

Niall glanced over his shoulder at Keenan and asked, "You'd keep him as *your* court pet now, wouldn't you? You'd look the other way far easier now that he is an asset. You'd let him bed your queen in exchange for the power he'd offer you."

"She makes her own choices as to her bedmates."

"Aaaah, your naïveté has always been amusing," the Dark King said.

Keenan exchanged a furtive glance with Seth, who now had a band of shadows covering his mouth, keeping him silent.

Niall turned his back to Keenan and walked toward his throne. "Tell your queen that she may still visit him. I'm afraid he can't speak to anyone but me, but I will let them enjoy each other in private . . . for a cost."

"Which is?"

"Your faeries will do as I request in a scuffle I expect to come sooner rather than later. I will have Bananach stopped." Niall looked at Seth, who was gesturing at them both now. "What's that you say? You think it's a brilliant plan? Sacrifice *their* faeries to do my work?"

Seth shook his head. His fingers were flashing wildly as if to convey words. Niall sighed, and black ribbons wrapped around Seth's wrists.

"You care for him," Keenan said. "He has been your friend. You *struck* me for him, offered your court's protection.

He is yours to protect."

"Sometimes such emotion is a weakness." Niall spread his hands wide. "Sometimes it's a useful tool. Look at us. We can take your worry for your queen, her worry for my pet, and we can find a way to work on my problem."

"This isn't like you. Listen to yourself, Niall."

"Sometimes a king has to do unpleasant things, kingling. Surely you understand that."

Kingling?

Keenan stepped forward. "You were my friend. For centuries you were family to me. Tell me what's going on."

Niall's lips curled in a wry smile. "I seem to be missing some *stability*."

"I am sorry you are hurting. I hadn't ever thought that . . . you would be so . . ." Keenan wasn't sure of a polite word. *Callous? Cruel? Broken?*

Niall sat silently for several moments. Finally, he stood and stepped around Keenan. "Go tell your queen my plan. I'll not injure my pet, and she can have her visits, but he belongs to my court now. Her ability to see him is at my discretion, and my discretion requires her court's support in a task. I want Bananach stopped."

A task? Fighting War was not "a task." It was a conflict that would echo through the mortal realm.

"We want her stopped too, but this is not the way. We can talk about this, approach it rationally. You, me, Donia . . . The Summer Court isn't as strong as Winter, but I have allies." Keenan pleaded. "We all want the same thing here.

None of us has declared war. She needs a declaration to start the kind of violence she seeks. There are rules that will prevent her from going any further if we all stand together."

The look Niall leveled at him was uncannily like his predecessor. "I sincerely doubt that."

"You're grieving, but you can't think—"

"Kingling," Niall interrupted. "Do you truly think questioning me is wise? Surely, you haven't forgotten the things the Dark Court can do. Have you forgotten what the Dark King has done to you? The curse that bound you for centuries? Shall I see if I can do it again?"

The friendship that Keenan felt for Niall was all that kept him from letting go of the rage that simmered at the allusion to the past. In as composed a voice as he could manage, Keenan asked, "And if Aislinn doesn't like your terms?"

Niall narrowed his gaze. "My court is too strong for her to attack. You know that."

Reluctantly, Keenan nodded. "I do."

"And there is another court, one whose favor I'm quite sure I can gain." Niall let the shadows in the room spring to life, and the dark figures began dancing and contorting in ways that no solid body could. "My court has long offered many things to the Winter Court. If you knew, kingling, it might disgust you. I had difficulty experiencing desire for the last Winter Queen, but a regent will do what he must for the good of his court . . . and truth be told, I'd find myself far more eager to offer whatever the new queen desires."

Keenan's carefully controlled emotions threatened to surface; his skin brightened despite his best efforts, but he forced himself to speak evenly. "Think about what you're doing here. We are not enemies. If you hurt Donia—"

"As you have?"

"You're caging your friend, threatening insane things . . . think for a moment." Keenan shook his head. "You weathered centuries of trouble with me. I can be here to help you without you resorting to cruelty against Seth or threats to my court. Please stop to think."

"I will do as I've done for *centuries*, little king. I will protect my court and those I love." Niall advanced on Keenan. "Once Bananach is dead, we can negotiate. Until then . . ." He shrugged.

Keenan gripped Niall's arm. "I will help you because you are my *friend*. You might not have forgiven me yet, but you *do* know how to forgive—or you wouldn't be so crazed over his death. I will talk to my queen and to Donia."

The Dark King frowned.

"This"—Keenan pointed at Seth and then at Niall's battered body—"is not you, Niall."

"Really?" the Dark King needled. "Who is it then? Who exactly do you think I am if I'm not Niall?"

For a moment, Keenan paused, trying to make sense of the challenging tone in Niall's voice. *Has he gone completely mad?* Cautiously, Keenan said, "I'm not sure what's going on in your head right now, but you need to step back and figure it out. If you think that you have to be vile to replace Irial, you're wrong."

The Dark King snorted, but did not answer.

"Think about what you're becoming," Keenan urged.

But Niall only motioned for him to depart.

In almost grateful silence, the Summer King did so. As he crossed Huntsdale to return to his own court, he considered the bizarre behavior Niall had demonstrated. His once-friend-and-advisor was acting *wrong*. Admittedly, the Dark Court wasn't a place Keenan understood, but he thought he'd understood Niall.

Is it grief? Being their king?

If Keenan would've had to swear as to Niall's sanity or propensity for cruelty, the answer he would've given today would be different from the one he'd have offered in the past. *He has changed. And not for the better.* Summer might not be always predictable, but they weren't mad or cruel.

So far.

Of course, Keenan wasn't entirely sure if that would remain the case if Niall injured Seth. The Summer Queen carried her emotions on the surface—*as a Summer regent should*—and the injury of the faery who'd been her first love, who loved her and risked death for her, would not be something Aislinn would accept gracefully.

Nor would I if it were Donia caged by Niall.

The thought of Niall's casual remarks about Donia sent Keenan's own temper flaring to life again as he reached the building that housed their loft.

Tavish stood in the street, perhaps on guard duty,

perhaps waiting for Keenan's return. The Summer King couldn't care less *why* his most trusted friend was there. What he cared about was that Tavish was there. The older faery had the wisdom and composure that Keenan and his queen would both lack just then.

Tavish looked at him, and Keenan gestured for him to follow.

Neither faery spoke as they walked to a seldom-used conservatory on one side of the park. Two rowan in the room looked to their king and his advisor. At a gesture from Tavish, the rowan both departed. The glass door closed with a barely audible click.

"He is unwell?"

"That's one way to put it," Keenan said, and then proceeded to fill Tavish in on the conversation with Niall.

"Killing War is not likely to be an easy task, if it is even possible." Tavish pursed his lips.

"Containing Ash isn't going to be particularly easy either."

"The boy is a seer?" Tavish mused. "There's use in such an asset. He's loyal to the queen. . . ."

"And loyal to Sorcha and, presumably, he is still loyal to Niall despite the Dark King's current madness." Keenan cupped an orchid in his hand and watched it blossom. The plants nearby stretched toward him as well, responding to the heat that radiated from his skin.

Tavish glanced behind him to the doorway, where the guards blocked them from sight. "Bananach has put us all in a position that we cannot ignore. We should stand with Niall."

"I intend to. He didn't need to threaten me for that to happen." Keenan scowled. "He stood with me for nine centuries. Even if he cannot put aside his current anger, he is my friend."

"And Winter? Do we need to speak to her?"

"She'll stand with Niall," Keenan said. "Regardless of what I do."

"You are sure?"

"I am." Keenan sighed. "She is a wise queen, Tavish. She would've led our court beautifully. I see it—the way she puts herself before her court. They would gladly slaughter anything and everyone for her smile."

"And you?"

Keenan startled. "I wouldn't hurt my court for her."

Tavish said nothing, but his silence said enough that words were unnecessary.

"Ash refuses me," Keenan said.

"Because you have backed away when the chances presented themselves." Tavish shook his head. "She might believe your excuses, but I've known you since birth. You've chosen to restrain yourself. *Repeatedly.*"

"She needs time," Keenan protested.

"No. When Seth was mortal, she needed time, but he's not mortal anymore. You *left* for months, during which you allowed Seth to have all of her attention. Even last night, you did not press her. The queen would be yours in all ways if you wanted her to. Instead, you've offered her every opportunity to refuse you. As an advisor and as a friend, I'm telling you that the time for prevarication has ended. Your father was too stubborn to listen to me where your mother was concerned. Be wiser than him."

"Beira tricked—"

"No, she didn't," Tavish said. "He knew what she was, knew she doubted him, yet he still tried to treat her the way one treats a summer faery. Aislinn would let you lie with her. The court knows it; you know it. Even now, with her Seth returned to her, you could seduce her. *Seth* knows this of her. He loves her still."

"I understand, but now is not the right time. She will be worrying over Seth's capture once she learns of it and . . . it would be wrong." Keenan heard the objections in his words, knew they sounded weak. Once, he would've done anything to woo the destined queen. He had done and said things that made him cringe afterward.

It's different. I know Ash. I respect her.

Tavish kept his gaze fixed on Keenan and asked, "How would you feel if Donia took a lover?"

"*She* hasn't," Keenan snapped. "She's not like summer fey."

"You are not *only* Summer, my King," Tavish reminded him. "There is more of your mother in you than you like to admit. You cannot look at me and say that you are truly trying your best to lure your queen to your side, that you are doing all you could to strengthen this court. Can you?"

"I've not objected to the pleasures of Summer before. The Summer Girls . . . and the revelries . . ." Keenan's words died at the chastising look on his friend's face. "If Aislinn accepted me, I would lie with her now even though she loves the morta— *Seth*."

"You would, yet you haven't. You refused her when she offered herself to you; you chose not to seduce her for months when he was away. She wanted you, still does, yet you do not take her into your bed." Tavish folded his hands in his lap and stared at his king. "You didn't love the Summer Girls enough to mind sharing them. Nor do you love my queen enough. It is not her connection to Seth that bothers you. Since you spent the Winter Solstice before last with Donia, you haven't—"

"I've lived my life to reach the point of strength for this court," Keenan interrupted.

"I know." Tavish reached out and gripped Keenan's shoulder.

The Summer King looked at the faery who'd been the closest thing to a father that he'd ever known, and he knew that any further protestations he could offer would be pointless. Tavish knew him, saw through any illusions that Keenan would like to embrace. Keenan had *not* pursued Aislinn as truly as he could have. He'd pursued her until she accepted the challenge of becoming queen, but after he'd spent time in Donia's arms, he had accepted Aislinn's rejections, had even helped her create them.

"Don't try to deceive either of us, my King. You've done

what you needed. You were steadfast in your devotion to the court. You became everything you had to be in order to be your father's heir. Having the faery you love in your arms has changed you. I can see it, even if most of the court cannot." Tavish's voice was gentle, helping lead them both to the sentences that had never been spoken, admissions that Keenan had considered in silence. "There are those meant to be sunlit and those who are not ever going to be at peace with the way things are in this court. Maybe you would feel differently if Aislinn were the Summer Queen in truth, if she gave up her lover."

"She might."

"Keenan?" Aislinn came through the doorway. "Why are you out here?"

"You need to make a choice, Keenan." Tavish squeezed Keenan's shoulder. "I would not fault you for either one, nor should you. If the court is to be strong enough to stand against Bananach, the time is here. No more prevarication. No more excuses. Sorcha is locked away; Niall is unwell; Donia is new to ruling; and our court is not as strong as it must be."

Keenan turned his gaze to the Summer Queen. He felt a nervous excitement build in his skin. His entire life had been about finding her. He'd thought it was that simple. His lips curled in a smile. *Simple?* Nothing about this curse had ever been simple.

After nine centuries, it all comes down to one day.

CHAPTER 27

Aislinn looked from her advisor to her king. The serious-
ness in Tavish's expression was not unfamiliar, but Keenan's
strangely bemused smile worried her. "Tavish? Keenan?"

Her advisor bowed his head. "I will be with the Summer
Girls," he said, and then he left her there in the humid conservatory with Keenan.

Once it was just them, Keenan walked toward her slowly.
"I need you to do something, Aislinn."

"Okaaay. . . ." She reached out and stroked her fingers
along a vat of soil. Under her hand, plants began to sprout.
She wasn't sure yet what they were, but she was unable to
resist touching the soil. "What's up?"

He took her hand in his. "Walk with me?"

The nervousness Aislinn felt grew as they left the conservatory. *The Summer Court's space, where we are strong.* She
squeezed his hand. "Talk to me. Please?"

The Summer King released her hand and stepped away

from her. He looked only at her and asked, "Do you trust me?"

"Keenan—"

"Aislinn, please," he interrupted. "Do you trust me?"

"I do," she assured him. All around them, the park was empty. The Summer Girls, the rowan, all of the faeries of the court were out of sight.

As they stood face-to-face in the park where they'd once danced, where they'd kissed, where they'd argued, and where they'd both led their court in revels—together and separately—Keenan said, "I've misled you."

She bent and trailed her fingertips over the dark soil, letting heat into the earth, refusing to look at him for a moment. "I know."

"I've manipulated you," he continued.

She paused and looked up at him. "Not really helping, Keenan."

"Do you trust me?" he asked again.

Aislinn straightened and faced him. "I do."

"Do you want to be near me?" He didn't approach her. Unlike his aggressiveness since he'd returned—and when she'd first met him—he was almost reserved now.

Still, she had to pause for several breaths before she could answer: "I do."

"Why?"

"You're my king. Something inside of me insists that I reach out. I can't even stay mad at you when I know I should be." She wiped the soil from her hands onto her jeans and paced farther away. "Never mind. . . . I want to know what you learned while you were out. Now is not the time for *this*."

"Actually, it is." Keenan watched her with an intensity that made her want to run. "The time for waiting has ended."

"You can't mean . . ." She shook her head. "You *just* got back."

Keenan stayed out of her reach as he spoke. "Will you let yourself love me, Aislinn?"

"You're my king, but . . . I *love* Seth."

"I need to belong to one person, who belongs only to me. I have done as I must for centuries, but there is a part of me that is not as fickle as Summer can be," Keenan said. "I need all or nothing. Either we are truly together, or we are truly apart."

She shook her head. "You're really asking me to choose *now*?"

"I am." He reached out, but didn't touch her. His hand was in the air next to her face, but he didn't close the distance. "I need you to decide. Now. The court needs to be as strong as possible."

"Whatever you learned . . . Talk to me," she pleaded. "Maybe there's another way, maybe . . ."

"Aislinn," he said evenly. "I need you to decide. Do we go away together or do I go alone?"

She felt warm tears trickle down her cheeks. "Yesterday, you told me I had a week. You told me *yesterday*."

"Would your answer change if we waited?"

Aislinn hated the understanding in his voice as much as she had hated it when Seth offered it to her. They were both wonderful, both good, both people any girl would be lucky to know—but she only loved one of them. If she could save her court and keep Seth in her life, that's what she would do. If Keenan wasn't near her, she wouldn't feel the pull to be with him. She hadn't felt it—*much*—these past six months, not like she had when Seth was away.

"Would you want it to change?" she asked.

"I want to be loved; I want to be consumed by it." Keenan traced her jaw with the barest touch of his fingertips. "I've loved Donia for decades, but I've lived for my court for centuries. I need more than an 'I think' this time, Aislinn. Do you want me enough to be mine? Do you care enough to try to love me? Do we become *truly* together for our court? Claim me as your king, or set me free to try to be with the faery I love."

"I do want you," Aislinn admitted. "Not just because of the court. You're my friend and . . . I *do* care for you. I can't imagine never seeing you again."

The Summer King stroked her cheek with his thumb. "Can you offer me your fidelity? Your heart and your body and your companionship for eternity? Do you want *my* fidelity? Either love me or kiss me good-bye, my Summer Queen."

She felt tears slip down her cheeks. He'd looked for her for almost a millennium, but she couldn't give him what he needed. She'd returned strength to their court, but the love she felt for the Summer Court wasn't the sort of love he wanted from her. She leaned into his caress. "Why do I think that what happens next is going to be . . ."

"To be?" he prompted softly.

"Something I'm not ready for," she finished.

Her earlier fears of ruling the court without him crashed around her. He'd been their king for centuries, and she had only been fey for a bit more than a year. *How do we rule from separate areas? Split the court? Can we even do that?* She bit her lip.

"How is this going to strengthen the court? I'm not sure—"

"Ash," he interrupted. Without looking away from her face, he reached out with his other hand and entwined her fingers with his. "Tell me you're truly mine, or tell me goodbye."

"You're really leaving for good if I say no?"

Mutely, he nodded.

"I can't be only yours. You'll always—"

The rest of her words were swallowed as the Summer King leaned forward and sealed his lips to hers. Sunlight filled her mouth. It covered her skin and trickled over her like a million tiny hands. Her eyes were open. The blinding brightness of the Summer King as he pressed against her was too beautiful to look away from.

He pulled away briefly, and she realized that they weren't touching the ground anymore. The air burned, crackling with heat lightning.

"Are you sure?" he asked.

"I am." She hadn't asked to be fey, hadn't wanted the future she had, but she cherished it now. She was *happy*—to be a faery, to be the Summer Queen—but she wasn't Keenan's beloved. "We would be making a mistake. I am never going to be *that* faery for you . . . or you for me."

"I'm sorry," he said.

"Me too."

And then he kissed her again.

The sunlight pulsing into her body made it impossible to keep her eyes open any longer. She felt like an eternity of languid bliss were seeping into her every pore, and as on the night that Keenan had healed her, she felt too consumed by it to object. His arms were the only things that kept her from tumbling to the ground, which was now far below them.

Aislinn wasn't sure how long they hovered above the park kissing. She only knew that her king was kissing her good-bye.

Finally, Keenan pulled away. "Think of the soil, Ash."

"The soil?" she echoed.

"The earth. Think of sunlight falling—" They plummeted, and Keenan said, "*Gently.* Falling gently, Ash."

She nodded, and they slowed. "I'm doing this."

"You are," he confirmed. "Sunlight isn't bound to the earth. Neither is the Summer Queen."

Her feet touched the soil, and Keenan released her. She would've fallen to her knees, but he steadied her. Carefully, he helped her sit on the ground.

As her hand touched the soil, vines shot out and wove together into an elaborate flowering throne. It lifted her from the ground, and she looked toward him. "Keenan?"

He backed away from her. "It'll be okay, Ash. Tavish will tell you what you need to know. You can do this. Remember that."

She blinked and looked past him to the park. The trees were a riot of blossoms. The hedges had grown as tall as trees, creating a formidable barrier. It was not yet full spring, but the area outside of the Summer Court's park was in bloom. All through the park, her faeries now stood waiting. She felt connected to each one of them more intensely than ever before.

Except Keenan.

Her gaze went to him. Her Summer King was . . . not Summer. She held out a hand to him. "Keenan?"

He took her hand and knelt. The sunlight that usually pulsed back when they touched, that had all but drowned her in pleasure barely a moment ago, was absent.

He lifted his head to look up at her. "I would hope to be welcome in your court, but this is not where I belong now."

Aislinn was speechless. The faery who had remade her, who had been the other half of the embodiment of summer, was no longer sunlit. In their good-bye kiss, he had somehow given her the sunlight that had been his own.

I am the only *Summer regent.*

"I would've given up the faery I love, devoted eternity to you, to them"—Keenan glanced to her left, where Tavish now stood, and then looked back at her—"but I need the love and passion you do not offer me. So do you. The lack of passion, of love, of *happiness* weakened my . . . *your* court. The court is now stronger than it's been during my life."

"But . . ." Aislinn tried to stand, but found her legs still too weakened to support her. Tears slid down her cheek, and she saw rainbows arc across the sky, matching the trail of her tears. "If you could walk away . . . I don't understand. Why couldn't I? This is what *you* always were."

Keenan pleaded for understanding with his expression. "I was born of two courts, Aislinn. There was a choice for me. One I couldn't make before, but now the Summer Court is in capable hands."

"And you are what?" She tugged on his hand, trying to pull him to his feet, but he shook his head.

"Dismiss me," he requested. "As the *only* Summer Court regent, give me your first command."

Tears clouded her vision, and rainbows flared all over the sky. "Keenan . . . you are ever welcome in my court should you need solace or a home. You remain a friend of my court . . . under our protection should you need it." Then, in a shaky voice, she added, "You are dismissed."

He stood and silently left the park. As he passed, the rowan knelt. The Summer Girls curtsied as one; their vines became like solid ink on their skin as they stood, no longer depending on their king-no-more. The curse that had bound them to him was ended.

They're free.

CHAPTER 28

After Evan's death, Donia felt numb. Evan had watched over her since she'd first become fey. He had been her guard and her friend for decades. To some, that was but a blink. *For him, it was a moment.* To Donia, it was the whole of her second life. There was rage, grief, heartbreak, but she kept those emotions submerged in the weight of the snow and ice inside of her. *I cannot wail, not yet.*

The Hound Chela had deposited Donia and Evan's body at the Winter Queen's home, and then elicited promises that Donia would not cross the line of guards and Hounds stationed outside—not that they alone would be enough to stop Bananach.

Which leaves the king-in-mourning, the fey-only-a-year queen, the Summer King, or me.

Donia thought of Beira, the late Winter Queen, with an unexpected pang. Beira was diabolical in many ways, but she was strong enough, cruel enough, and skilled enough to fight Bananach. *And dead.* Donia sighed. Beira's death

had saved lives—*including mine*—but it had eliminated the
most powerful of the regents on this side of the veil.

A veil that is now closed.

With a solemnity that she used to hide the sorrow inside
of her, Donia stared at the earth; then, with a breath, she
lifted all of the snow from the tree beside her favorite spot in
the winter garden. The Scrimshaw Sisters, Hawthorn people, lupine, and myriad other of the Winter Court faeries
clustered in the garden. Several of the guards carried Evan
to the spot she'd cleared.

Silently, they arranged his empty shell on the wet soil.

When they were done, Donia pulled the remaining
moisture from the soil on which he rested, and Evan's body
sank into the earth. Tears slipped down her cheeks as the
ground accepted him, and as she wept, snow fell from the
sky. "Good-bye, my friend."

She bowed her head, and her faeries began to depart.
They were mostly all gone from her presence when three
of the Hawthorn stopped. One of them asked, "Would you
prefer solitude or companionship for your mourning?"

"Solitude." She lifted her gaze to them. "Unless business
requires it . . ."

With soft brushes of their hands over her arms and
shoulders, they left her alone in the winter garden where
her friend, guard, and advisor was now buried. As soon as
they were gone, she parted her lips for the shriek of hurt and
rage that she'd held inside. The sky tore open, and a winter
storm whipped around her. The wind lashed her cheeks; the
ice hammered her upturned face; and the snow wrapped her

in its much-needed embrace.

The Winter Queen knelt on the again-frozen earth and wished there were more she could do to avenge the death of the faery who had protected her in her years as Winter Girl, who had helped her adjust to being Winter Queen.

I want her death. She paused. *This is what Niall feels. What Gabriel feels.*

There was no doubt in Donia's mind that the actions Bananach had taken were planned: she wanted their pain and rage.

Why?

Donia forced her emotions back under the calming press of the snow she carried inside her and walked into her home. She was a faery in mourning, but she was also a queen in conflict. She wouldn't allow her emotions to keep her from being a good queen. Evan might not be there advising her, but he had counseled her often enough that she knew what he would tell her: understand Bananach's motivations, study the patterns.

Inside her house, Donia sat before the vast stone fireplace in one of the lesser-used rooms and started writing down what she knew. The activity had the added benefit of distracting her.

She was shifting through Evan's piles of letters and papers, hoping for more information to add to her puzzling-out of Bananach's behavior when one of her fey came into the room.

"Donia? My Queen?"

She looked up at Cwenhild, the Scrimshaw Sister who waited in the doorway. "News?"

"A guest." Cwenhild frowned. "He waits to see you."

Donia motioned for her to continue. "Who?"

"He . . . the faery . . . the . . ." The Scrimshaw Sister shook her head. "I'm sorry, my Queen. He's in the garden. I can bring . . . him if you . . . I didn't think."

"No," she said firmly. "I find peace in my garden. That has not changed."

Cwenhild nodded, and Donia went to her garden. Once there, she understood Cwenhild's inability to answer her question. The faery who waited for her could no longer be named by the title they had always known him by. Keenan sat in the center of her garden, peacefully waiting on her favorite bench—and his sunlight was gone.

The snow in her garden didn't burn away as it fell near him. Instead, it collected on his no-longer-sunlit skin. The copper of his hair was unchanged, but the glints of sunlight were replaced by a sheen of frost. He looked up. "I've never felt at peace here, you know."

"What happened?" She stared at him. The sunlight that he had wielded as a weapon, as an extension of himself, as a part of his very being, was gone. He was still fey, but he was not filled with light.

He slid over and patted the bench beside him. "Would you sit with me?"

"What have you *done*?" The cold air from her lips didn't steam away as it touched him.

Keenan smiled tentatively. "Changed."

"I can see *that*." Without meaning to, her hand lifted as if to touch the glitter of frost on his skin. She lowered her hand almost guiltily.

And he sighed. "I've given my sunlight to the Summer Queen. I am not of that court anymore."

"Is it . . . *real*?"

He nodded. "I came here as soon as I was . . . free."

For a moment, she looked at him, the faery who'd stolen her mortality, whom she'd been willing to die for, whom she still dreamed of—and she couldn't help but marvel at him. After all the things she thought she knew about the world, this was new. *He* was new.

Yet he was still the faery she'd known, and as they sat there, she realized that she needed to tell him about the loss that had left her in sorrow. "Keenan?"

He looked at her, and she said softly, "Evan's . . . gone."

"Gone how?"

"Bananach kill—"

"*When?*" Keenan's no longer summer-green eyes widened. Icy blue filled them, reminding her of the other side of his heritage.

The side that makes him able to sit in the winter garden so comfortably.

"When I left the loft," she admitted. "Bananach was waiting for me. The Hounds came; my guards came. Including Evan, we lost just over a dozen faeries."

As calmly as she could, she told him all she knew, all that

had happened. She did not weep on his shoulder, although the temptation was there.

"She's taken Irial, Evan, and . . ." Keenan exhaled a cloud of frost, but didn't seem to notice that he'd done so.

He belongs to my court. He is the last Winter Queen's son.

Donia was speechless at the revelation, and at his seeming obliviousness to it. He was never as unaware as he appeared, though; he was merely skilled at disguising the things that he would rather not share.

For several moments, they sat in silence, and then he looked at her with now winter-blue eyes and said, "I have no right . . . to be here or to touch you. I know that."

"You don't have the right to touch me," she agreed, but she wanted him to claim the right to do just that. *He's hurt me. He's failed me. He's promised things he couldn't do.*

"I want to hold you, not just because you are hurting but because I *can* now," he admitted. "May I?"

He held open an arm, and she slid closer. Cautiously, she leaned her head against his shoulder. The rightness of it, the way her body felt against his, filled her with a sense of completion that she'd never known.

They sat there together for several moments in silence until he said, "I am sorry for your loss."

"And yours." Donia lifted her head and looked at him. "He was your faery first."

"I was relieved that he came to you when you became queen." Keenan kept his arm around her. His fingers were curled around her shoulder still, holding her to him as if afraid she'd flee. "I knew he would keep you safe the way I hadn't."

She couldn't stop herself: she reached up and ran her fingers through Keenan's hair. It felt different, not sharp enough to hurt, but soft. There was no pain, no steam, no clash—so Donia continued trailing her fingers over his changed body.

He closed his eyes. He stayed perfectly still as she caressed his cheek and traced her fingertips across his jaw. In several decades, she'd only had one Winter Solstice, over a year ago, in which she could touch him without pain to either of them.

"You're not a king now. What does that make you?"

His lips curved in a smile, and he opened his eyes to stare directly at her. "I have absolutely no idea. I've not offered fealty to anyone. *Yet.* I would. I would offer anything I have to the right queen."

"Oh," she breathed.

"I don't belong in the Summer Court, not now, not ever again." He ran his fingers through the snow that had accumulated on the bench on the other side of him. "When I was a child, I could exhale frost into the air, and then melt it in the next breath."

He knew. He wasn't oblivious, but he wasn't hiding it either. *At least not from me.* Keenan carried his other parent's heritage, had buried it under sunlight for centuries. "I didn't tell anyone. My mother knew, but she didn't tell anyone either."

"You are of my court," Donia said, her words as much a

question as a statement. "You are heir to the throne I hold."

"No. I don't want your throne, Don; I only want *you*." Keenan stared into the snow-covered garden. "My mother told me that she'd loved only once. She would've done anything for him, but he betrayed her. She didn't recover from that."

Donia moved away from him. In the midst of everything going on, on the edge of war, with faeries defecting and faeries dying, Keenan was sitting in her garden telling her about his childhood.

"I don't understand what's going on," she told him.

Several moments passed, and he said, "I am going to see Niall. I need to help him if I can. After that"—he stood and turned to face Donia—"I will be back. I'm a solitary faery now, strong enough to be . . . whatever you are willing to let me be. You see what I am. Both summer and winter lived inside me as a child. I chose one because my father was slain and his court needed me, but I've left the Summer Court. Once Niall is well again, I will swear fealty to you, or I will remain solitary. I will be your subject, your servant, solitary but not of your court. Whatever it takes to have the chance at being yours, truly and forever—that's what I want."

He bent down and pressed his lips to hers. Then he said, "I am my mother's son in some things, Donia. I would've tried to be loyal to my queen if I had to, but she knew—and *you* know—that she was never first for me. I know I don't deserve you. I never have, but I want to find a way to be worthy of you."

"Keenan, I don't—"

"Let me say this." He knelt in the snow that drifted around the bench. "When I told you I wanted to try, I spoke the truth. When I turned away, it was for my former court, and when I tried to make another faery love me, it was for that court. I've lived for my whole life trying to bring the Summer Court back to the strength it once was. In all of those years, in *centuries*, I've only wished myself free of duty because of one reason. You."

"What if—"

"Please?" he begged. "The only thing that stood between us was a court that is no longer my concern. Tell me what vow you want me to offer you, what promise. Anything."

Donia thought back to the times when he'd looked at her with that same raw hope—and the times *she* had felt that hope. They'd been in this moment so many times. *This time is different.* She felt it, knew it the same way she'd known they would fail before.

She took a breath, exhaled slowly, and then told him, "If you fail me, I'll kill you. I swear it, Keenan. If you fail me, I'll rip your heart out with my own hands."

"If I fail you, I'll cut it out *for* you." He stared up at her. "Let me love you, please? Tell me you're saying there's still a chance, Don?"

She couldn't breathe around the pain in her chest. "Tell me I'm the only one."

"You are the *only* one. I love you," he swore. "I have loved you for years, and if I could've, I would've made you my queen. You know—"

She leaned down and kissed him, stopping his words, and tumbled to the snowy ground and into his arms. It wasn't Solstice, but that didn't matter anymore. He was here, in her garden, in her life.

Mine.

For now and for always.

CHAPTER 29

After the king-no-more had left, Aislinn remained in her park, surrounded by her faeries, and wondered at the intensity she felt. If she'd thought being coregent was overwhelming, having the other half of Summer fill her was soul-melting.

I can't imagine if all of this had hit me at once. How did Donia do it? How did Niall?

At the thought of the other recent regents, she straightened. They *had* done it; they'd taken control of their courts, led them, guarded them. Undoubtedly, they'd had struggles she hadn't known of, but they'd done it.

And so will I.

She squared her shoulders and looked at her court. *First things first. You've been doing this with half the strength and handling it while he was away. You can* do *this.* The Summer Queen smiled at her faeries.

Tavish came to stand beside her throne. Several of the

Summer Girls stepped forward. Some of the rowan took position as guards; others moved throughout the crowd. Three glaistigs who were attached to the court under temporary vows of fealty divided into other positions—one to either side of the throne where she sat and the third to the far edge of the park. Aobheall had stepped outside her fountain and stood between the Summer Girls and rowan people.

Her court waited for her to lead them.

"I'm guessing all of the Summer Girls"—she let her gaze drift over them—"are free to leave the . . . *my* court, but I would like you all to stay."

Most of them nodded or smiled; a few looked unsure.

"You do not have to decide today," Aislinn added. Then she sought two of the girls who had been instrumental in helping her understand what it took to lead the court. "Siobhan? Eliza?"

"My Queen," they said in tandem.

"I'd like you to join Tavish as my court counselors," she said.

Eliza gasped quietly, but Siobhan grinned.

"Summer Girls are foolish, spinning things, my Queen," Siobhan said lightly. Her eyes widened in a faux attempt at naïveté.

Aislinn laughed. "If you wanted me to believe that was *all* you were, you shouldn't have advised me when Seth was missing. You can all remain exactly as you were before. I expect that you will still rejoice and frolic. *All* of my court will do so. . . . First, though, we will consult with the Winter and Dark Courts, and we will figure out how to contain Bananach."

The Summer Queen turned her attention to Tavish. "You will be sole commander of guards in addition to advising me with"—she glanced at Siobhan, who nodded, and Eliza, who shook her head—"my new advisor, Siobhan."

After a brief proud look, Tavish bowed his head. "It is my honor."

Three matters resolved. She had her guard, her new advisor, and had extended welcome to the Summer Girls. Now, she needed to deal with a situation that had grown unacceptable.

"You"—Aislinn turned her gaze to Quinn—"need to answer some questions."

Quinn had stood silently while she selected his replacement. He hadn't approached when she began tending business, nor had he functioned as a guard. Instead, he had stayed at the edge of the group of assembled faeries. "My queen?"

"You've questioned me." She advanced toward him, noticing that bands of flowers rippled out from wherever she stepped and making a mental note to figure out how to turn *that* off.

Quinn watched her approach without backing away.

Point for that. She paused. *Or not. Is it courage or disdain?*

"You do not treat me with the respect one accords his queen," she said softly.

Quinn locked his gaze with hers. "I serve my court."

"The question is if you serve *my* court," she countered.

When he didn't reply, she pressed, "Do you serve the Summer Court?"

As Quinn stared at her, Aislinn felt the heat of the Summer Court burning in her skin. She put her hand on his shoulder. At her touch, his shirt burned away, and his skin sizzled.

Turn it down, she cautioned herself. Her expression showed nothing, but a brush of guilt slid across her chest. *I didn't mean to. . . .* She steeled herself. *These are faeries, and I am their queen. Seeing me falter will do more harm than good.* She forced Quinn to his knees. "What court do you serve, Quinn?"

"I am the advisor to—"

"No," Aislinn said quietly. "What *court* do you serve? You are not here to serve my wishes, so whose will do you serve?"

"Sorcha's," he admitted. "The High Queen sent her representatives and . . . she wanted word of our court."

"*My* court," Aislinn corrected. "If you were spying on *my* court for another regent, this is not your court. Go."

"Go?" he echoed.

Aislinn gave him the faery-cruel smile she'd learned when she became Summer Queen. *When Keenan taught me to pretend I was not overwhelmed.* The smile did not falter, nor did her voice as she said, "She wants you, go serve her court. My faeries do not serve the wishes of other regents without my consent."

"But . . . but the veil is closed. I *can't* go to Faerie."
Quinn's usual self-confident expression was absent as he
looked up at her. "I . . . beseech you: grant me your mercy,
please."

The Summer Queen stared at the kneeling faery. Around
her, the court was silent. *Mercy?* She didn't want to be cruel,
but she now understood what it meant to lead. Sometimes,
a regent had to do things that would keep her up at night. It
wasn't always clear, but absolute good and evil were the stuff
of children's fairy tales.

Firmly, she told him, "I don't trust you, Quinn. You put
another court's interests ahead of *my* court while claiming
to serve me. The safety of my faeries is my first priority. It
must be."

"But . . ." He bowed his head. "I cannot go to her, and
out there . . . *War* is angry. Please?"

Aislinn sighed. "Advisors?"

"He cannot be allowed to remain in the loft or within
the upper levels of the building," Tavish said.

"Or to attend any meeting or to know the touch of any
of the summer fey," Siobhan added.

"Or to serve as guard," Tavish said.

"My advisors seem to be leaving the option of mercy
on the table, Quinn." The Summer Queen looked at her
advisors and smiled. Then she looked down at Quinn. "You
carried word to another court. You were not truly *my* faery.
You are no longer Summer Court, but if you are solitary,
you may linger among us for your safety until such time as

you find a new court—if my advisors can find suitable use
for you."

"You are merciful," Quinn said, with gratitude plain in
his expression.

Aislinn caught his throat in her hand and let just a
little heat into her touch—not enough to truly wound,
but enough that her handprint would remain when she
released him. "If your actions endanger my faeries, my
mercy will end."

"Yes, m—"

"And if your actions"—she squeezed—"continue, you
will be the one to see how much damage a fully capable
Summer regent can do." Then, Aislinn released him. "Get
him out of my presence."

Eliza stepped up along with two rowan. The Summer
Girl said quietly, "I would ask to join the guard, my Queen."

"I don't see why not. If"—she shot a glance at Tavish—
"the head of the guard approves."

"Training will commence after we escort Quinn to a
comfortable cell." Tavish motioned for Eliza to grab Quinn's
arm, and then he added, "I think we might have a job for
you, Quinn. How do you feel about being a training aid?"

The fastidious ex-advisor scowled, and then said, "If the
Summer Queen would like me to do so, I will do so."

Aislinn nodded. "I think a number of the Summer Girls
could use some basic defense—"

"And offense, my Queen," Siobhan interjected.

"Defense *and* offense training. Quinn will make a fine

dummy to practice their skills on." Aislinn didn't bother smothering her smile.

Quinn gritted his teeth. "As you wish."

And with that, Eliza and Tavish led him away.

Aislinn sat back in the vine-wrought throne and told her court, "I want to celebrate, to dance with you, to lose ourselves in weeks of revelry, but the king-no-more has made a sacrifice in order to give us the strength to stand with the Cold and the Darkness. Once we find a way to contain War, I promise you we will celebrate as I want to right now."

Her faeries smiled and cheered.

"The park is safe. Bananach cannot enter it without my consent. No one can," Aislinn assured them. "You may stay in the park or you can stay in the Summer Court's building, but without my leave, you may not go anywhere else. Dance or rest, make love or make music, but remain within the space where you are safe."

Despite the restrictions she'd just imposed—or maybe because they were summer fey—her faeries seemed perfectly content with her command. *They are.* She felt tendrils of connection to each of them, and she knew they weren't feigning their cooperation. They trusted her and her judgment.

Please don't let me fail them.

CHAPTER 30

"I am not taking care of the court." Niall straightened the sheet that he'd draped over Irial. "It's better today, but I can't remember all of the minutes."

On the bed in front of him, Irial's body was immobile. They were alone. A Hound guarded the door, but like the other guards, he was forbidden to enter the room. Aside from Niall and Gabriel, no one had entered the room since Irial had died. The body hadn't changed. It looked as though Irial only slept, but when Niall touched his arm, the flesh was cold.

"I am not sure if I'm glad that you aren't here to see my descent into madness. I still dream of you. The first time I left you, I dreamed of you—memories of things." Niall laughed bitterly. "Apparently, I am not any better at losing you this time. Who would've guessed?"

Ink-black tears dripped onto the corpse as Niall kissed Irial's forehead. "I'll be home later."

Then the Dark King left the house and went to the ware-house. Faeries watched his approach with a degree of fear that seemed out of character. *They see my madness. They fear me. Because Irial is dead.* Niall tried to smile encouragingly at them, but the emotion that rolled off of many of them was still fear.

"Go. Tonight, I want to be alone with the betrayer." He looked at each of the guards that lingered outside the ware-house. "Tell all of them. As your king, I order you to seek your pleasures among whatever faeries you want. Nourish yourselves. I need you all to be at your strongest."

Inside the warehouse, Niall repeated his order, and glee spread through the Dark Court faeries. As the Dark King looked on his rejoicing faeries, a voice in his memories trickled to the forefront.

I am not depraved; I do not allow unforgivable acts.

Niall stopped in the middle of the warehouse, lifted his voice, and added, "Take pleasure *only* with the willing, but revel in fights, revel in debauchery as you mourn your dead king."

Once they left, Niall walked over to the cage suspended in the middle of the room and stared at the betrayer.

Seth killed Irial.

The Dark King paced away. He stopped in front of one of the fires that burned in the warehouse. It did little to chase away the chill that seemed to have filled him since Irial died. Angrily, he stirred the embers with a fire poker, but the cold didn't abate.

"You could have saved Iri. Could've saved me from this"—Niall tossed the poker onto the ground and looked up at Seth—"madness that threatens me."

As Niall stared up at the cage, Seth wondered if their friendship would be the death of him.

"We are friends, Niall. Let me out," Seth said quietly.

Unfortunately, Niall was more Dark King than faery friend in the moment. Muttering quietly to himself, he paced the empty warehouse, then paused and looked at Seth.

He is grieving and unbalanced.

"Have I become as mad as Bananach?" Niall asked.

Inside his prison, Seth chose not to answer that particular question, so Niall kicked the iron bar that held the cage's chain. The cage plummeted to the ground. "Tell me, Seer. Am I a madman?"

Seth righted himself from the floor, where he'd fallen as the cage dropped. "Caging your friends isn't high on the sane list."

"I don't cage friends." Niall grabbed the fire poker from the ground and pointed it at Seth. "You misled me, infiltrated my court—"

"Okay, *now* you sound crazy." Seth stretched and looked around the dimly lit room. "What time is it anyway? We could go out. Grab some breakfast or dinner. Then you could catch a much-needed nap. What do you say?"

"You killed Irial."

"No," Seth drawled. "That was Bananach. I fought *with*

you. You remember that, Niall. I know you do."

"Murderer." Niall stabbed the poker deep into the fire. "The Dark Court doesn't tolerate betrayal. I don't tolerate it."

"Not going to be much of a court if you don't get your head out of your ass, Niall." Seth came to his feet. "Where's Gabe? Where is everyone? Bananach is gathering forces, Niall. You need to *do* something."

"I am about to," Niall said.

"If you're going to do what it looks like you are, that's high on the crazy list." Seth watched the tip of the poker heat up. "I'll forgive a lot of shit, Niall, but you're starting to tap into the unforgivable list here."

The Dark King shook his head. "I've watched them blind Sighted mortals."

"Not mortal."

Niall lifted the poker and walked toward the cage. "I didn't understand it, but Sorcha follows the old ways. Maybe she knows things. Does she, Seth? Does she know things I'm lacking?"

"She sees the future, so yeah." Seth backed away from him. "You got to know that's a bad idea. You offered me your court's protection."

"I did." Niall stared at the hot iron tip. Then he lifted his gaze to Seth as he wrapped his hand around the metal.

"Stop!" Seth surged forward, arm extended through the bars of the cage, but he couldn't reach Niall.

Niall didn't reply. The sizzle and scent of burnt flesh were the only signs that the Dark King was, in fact, injuring himself.

"Stop!" Seth repeated.

"Fine." Suddenly, Niall released the burning tip of the poker and shoved it toward Seth's face.

With the faery speed he was extremely grateful for, Seth moved—but not fast enough. Searing pain rocked him back as the poker grazed his face. His eye was intact, but a burn across his temple left him in agony.

"Damn it, Niall." Seth forced back the pain that threatened to make him vomit. "You can't do shit like that."

The Dark King's voice was dull as he asked, "Why?"

"Because . . ." The voice behind them made both Niall and Seth turn. Standing in the shadows of the room was the only person in the world who might be able to reason with the Dark King since Irial's death. The still-too-thin, soft-spoken mortal walked toward them. Her footsteps were sharp echoes on the cement floor.

"You are not this person," Leslie said.

Niall dropped the poker to the warehouse floor.

She walked farther into the room; her posture and expression said she was perfectly at ease with the scene in front of her.

Leslie stepped in front of the cage. "Niall? You don't really want to hurt yourself . . . or him."

Niall no longer looked like the fiend he'd been about to become mere moments ago. He looked like a faery who needed things that no one there could give him. "Seth *sees* things. He knew and . . . He knew that Irial . . ."

"I heard what happened." Leslie approached Niall with her hand outstretched. "Ash called me. Donia called me. . . .

You sent for me. Do you remember that, Niall? You sent Hounds."

Niall stared at Leslie with something between terror and hope. "I didn't want to tell you."

"I'm here." Leslie looked over her shoulder to where a Hound stood in the open doorway. "I am here with *my* court. I am here with *you* . . . because you needed me. *They* need me to be here with you."

The Hound said nothing even as his king looked at him, even as he saw the fire poker and the fact that Seth was caged. Seth didn't think for an instant that the Hound would set him free, so he was unsurprised when the Hound merely nodded at him before he turned and left.

Leslie took Niall's uninjured hand in hers. "Irial wouldn't want you to hurt. You *know* that."

"He died, Leslie. He's *gone*. I'm so tired, and he's gone."

"I know. That means you need to take care of the court and of yourself now." Leslie touched his face with her other hand. "Come rest with me."

"Seth *knew* and he—"

"Seth is not my concern right now . . . or yours." Leslie reached up and kissed Niall tenderly. "You're hurting. *I'm* hurting. Do you want to stand here and torture Seth or hold me so I can cry?"

"I don't want you to cry." Niall pulled her into his arms, though. "I couldn't save him. I tried, Leslie. I tried, and . . . I failed."

"Come on." Her voice was muffled by how tightly he

held her. "Will you rest with me, Niall?"

"I can't. If I sleep, I dream about Irial," Niall confessed. "I don't want to sleep."

Leslie leaned back and looked up at him. "I will be with you. I'll wake you if you need. Just take me to the house. Please?"

He hesitated. "I . . . inside . . . I was upset."

Leslie caressed his cheek. "You're in pain, and Irial is dead. Do you honestly think I care about anything other than that?"

With one arm around Leslie, Niall grabbed the chain with his injured hand and yanked. Seth's cage ascended. Once it was up at the rafters again, Niall fastened the chain to the bar.

Then, without another word, he and Leslie walked into the shadows of the warehouse and left Seth alone in the dark.

Unfortunately, he wasn't alone very long. A few hours later, he was awakened by a caw of laughter.

Bananach walked across the empty warehouse. Behind her was a parade of faeries, familiar and unfamiliar to Seth.

Bad to worse. Seth watched the mad raven-faery stroll into the Dark King's domain with enough blood on her that he knew someone was dead or severely injured. *Ask or wait?* He didn't know Bananach well enough to know which path was better.

Her steps were even as she crossed the warehouse to the Dark King's throne.

The raven-faery herself looked up at Seth as he stood and gripped the bars of his cage.

"My, my, little lamb. Aren't you a pleasant surprise?" She opened her wings full-width and lifted up to hover in front of him. As she did so, Seth could see that one wing was badly torn. Logic said she shouldn't be able to rise with such an injury, but he didn't think that pain was much of a deterrent to Bananach.

"Look, my lovelies: the old king left me a coronation present."

Seth wondered if she could taste emotions as Niall did. *Does she know I'm terrified?* He hoped not. He held his voice even and told her, "The Dark King—"

"Is gone." She dropped to the ground in front of the throne.

Did she kill Niall? Between the blood and her words, Seth wasn't sure. He searched to see Niall's threads, but there was only darkness. *Which doesn't* prove *anything.*

The assembled faeries were silent as Bananach stood before the empty throne. Their collective breaths sounded as a gasp as she stepped onto the dais and reached out to touch the arm of the chair.

She turned, her gaze sliding across the faeries watching her, and then she sat in the Dark King's throne. For a long moment, she closed her eyes and was silent. Then her eyes snapped open. "I am the Dark Queen. This is my throne, my court, and you"—she spared him an unsettling look— "are my prisoner."

Seth's eyes widened. "You can't just *declare* yourself queen. There are rules, processes, and—"

"Those are for subjects, and I, my lovely little lamb, am *over* being anyone's subject. When a regent is *meant to be*, she can make it so, and I am meant to be queen. I *am* the Dark Queen." She lifted her voice then. "My subjects? Come."

The room began to fill with even more faeries. Faeries that should belong to the Summer and Winter Courts joined Ly Ergs, some thistle-fey, and solitaries that Seth had seen around town. They all came crushing into the warehouse. With mad grins and bloody hands, they expressed their joy.

Bananach sat in the regent's place and gestured regally. "Come, my errant ones, and offer me your fealty."

To Seth's horror, they did. One after the next they knelt before her and bowed their heads. They retracted their oaths to Niall and called Bananach "my liege," and they offered vows of fealty.

At least he's alive. . . .

Seth had seen Niall fight Bananach twice, and he doubted that anyone else had the skill to do so—especially if Bananach had control of the Dark Court—but the unbalanced Dark King was currently in no shape to fight anyone successfully.

I don't want to oppose Niall.

No other High Court faery remained on this side of the veil.

When a regent is meant to be, he can make it so. Seth pondered the words that Bananach had used to explain her ability to become queen. *Either she's wrong, and it doesn't matter; or she's right, and this will work.*

When Bananach's hordes were done offering their promises to the raven-queen, they watched her with rapt adoration.

"I *am* the . . . Dark King's balance," Seth said as quietly as he could. "I am the faery that will balance Niall. I am the son of Order; I am made of the High Queen; I am your *brother*, Niall."

He felt ridiculous, but he kept repeating the words over and over as he looked down at the faeries that stood before the self-declared Dark Queen.

"I balance you, Niall . . . order to your darkness," Seth whispered.

Bananach stood and took two steps away from her throne.

"I am Order on this side of the veil." Seth stood and gripped the bars of the cage. "I am the Order to your Darkness."

The raven-faery let her gaze travel over the assembled fey. She glanced up at Seth briefly.

"The other regents would not give me the word I needed; they refused my hunger for war; but *I* am a regent now." Bananach lifted her voice and said the words that the other courts refused: "The Dark Queen, *your queen*, speaks War. They will bow before us, or they will be trampled under our feet."

CHAPTER 31

When Donia woke, she looked upward to see icicles and snow arches. For a moment, she wondered if she'd slept outside, but sheets were tangled around her legs. *My home. My bed.* She sighed happily. A wintery heaven filled her room to the point that she could hardly believe she was inside a house. She looked up at the crystalline ceiling over her head, and then at the faery sleeping beside her.

I want to stay right here forever.

Unlike the previous times she'd touched Keenan since she'd been fey, this time his skin was unbruised. Her ice didn't injure him as it had when he was the Summer King. She propped herself up on one arm, and with the other, she carefully slid her fingers through his hair, and then on to his bare shoulder. No steam lifted from his skin as it had when they'd spent Solstice together; no bruises formed as they had when she'd touched him other times. After decades of wanting this, of believing it could never truly happen, they were together.

"If I pretend to be asleep, will you keep touching me?" He kept his eyes closed, but he reached out and slid his knuckles down her bare arm.

When she didn't answer, he looked at her. "Don?"

"Tell me again."

With the same wicked smile that had stolen her breath when she'd met him, he pulled her into his arms and rolled her under him. He braced himself over her and stared into her eyes as he reminded her, "I love you, Donia."

Snow fell on him from somewhere above the bed as he lowered his lips to hers and told her, "And I will spend the rest of eternity loving you. Every day."

"And every night," she added with a smile.

"Mmmm, and every morning?" he asked.

To that question, there weren't any words that would do justice the way actions would, so Donia answered him with her touch and her kisses.

Afterward, when hungers of other sorts necessitated leaving the pleasures of the bed—and the snow-covered floor—Donia couldn't stop smiling. They walked through the house hand in hand.

Her faeries looked on approvingly, much to her surprise.

"I want you to stay here," she blurted.

Keenan paused. "Right now?"

"No." Donia turned so they were face-to-face. "Stay here, live here, *be* here."

The look of joy on his face made her realize that the

things she'd thought alluring when he was filled with sunlight were only a fraction of what he was now that he had only Winter within him. His eyes glimmered with the sheen of a perfect frost; his features seemed somehow sharper as she looked at him.

And I don't have to resist now.

With a satisfied sigh, she pulled him to her and kissed him. When she stepped back, his lips parted and his eyes widened in surprise.

"Say yes," she urged.

"I'm yours, Donia." He leaned his forehead against her head. "You don't need to offer anything you aren't ready—"

"Are you serious?" She laughed. "I've waited most of my life for you."

"You're a queen. I'll accept whatever you—"

She kissed him again, and then asked, "Do you want to live here?"

"Yes."

"Then don't be a fool, Keenan. I want you here."

"Once Niall is stable, and we know that Bananach won't slip in at night and kill us in our beds . . ." He scowled. "I don't know what we're going to do about her."

Donia interlaced her fingers with his. "You're not a king. It's not your duty now."

"Oh." He paused and then nodded. "I will fight . . . or what do you need?"

"You were going to go to Niall," she reminded him. "Have you changed your mind?"

"No," he said very carefully, "but I want to . . . I didn't know Evan was gone, and I don't want . . . Not that you can't defend yourself, but . . ." He raked his hand through his hair.

Gently, Donia suggested, "You're a solitary faery, Keenan. Not my subject. Not anyone's subject. You can do as you will."

He nodded.

"What are you going to do? What do you *want* to do?" she prompted.

"I'm going to go try to help Niall. He's not acting like himself, and I have a theory on what's wrong," he told her. "Then afterward I'm going to ask you to marry me."

She stepped backward, her knees strangely weak. "Faeries don't . . . That's not exactly *done.*"

"I've dreamed of it. The ceremony, the vow"—he stared at her with an intensity that made her sit down suddenly— "I thought about it a lot. Faery vows are unbreakable. If I phrased it right, you'd *know* that I belong to you. Only you. Always."

She blinked several times, and as casually as she could manage, pinched her wrist. *I am awake. Keenan is here in my home telling me he wants a faery vow and a wedding.* This was the part where she was to say something encouraging; she was sure of that. Instead, she stared at him silently.

He knelt, like a mortal man, on one knee before her. "Faeries don't make fidelity vows often, but we can. *We* can."

"Yes."

But he misunderstood and continued, "When I come back, I'll get a ring. First, I am going to help Niall. Something is wrong with him, and I'm going to try to figure out how to get him back to himself."

Too stunned by the utter unexpectedness of the morning, she nodded and repeated, "*Yes.*"

"We can do anything, Don. We'll defeat Bananach, help Niall. . . . Everything is possible now. *You* make me believe in the impossible. You always have." He stood and kissed her until she really wasn't sure if she was awake or dreaming, and then he said, "I'll be back. We'll stop Bananach, and then we'll have forever."

And he was gone before she could think clearly enough to explain that her yes was a *Yes, I'll marry you.*

CHAPTER 32

This time, Keenan sought the Dark King at his house. It was a place he'd never thought to visit voluntarily, and he wasn't sure that he would be able to gain entry. However, the Dark Court fey he'd seen had all suggested that Niall would be at the house. Of course, they'd also all suggested—with varying degrees of humor and fear—that Keenan had better be prepared to bleed if he was going to enter the Dark King's house.

Keenan arrived as a thistle-fey was leaving, so he avoided the awkwardness of getting past the gargoyle at the door. Inside the house, the evidence of Niall's rage was everywhere. Shattered glass and broken furniture were intermingled with twisted bits of metal. Dark stains made obvious that the damage wasn't merely to the inanimate.

The former Summer King walked through the debris until he stood in the doorway of the room where Niall sat.

"I don't think you were summoned, kingling, or"—the

body that was Niall's looked up at him—"that you're strong enough to withstand the Dark King's rage."

"I know Niall, and *you* aren't him." Cautiously, Keenan peered into a face that he knew as well as his own. "Tell me that you are truly Niall, or tell me what you've done to him."

"Curious theory," the imposter said.

Keenan stepped closer to the body that looked like his friend, but was not him. "Who are you?"

"I am the Dark King, and you"—he leaned back and stared at Keenan—"ought to know better than to question me. Do you forget what the Dark King can do? Do you miss that curse?"

The faery opened the cigarette case on the table and extracted one of the noxious things. The motions were decidedly *not* Niall's. Niall was many things, but he wasn't that easily arrogant.

Or dismissive. Or deliberate.

"Irial?" Keenan asked, testing his theory.

The Dark King leaned back and offered Keenan a sardonic smile. "War killed Irial."

"You don't appear to be *dead*." Keenan shook his head. "Is that why he's acting so . . . vile? You've taken his body and—"

Irial snorted. "No. He's grieving. Believe it not, kingling: he's mourning my loss."

"Yet you're here."

"You are observant, kingling." Irial pointed at Keenan with the unlit cigarette. "In his dreams and when I can get through in his waking hours, I've tried to explain that I'm really here, but he's struggling. He refuses to sleep properly since my death, and I was unable to speak to anyone to reveal my presence to the living until someone figured it out."

"Why?"

Irial gave Keenan a decidedly droll look. "Because he's *mourning. . . .*"

"No, *why* couldn't you tell anyone you were in there?" Keenan asked as patiently as he was able.

"There are rules, kingling. I hinted as best I could, but I forgot how *slow* some of you lot can be. I all but told you when you were at the warehouse," Irial said.

Only Irial would find a way around truly dying. The former Summer King felt a grudging respect for the dead king.

When Keenan gestured for Irial to continue, the dead Dark King inhabiting Niall's body added, "It's like lying: there are unbreakable *geasa*. Shades—even those of us not fully untethered—cannot tell the living of our postdeath experiences or presences unless the living call us out by name. It's only in Niall's mind that I can speak freely, and he's been obstinate."

"But you can talk to him in his dreams because . . ." Keenan rubbed his temples. "How are you dead, but here?"

The body that was Niall smiled a mocking smile that was pure Irial. "Before I died, our dreams were stitched together. I was dying, and I saw a chance"—Irial shrugged in faux modesty—"so I took it. Unfortunately, Niall has half convinced himself that if he's dreaming of me now, perhaps the dreams we shared after my stabbing but before my death weren't real either."

Keenan couldn't imagine what the two Dark Kings had dreamed that Niall wished were real—nor did he *want* to imagine those dreams. He might accept Niall's forgiveness of Irial some day, but the truth was that Keenan loathed Irial. The former Dark King had bound Keenan's powers; he had hurt Niall; and now he was possessing Niall. None of that evoked *positive* emotions.

"Could you go away?" Keenan asked.

"If Niall wanted me to, yes." Irial tapped his still-unlit cigarette on the table. "First, though, he needs to accept that I'm *here* before he decides whether or not to cast me out."

"Can you take"—Keenan gestured awkwardly—"the body at will?"

"Not unless he lets go of his control." Irial lifted the cigarette and lit it. After he took a long drag, he exhaled a plume of smoke in Keenan's direction. "I'm surprised you noticed. Even with the hints, I was thinking you wouldn't get it. I'm glad you did, but surprised that *you* were the one to catch on."

"He is my friend," Keenan said simply.

Irial stood up and walked toward Keenan. When they were face-to-face, Irial said, "I hated your mother, you know, but her grief was great when your father died. It made her do things that were awful."

"He was dead because she killed him."

"Yes, well"—Irial gestured dismissively—"that is true. Still. She was grieving, and she was afraid."

Keenan wanted to strike out, but it wasn't truly Irial: Niall's body would feel any blows. "Do you have a point?"

"I don't fully regret binding you. I did what I had to do for my court, but I respected Miach enough to be sorry that I had to hurt his son. Beira's grief led to troubles. It's why Bananach manipulated your parents. She has been manipulating us as she did them." Irial blew smoke in Keenan's direction again. "Niall's grief would be more deadly, if not for actions I took. He is unbalanced and grieving. He needs friends. Allies. *You* need to help him."

"I know." Keenan waved the smoke out of his face. "And I'll tell him you're . . . here—assuming he listens. I gather that's what you want."

"Yes." Irial smiled, and seeing the familiar half-laughing smile of the former Dark King on Niall's face was disconcerting. "You do know, of course, that he's not forgiven you. He's a grudge holder, so you'll need to try to convince him. Ahhh. I could tell you something delectable that no one else would know. A little detail to convince him our dreams were real—what do you think?"

"Go away, Irial."

Laughter greeted Keenan's discomfort, and then Irial said, "If you're sure . . . I'd take a step or two back if I were you. Then again, I never did like you, so . . ."

Keenan rolled his eyes, but he retreated all the same as Niall came back into possession of himself.

Confusion flickered over Niall's face. "You cannot just walk into my home." He shoved Keenan against the wall, and then paused.

He peered into Keenan's eyes. "What did you do? You're . . . different."

"I gave up my throne."

Niall's anger fled under shock, but he still had one hand pressing Keenan against the wall. "Why?"

"The Summer Court needed a stronger regent." Keenan ticked the reasons off on his fingers. "I needed to be with the faery I love; the Summer Queen needed to be with the one she loves; and *you* need a temporary advisor."

"A temp—*you* . . ." Niall looked from Keenan to his own hand. He released Keenan and frowned, seemingly confused by the sight of the lit cigarette between his fingers. "Why would I accept *you*?"

Keenan kept his voice even. "You were there for me, Niall. Let me be here. The courts *all* need to be strengthened. Bananach will destroy us all if we don't do something. Irial wants you to know—"

"No!" Niall slammed Keenan into the wall a second time. "Irial—"

"Is inside your body somehow. I just spoke to him. You. Him in your body. He wants you to know he's still here." Keenan stayed perfectly still. "Do you remember me arriving?"

"No, not really." Niall's voice held a thread of hope as he asked, "Irial is here?"

"He is. Inside you."

"I'm not mad?"

Keenan shook his head, and then looked pointedly at the cigarette that was now burning a hole in his shirt. "I won't swear to *that*, Niall, but you're not mad for thinking Irial is here . . . there. With you somehow."

Silently, Niall released him. "I hear him. I thought . . . I thought I was *fractured*."

"You imprisoned Seth. You skewered your faeries." Keenan shook his head again. "I'm not going to pretend to understand what you are doing, but whatever else is going on, you're not imagining him. He said something about stitched dreams. Does that make sense?"

Niall turned his back to Keenan, but he nodded.

"He also said your shared dreams were real," Keenan added.

The Dark King tensed at that revelation. His sudden stillness alarmed Keenan, and the awkwardness of the moment stretched out. When Niall finally spoke, he said, "I don't expect you to understand."

"He hurt you," Keenan said simply. "When I was a child, I remember the way you looked when I asked about your scars. He let them hurt you, did *nothing* to keep you safe. I don't understand how you can forgive him for failing you."

"Donia almost died for your mistakes." Niall turned to face him. His expression was unreadable. "You used me like a weapon against the Dark Court. Are you so sure you want to discuss forgiveness?"

"I made decisions that I thought were best for my court and my subjects—including *you* then." Keenan didn't flinch away from the censure that had entered Niall's eyes as he spoke. "Kings aren't always at liberty to let emotions overrule duty."

"Exactly," Niall said.

They stood at an impasse. Keenan clung to his hatred of Irial, but he was relieved that Niall was speaking to him civilly.

Niall walked away, and Keenan followed him farther into the wreckage of the Dark King's home. The destruction was somewhat expected: he'd known that Niall wasn't dealing well with his grief. What was *unexpected* was the sight that greeted him as they entered what appeared to have been a study: in the doorway stood the mortal who had been the source of Niall's ire at Keenan.

"What is *he* doing here?" Leslie folded her arms over her chest.

The Dark King turned his back to Keenan. "Les? I thought you were still sleeping."

The mortal marched across the room with a self-confidence utterly at odds with the broken spirit he'd last seen in her. She stepped in front of Niall, putting herself between the two faeries, and pointed at Keenan. "Don't you upset him."

Keenan held up his hands disarmingly.

"He's . . ." She glanced over her shoulder at Niall, and her ferocity vanished. "He's going to be fine. He's already *much clearer* today, so you can just walk out of here."

"Les?"

She looked at the Dark King.

"Did you know?" he asked. "About Iri?"

"That he died?" Leslie took Niall's arm and led him farther away from Keenan. "You told me, but I knew when I
got here." She shot a glare back at Keenan. "We talked about
this. When you woke up, Niall, you were better than before.
You weren't thinking right because of fatigue, but it's better.
You're better, and I'm going to stay a few days, help you get
settled with the . . . things that he handled."

"He's not dead," Niall told her. "He's still here. Keenan
said—"

"Get out," Leslie snarled at Keenan. She stepped away
from the Dark King faster than a mortal should be able to
move and advanced on Keenan. "He's upset, and whatever
you did or said made him worse—"

"Irial is *inside* Niall," Keenan said.

"Get out!" Leslie grabbed Keenan's shirt and started to tug
him toward the door. "Get out. Stay out. Just leave us alone."

"Shadow Girl? Leslie, love?" Irial-Niall grabbed her hand
and tugged her away from Keenan. The Dark King kept
hold of her as he turned her to face him. "The kingling is
telling the truth. I couldn't tell you last night. I wanted to,
but there are rules."

"Iri?" Leslie gaped at the Dark King. "Honestly?"

"I'm here." He pulled her into his arms. "I've been here
since I died. Every moment."

"Iri . . . oh gods, I thought . . . He . . ." She leaned against him, and whatever she said next was muffled against his chest—or Niall's chest, in actuality.

"Far Dorcha is still in town because of you," Keenan announced. The missing detail suddenly became clear. The head of the death-fey had come to Huntsdale because of the peculiarity of Irial's state of death.

As Irial-Niall turned, he kept one arm around Leslie, and for an odd moment, Keenan wasn't entirely sure which of them was currently in possession of the Dark King's body. "Yes."

Leslie looked at Irial-Niall. "Who?"

"Death," Keenan answered. He sat down on the edge of a relatively clean table near the unlit fireplace. "I will do whatever Niall needs, but we have to have a plan. Far Dorcha can't stay in town. Bananach is already trouble enough."

"Her," Leslie muttered. "She needs to die an ugly death."

"My bloodthirsty girl." Irial smiled at Leslie, and the proud darkness in that smile made quite clear that it was the former Dark King in control.

Leslie scowled. "I'm not bloodthirsty, but . . . seriously, she *killed* you. She needs to be dead."

"Except killing her could kill *every* faery, love," Irial pointed out. He glanced at Keenan and added in a level voice, "That's the problem. It's the only reason our boy hasn't gone after her. Perhaps you might take it up with your ex-queen's . . . What is he?"

"Ex-queen?" Leslie's eyes widened. "Ash isn't Summer Queen now?"

"She is," Keenan said. "I'm no longer Summer King, though."

Leslie leaned her head against the Dark King's shoulder. "How about we start at the beginning?"

Irial tilted her chin up so that he could stare at her. "In a moment."

Without looking at Keenan, Irial made a shooing gesture with one hand.

And Keenan walked out to give them their privacy. He'd only left the Summer Court a day ago, but embracing his Winter Court nature meant that the complicated relationships of the Dark Court were unsettling now. After centuries of spending much of his free time pursuing girl after girl, the idea of eternity with only one faery was his sole desire.

Before he could begin that eternity, Keenan needed to help his former advisor—and the dead faery who'd once helped bind Summer—figure out how to nullify Bananach, and convince Far Dorcha to depart.

Keenan sighed.

No problem.

CHAPTER 33

A block from the Dark Court's warehouse, Chela held up one gloved hand. Three faery messengers and one Hound directly behind her paused. She told the messengers, "Obey him."

The messengers nodded.

"Once they're gone," she told the Hound, "you will fight, but until the messengers go, you wait."

The thought of missing any of the battle obviously wasn't appealing to the Hound. His scowl deepened, but he nodded. "I'll make up for lost minutes, Gabr—*Chela.*"

"I know you will, Eachann. Gabriel will be pleased when he comes back," Chela said, and then she urged her steed, Alba, forward. No one would declare her mate dead if she could hold even a sliver of hope.

Some Hounds are daft, Alba muttered in her mind.

Instead of answering, Chela urged aloud, "Faster."

In only a matter of seconds, Alba battered down the

warehouse door with his front paws. Unlike her mate's steed, Chela's shifted shapes the way some people changed clothes. Alba wasn't frivolous, merely awkward with emotions. He chose to express his feelings with his shape. The fact that their Gabriel was missing meant that Alba was leonine, feral and ready to hunt.

Me too, Alba. She stroked one hand over her steed's close-cropped fur, and then she extended her voice to the rest of the Hunt and added, *No mercy if Gabriel is . . . gone.*

None of the Hounds replied, but they all knew that their Gabriel was either dead or severely injured. As his second, Chela wouldn't be able to communicate nonverbally with the pack if he were safe. She held hope, though. She and Gabriel might have had a few difficulties—including those over his tendency to sire half-mortal children during their times apart over the years—but they were as faithful as Hounds ever were.

He is not dead yet, she told Alba once again. *If the words were lies, I couldn't speak them.*

Her steed was too kind to remind her that opinion didn't follow the truth rule, but they both knew it. If Gabriel was gone, she'd do what she must. Gone or not, he'd been injured enough that she was acting in his stead.

She will suffer, Alba growled. *We will not stand down.*

The faery courts had let things go too long. The Hunt had no such patience. Gabriel had pursued Bananach. That told them where their Gabriel stood on the issue of striking War.

We will finish the fight our Gabriel began, Chela told them all as they followed her into the Dark Court's warehouse.

They were silent as they saw confirmation of one of the fears that had brought them here: Bananach sat on the regent's throne. The raven-faery snapped her beak at them as the Hunt continued to thunder into the vast room. She stayed spine-straight, ankles crossed and hands dangling carelessly over the arms of the black throne. Her wings curled forward on either side, so she appeared to be surrounded by a giant shield.

All around her, Ly Ergs and unfamiliar faeries waited. A few Dark Court faeries were in the crowd, but they did their best to duck behind others as the Hunt poured in. Sparks glimmered in the shadows as the steeds' claws, hooves, and talons struck the cement floor.

Stay mounted, Chela ordered.

Where is the Dark King? one of her Hounds asked.

Seth is caged, another reported. *Left and above the throne. Birdcage.*

Is Seth injured? Chela asked.

Yet another Hound replied, *Can't tell. Not moving. Think he's alive, though.*

If he is dead, it's recent, said the first Hound.

Despite the flurry of reports that joined these in her head, Chela's outward expression was implacable. She faced War, who had apparently staged a coup.

Straight up the center, Alba.

Chela's steed stalked toward the raven-faery.

"Gabriela!" Bananach crooned. "Have you come to show your support of your queen?"

Chela stared directly at Bananach. "I am Chela, mate to the Gabriel, second-in-command of this Hunt."

"*You* are Gabriela, and I am the Dark Queen . . . and this"—Bananach opened her arms wide—"is my court."

"No. There is no Dark *Queen*," Chela ground out.

Underneath her, Alba growled his accord. The assembled faeries—the whole mutinous lot of them—shifted nervously as other steeds and Hounds echoed Alba's growl.

"Yet here I am." Bananach paused as if confused. "No, I'm sure of it. I am the queen here, and I could use the Hunt. As I killed him—the last Gabriel—that would be your decision, Gabriela."

Gabriel is dead. My mate. Chela's hand tightened on the hilt of the first sword her mate had given her. She drew it from the scabbard with a slide of metal on metal.

Draw weapons, she demanded.

As the Hunt complied, Chela lifted her voice and her sword: "The Hunt, with Gabriel at the helm or with me, will stand with the Dark King. If you are here with this imposter"—Chela did not look at the assembled fey, but instead sneered at Bananach—"you are declared enemy to the Hunt."

"You challenge me, whelp?" Bananach tilted her head to one side and then to the other as if studying Chela.

"Do you declare yourself queen of this court?"

"I do," Bananach said.

"Then the Hunt challenges you." Chela added silently to her Hunt, *On my word . . . Ready . . .*

"Fair warning," Chela said aloud. "The Hunt comes here as sworn support of the *rightful* regent of the Dark Court. Stand against us, and be found our enemy."

She focused on each of them, marking their faces and scents in her mind.

Know them. Remember them, she told the Hunt. *They stood with the one who killed our Gabriel, who killed his daughter, who killed Irial. No mercy. No survivors.*

The bemused expression on Bananach's face was unfaltering. She looked only at Chela, but she told the assembled traitors, "You've sworn fealty to me, and I've spoken War. They stand with our enemies, and as your *queen,* I order you: kill them all."

Now, Chela growled to her Hunt.

Then Bananach launched herself at Chela in a blur of feathers and talons, and there were no more words.

Hounds and faeries and steeds filled the Dark Court's warehouse with screams and blood. Bodies crashed together in a fight that had been too long in coming.

Send the messengers for the faery courts. This is the end.

CHAPTER 34

Keenan had just listened to Niall and Irial explain that because of Faerie being closed they could—*possibly*—kill Bananach. Everyone knew that Bananach wasn't going to stop, but killing her on the basis of the new seer's word . . . that was a bit of a leap.

"I'm not sure we *can* kill her. She's strong," Irial pointed out. "She killed me and cut through Devlin like he was untrained. We've got us, the Hounds, and those we can round up from the other courts."

"Could we contain her?" Keenan asked.

Before anyone could reply, one of the thistle-fey came into the wreckage-strewn room unannounced. "My King!" He half pushed, half dragged another faery in front of him. "War has come."

Before they could reply, the faery that had been shoved into the room said, "The Hunt has begun the battle, Your Majesties." He looked from Niall to Keenan and back to Niall. "The Huntswoman sent us to each of the three courts. The fight . . . Bananach sits on your throne, has declared herself Dark Queen."

"She *what*?" Niall—*or perhaps Irial*—asked.

Keenan repressed a shiver at the darkness in that voice. He'd seen Niall angry, understood the horrible depths that both kings were capable of separately, and now wondered what it would mean to have both of those tempers in the same body.

"We have our answer." Niall-Irial stood. The Dark King caught Leslie's hand, and the terrible darkness vanished. "Will you stay here? If things . . ."

"I'll be here. Not forever, but for a couple days until everything is sorted out." The mortal girl embraced the Dark King. "Go kick her ass."

With something like awe in his expression, the Dark King—whichever of them—looked at Leslie and then kissed her briefly.

He turned to Keenan. "Will you fight? Or now that you have no sunlight . . . are you able?"

Instead of answering, Keenan let winter fill his eyes as he looked at the Dark King. "I am not skilled with *this* element, but I am not exactly defenseless."

Irial—because that dry tone was clearly not Niall—said, "Well, wouldn't Beira be . . . shocked?"

"No." Keenan shook his head. "She knew all along what I could do. I *chose* to be Summer, and she knew it every day of my life."

The Dark King smiled. "Your father would've been proud."

Keenan paused and admitted, "I hope so. . . . Niall?"

"No. . . . That was Irial." Niall shook his head. "I hear him when he speaks now. I hear him speaking in my head to only me, and I hear him when he speaks to you with . . . *through* me."

Keenan stared at Niall. "Can you fight like this?"

"I can. I feel better now than I have since he died." Niall frowned. "I don't know if it's from sleeping or knowing he's still with me or . . ." Niall's words faded as he put aside whatever thoughts he was trying to make sense of. He looked at Keenan. "Donia knows about your capacity for Winter?"

"She was the only one alive who *did* know until now." Keenan looked around the room. The mortal, the Dark Kings, the messenger, and the thistle-fey all stared back at him, and the former Summer King felt like a carnival curiosity. "Do we have a plan?"

"Weapons," Niall called. "We fight War. *Now.*"

Dark Court faeries came trooping into the room as if utterly unconcerned by the king's declaration that they were going to fight War. One tossed a halberd to—or possibly *at*—Keenan. They were nothing like the faeries he had been surrounded by his whole life. Several of them paused to smile at the mortal girl; Leslie sat peacefully in their midst as if they weren't loathsome. None of the thistle-fey touched her, but most every faery that crossed the threshold beamed at the sight of her, and many of the not-painful-to-touch faeries stroked her cheek or arm as they passed her. Through it all, Leslie said nothing.

The messenger looked far less at ease.

The messenger . . .

Keenan passed the halberd off to a thistle-fey and grabbed the messenger. "Go to the water, the river, and tell them that the *bestia* brings deaths. Tell them that Innis promised to aid me. Go."

The Dark King hefted a broadsword. "You weren't merely out sulking after all."

A group of three faeries came in with arms full of weapons—many bloodstained—and tossed them onto the floor. Other faeries sifted through the weapons. The flow of armed faeries started toward the street. They were chortling and grinning.

The messenger fled, and Keenan shrugged. "Having allies seemed wise."

"Are we allies now, kingling?"

"I'm not a *king*, but I will fight with the Dark Court and any of those who stand against Bananach, and not"— Keenan stared directly at the Dark King and grabbed several throwing knives from the stack of weapons—"because of a *threat* by either of you."

"You are your father's son," Irial remarked.

Keenan looked back at the faery who had bound him, who now possessed the king he'd offered to advise. "I won't ever like you, but my father saw something worthwhile in you, and so does Niall. Summer will, undoubtedly, be there, and I know Winter will."

"Then let's move so we're not last to the party."

"My Queen!" Tavish's voice rang through the loft.

Aislinn felt as much as heard the panic bloom in her seemingly imperturbable advisor. She hurriedly pulled a sundress over her head, but she was barefoot when she rushed to the main room of the loft. The onslaught of full Summer inside of her made it hard to stand still, so at the least, the burst of speed to her advisor's side was refreshing.

"What's wrong?"

"A messenger arrived, my Queen." Tavish was moving toward her even as he spoke, and he stood at her side before he continued, "The war has begun."

The messenger flinched and turned her face from the flash of light that filled the room. *New powers; not really the best time to go diving into battles.* Aislinn sighed, and eddies of wind tore books from the shelves. With effort, she spoke softly. "Where? Who fights?"

"The Dark Court's warehouse, my lady." The doe-eyed faery moved aside as a torn bit of curtain floated to the floor beside her. "The Hunt started the fight when Bananach declared herself Dark Queen . . . and the Gabriela bade me tell you that War has Seth."

"She has Seth," Aislinn repeated, with a stillness that was the polar opposite of her emotions. "Has him *how*? Where?"

"In a cage." The faery stepped backward even as she spoke. "Gabriela—"

"Gabriela?" Tavish interrupted.

"Hound that was Chela. The Gabriel's dead, so she's Gabriela." The faery shivered as rain filled the room. "I am blameless, Summer Queen."

"I'm not angry with you," Aislinn muttered. Every bit of self-control she had was going into keeping her temper in check.

So really *not the time to do this.*

Tavish advised, "The rain is fine, my Queen, but the sunlight in here is growing dangerous to any not of our court."

"Oh." Aislinn concentrated specifically on dulling the light and heat. She inhaled the warmth with a steady breath and then stared at her advisor with sunlight still pulsing on her tongue. Carefully, she said, "Let's take it to where it can be dangerous to the right one then."

Tavish nodded. "The Summer Guard will be ready in fifteen minutes."

"Fine, but I'm leaving in five, with or without guards." Aislinn strode off.

The Summer Queen returned to her room to pull on boots and jeans. Getting her feet crushed by flailing faeries was an avoidable injury, and her wet sundress was far from ideal for movement. *Or fighting.* She shucked off her clothes and yanked on jeans. *I can't fight worth a damn.* She'd taken lessons from Tavish, trained with the guard after Donia had stabbed her. *It's not the same as centuries of experience.* The handles of her drawer turned to ashes in her hand. *Or any experience with all of summer inside me.* Ashes slipped from her hand to the floor.

Siobhan came in. "Let me help."

"Stupid wood." Aislinn wiped her hand on her jeans.

The new Summer advisor pulled out the charred drawer.

Aislinn blinked away sudden tears of frustration and worry. "How am I to do this? I can't control this yet."

"You don't need to keep it in check in a fight, Aislinn." Siobhan reached in to grab the blade nestled among the T-shirts and immediately pulled her hand back when she realized that the blade was steel.

"Got it. *That* I can touch." Aislinn wrapped her hand around the hilt. "I want you to stay here." Then she yelled over her shoulder, "Two minutes!"

"I can fight." Siobhan glared at her queen. "I've been—"

"Not doubting you." Aislinn pulled her hair back into a hasty braid. "I need someone to handle things here if we don't . . . If anyone gets past us, there are faeries here who are not designed for fights. You are in charge until I return."

Siobhan bowed. "I won't fail you."

"Hopefully, it won't come to that, but . . ." Aislinn shook her head, and then she looked at her friend and advisor. She took a deep breath and nodded. "I can do this."

"You can." Siobhan squeezed Aislinn's free hand. "You are the Summer Queen. The first faery to hold the full weight of Summer in more than nine hundred years. Trust your instincts."

Aislinn laughed. "My instinct is that I want to incinerate

Bananach. Summer is to rejoice. Threatening my faeries? Starting conflicts with my friends? Injuring *Seth*? Not encouraging much rejoicing."

"He's going to be fine." Siobhan stared directly at her.

"How can you say that? You don't know—"

"Neither do you," Siobhan said firmly. "And if he's not, we'll deal with it, but right now, your beloved needs rescuing."

Aislinn leaned in and kissed Siobhan's cheek. "I knew you would be a fabulous advisor."

Then the Summer Queen strode through the loft, calling, "Time's up."

Some of her faeries were still strapping on weapons, but Tavish was at the door. "Those not ready will follow in short order."

Admittedly relieved that he was at her side, Aislinn nodded, and together she and her advisor led the Summer Guard toward the Dark Court's warehouse.

CHAPTER 35

While the remaining Dark Court faeries assembled, the Dark King turned to Keenan. "Seth. He's still at the warehouse. If the Summer Queen learns . . ."

"Ash will meet us there, and unless someone speaks otherwise, she'll think it was Bananach who . . . caged him," Keenan said.

The Dark King nodded. "He was alive when I left."

"Let's hope he's still that way when we get there," Keenan muttered, "and when Ash gets there."

"Sorcha was ready to kill us all to protect him," Niall-Irial said almost absently as he walked over to a panel on the wall and opened it. "I didn't intend him to die . . . else I'd have given him to Far Dorcha."

"Am I the only one who hasn't crossed paths with the Dark Man?" Keenan asked.

The Dark King walked over to the mortal on the sofa. He knelt in front of her and handed her a gun and a spare clip. "Solid steel bullets. We can't use them, but you're still mortal enough that *you* can. Use them if she comes here. I think you're safer here than anywhere else, but . . ."

Leslie nodded.

"If I . . . *we* die . . ." The Dark King faltered. "Don't hesitate to ask them for help. Seth, Keenan, Ash, whoever lives. Whatever you need to do to survive. . . . I wish you didn't have to deal with this, Shadow Girl. This world, this—"

"If Bananach wins, she'll kill me." Leslie trailed her fingers over Niall's scarred cheek and added, "I love you."

"And we love you." The Dark King kissed her softly, and then he looked around the room at the assembled faeries. "Seth says we can kill Bananach. Let's go find out if he's right."

"And if he's not?" Keenan asked.

"We either die by her hand or as a result of killing her." The Dark King shrugged. "I'd rather go out in a fight."

The former Summer King lifted a short sword. "It's a shame we can't use guns. Walk in, shoot her, and be done with it."

Niall laughed. "You stop being king for all of what . . . a day?"

He glanced at Keenan, who shrugged. "About that."

"A day of being solitary and you want to throw Faerie Law aside." Niall gestured for the remaining faeries to precede him and slung an arm over Keenan's shoulder. "You might be qualified to advise the Dark Court after all."

"Assuming we aren't about to get slaughtered," Keenan added.

"Sure." Niall followed his faeries into the street. "Some of us will live . . . or we'll all die. Either way, I don't see the benefit of worrying about it."

Dark Court faeries laughed, and Keenan shook his head. He wasn't sure who he was anymore, what he was, or if there was a tomorrow, but now that Irial and Niall were shifting in and out of steering the Dark King's body, Niall seemed almost sane—or at least as sane as possible when they were off to fight War—and the faeries he would fight alongside were the most vicious of the courts.

Except Winter. Don will be there too. Other messengers had gone to Summer and Winter. *Not apart but working together.* It seemed like that should matter, but a dethroned Dark King, an untrained Summer Queen, and a former Summer King weren't the ideal group even if they were together.

Which leaves Donia . . .

With thoughts of his beloved on his mind, he ran across Huntsdale in the company of the members of the Dark Court who hadn't sided with Bananach, the Dark King who was possessed by the dead Dark King, and a few solitary faeries who joined their group.

Half a block away from the fight, they had to stop running. Even at this distance, the roar of the fray they were about to enter made more than a few passing mortals look to the sky as if a storm rode in overhead. *Be grateful you can't see,* he thought. Then he exhaled a gust of cold air toward them, hoping to send them farther from the fight that had spilled into the street in front of him. Some of the mortals scurried away.

The former Summer King put a hand on his once-advisor's arm. "I am no longer a regent. Her declaration of regency could mean that I am useless against her."

"She is *not* a regent," Niall snarled.

Then Bananach's troops swarmed toward them with weapons raised.

Niall's faeries fought against those who should be his. The Dark Court had been weakened by Bananach's machinations—*as Summer would've been if I'd tried to stay.*

Hounds and their steeds were already fighting, but far too many faeries had been called to Bananach's aid. Keenan looked around at the staggering number of faeries.

Where did they all come from?

War had been recruiting solitaries and faeries who should belong to other courts. He saw lupine and rowan and thistle-fey fighting alongside the Ly Ergs. He wasn't sure how they could tell enemy from ally, but one enemy was clear—Bananach. There was no doubt there. They just had to get to her.

"Safe hunting," Niall called as he launched himself into the fray.

Any answer Keenan could've offered would have been swallowed by the cacophony of violence. The loyal clashed with those who'd tried to usurp their king, and the result was already obvious: the dead, of both sides, littered the ground.

The Summer Queen and Tavish were three blocks from the Dark Court's warehouse when Aislinn found the composure to say the words she didn't want to speak: "If she hurts him or . . . worse, I will kill her."

"Even if she doesn't, she needs to be stopped." Tavish kept pace with her despite the increasing speed at which she traveled.

Aislinn's self-control was not as thorough as she would have liked: snow melted in floods in her wake; trees burst into bloom; and rivers of mud rolled into the street.

Finally, as they were almost at the warehouse, she asked, "Advice?"

He gestured for her to pause for a moment. As the Summer Guard raced up behind them, he said only, "Trust your instincts. If we can't stop her, we'll be looking at our deaths anyhow."

In front of them, Aislinn saw Dark Court fey fighting Dark Court fey, and she wasn't sure which was the side her court fought *with* and which was the side they fought *against*. "How do I know who to fight?"

Tavish lifted his sword. "If they swing at you, defend yourself."

"Right." She shoved sunlight like a blade into the chest of a faery running at them. "Did we have a plan? You're the one with experience at this."

"The plan? Thin Bananach's numbers, hope we can nullify or kill her, not die, and rescue Seth." Tavish swept a Ly Erg's legs out from under him, and then sliced open the faery's throat.

The sight of it gave her pause. "Is he . . ."

"Dead? Yes." Tavish no longer looked like the diplomatic advisor she'd known. Every semblance of civility was gone as he neatly cut down another faery without hesitation. "They knew the risk when they stood with Bananach. As do our faeries when they fight against her. . . ."

At that reminder—*my faeries or the madwoman's faeries*—the twinge of horror Aislinn felt was replaced by resolve. *I am the Summer Queen. These are* my *faeries.* She saw Keenan, cornered by three Ly Ergs—and holding his own. *My faeries* and *my friends.*

With a concentrated look, she sent a sunbeam sizzling at the chest of one of the Ly Ergs. The faery fell, and Keenan flashed her a grin before resuming his fight with the other two. As Aislinn started to strike another of the faeries Keenan fought, four former Dark Court faeries charged her and Tavish.

Several more Summer Court guards came up on either side of her. Tavish stayed slightly in front of her. As far as Aislinn could see, faeries engaged in fights to the death, and somewhere in that morass of violence Seth was trapped.

"Lead on," she told Tavish as she directed several more sunbeams at the seditious faeries.

Tavish nodded to one of the guards, and as a group they

advanced through the center of the conflict while the rest of her guard engaged the faeries fighting for Bananach. Blades of all sorts flashed in the sunlight that radiated from her skin. If it had been only Summer Court faeries fighting on her side, she could have let the full force of her light shine, but some of the Dark Court faeries were there to oppose Bananach. A solar flare would blind and injure allies too.

A storm wouldn't favor only her side either.

One at a time, then.

She didn't know how many faeries stood between her and Seth, or even where to look for him, but he was in there.

As are my faeries and my friends.

Aislinn, Tavish, and the rowan advanced slowly, and as they did, she aimed sunbeams and sent vines tangling the enemies. They weren't fatal strikes, but killing still made her squeamish. In defense, she could do it. *Or if Seth is injured.* She blanched as a thistle-fey skewered a vine-wrapped faery, but she continued as she was. Mercy wasn't the way of the Dark Court fey.

It won't be mine either if Seth is injured . . . or worse.

CHAPTER 36

The Winter Court was last to arrive. In front of her, Donia saw Summer Court and Dark Court fey. The crush of faeries extended from the warehouse to the edge of the street and spilled into the block around them. Various rowan and Summer Girls—*Summer Girls?*—fought the enemy. Others dragged mortals away from the violence.

"Summer, *move!*" Donia waited the count of three for the faeries to get to safety before she hissed a breath of ice into the street, chasing the mortals away effectively and quickly. The ice from her lungs wasn't thick enough to kill the Summer Court faeries who weren't out of her reach, but it did make a couple of them falter.

"Winter, *here.*" She let another, much stronger gust of ice coat the ground. She could keep the mortals from crossing the line into the faery war that had erupted.

Beside her several of the most dominant of the Hawthorns and Scrimshaw Sisters and lupine stood awaiting her decisions. She gave her faeries an icy smile. "Winter shows no mercy to Bananach. Push forward into the thick of the fight—but only if doing so does not make the boundary porous. No escapes."

At her word, all of the faeries beside her except for Cwenhild carried the word to the troops. The Scrimshaw Sister waited. Without any ceremony or drama, Cwenhild had stepped up to fill the role of chief guard and advisor.

Donia looked at her questioningly.

She shrugged and said simply, "I protect my queen."

"I *will* fight."

Cwenhild shrugged again. "So be it."

Donia hadn't had the years of fighting experience that the Dark Kings or the Hunt had, but what she did have was power that ached to be released. The sheer number of faeries fighting in the streets outside the Dark King's warehouse made it impossible for her troops to get inside, so Donia stayed with her fey. She felt the pain of loss strike her when her faeries fell, felt the cold satisfaction of their victories, and she shivered at both sensations.

Mine. They are mine to protect.

In the midst of the fight, Ankou and Far Dorcha strode through the bodies; the death-fey were untouched by the violence. No stray arrows or knives' tips pierced them. Their clothes were torn, and the hem of Ankou's winding sheet was heavy with blood and dirt and ice. She went about her macabre business, collecting the corpses, removing them from the fight—and for the first time, Donia understood the need for the death-faery's work. The fallen did not deserve to be left to be trampled; the living didn't need to see their comrades dead in their path. Ankou did necessary work in the midst of battle.

"My Queen?" Cwenhild prompted.

"None of Bananach's faeries are to get past you." Donia looked up, aware that both Far Dorcha and Ankou had stopped mid-step to look at her. The suddenness of their gazes made her falter. Seeing Death gazing back at her so studiously wasn't encouraging.

My faeries bleed.

"I go with you. I protect my queen first and always," Cwenhild insisted.

"No." Donia pulled her gaze away from the two death-fey. "You know how to lead them in battle. That is my order, Cwenhild. They need a general, and I need you to lead them, not guard me."

"I disagree," Cwenhild said, "but I will do as you order."

As Donia pushed through the fight, she saw Keenan near the door of the warehouse. He hadn't yet reached Bananach, but he was obviously trying. Frost and frozen flecks of blood clung to his skin like a dusting of silver and crimson glitter.

"What are you doing?" she muttered. Keenan wasn't a king anymore; he couldn't stand against Bananach if she was a regent in truth. Only regents or equally powerful faeries could kill regents, and Keenan had surrendered most of his power.

The Winter Queen had swords of ice in both hands, and when that wasn't enough of an offensive, she exhaled and encased faeries in sheets of ice. While she had been queen less than two years, she'd wielded Winter as the Winter Girl for almost a century.

Donia battled her way to Keenan, and then fought side by side with him. As she speared the chest of a thistle-fey, she told Keenan, "You waited for me. How sweet of you."

"I *am* a gentleman sometimes." The glee in Keenan's eyes reminded her that while he had never been as adept at fighting as he was at seduction, he was still far more experienced at fighting than either she or Aislinn were.

We can do this.

Donia turned so that she was back-to-back with Keenan; she erected a wall of ice in the path of the faeries who advanced toward them, effectively dividing the fight. All those who would come up behind them were now locked out. Her faeries, along with the dark and summer fey, would deal with the mutinous lot outside the ware-house. The Hounds, the rowan, and the Dark Court fey inside would stand against the faeries left on this side of her barrier.

She turned back to face Keenan, and for a brief moment, they were alone with a wall of ice behind them, and the chaos of violence in front of them. "Where's Niall?"

"Somewhere in there." Keenan motioned with a lift of his chin toward the warehouse. "He's a bit more determined."

"Nothing to do with his skills," Donia teased.

"Maybe a little, but"—Keenan gave her a look that was every bit the wicked faery she'd woken up next to—"I'm sticking to the 'waiting for you' answer."

"You sure you want to do this?" Donia glanced his way.

The impishness in his eyes was replaced by resolve. "Ash and Niall are in there. Bananach already killed Evan, Gabriel, Irial, possibly Seth if he was still in his cage. . . ."

"Seth was *caged* here?" Donia looked toward the melee. "Does Ash know?"

Keenan shook his head. "That's not something I'll be telling Ash either. It's not *my* business now."

The ease with which Keenan had slipped into non–Summer Court gave Donia a brief pause, but the truth was that Keenan was a faery, had only ever been a faery. His loyalty was to court first, and right now, he'd offered that loyalty to Niall—and to her. *Just like that. He is a subject . . . to protect.* Carefully, she suggested, "You could stay out here—"

"Don?" Keenan's glare was withering. "I'm not a king anymore, but I'm far from defenseless. Plus, I have plans for a future now . . . one that requires peace."

He stepped into the warehouse.

She wanted to be angry, but if he hadn't been the sort of faery who'd stood against impossible odds repeatedly, they'd never be where they were. She'd not be a faery; he'd not have found Aislinn.

And we wouldn't be together now.

But she was a regent, and he wasn't. She stepped around

him. "If you get killed, I'm going to be furious."

"I love you too. Come on."

Together they started to force their way through the fight. The Winter inside his skin wasn't as strong as hers, but he slammed what he had into a faery who came at him with a mace. Donia loathed the necessity of what they were doing, but the sight of two dead Hounds, dead rowan, and more dark fey than she wanted to count strengthened her resolve.

As they got closer, Donia spotted Niall and Bananach fighting. Aislinn was nowhere to be seen. *Let her be alive.* Chela—*now Gabriela*—was a vision of horror as she fought with a fury that befit the Gabriel of the Hunt. Friends, faeries she'd known for most of her life, and those whom her friends had sworn to lead and protect were in the midst of violence.

As they pushed forward, they reached the faery who'd raised Keenan and served as his advisor Keenan's entire life. Tavish wiped his sword on the shirt of a fallen Ly Erg. "Well, it's about time you got here."

"Ash? Seth?" Keenan asked him.

"My queen is over there." Tavish pointed to a crush of bodies with his sword. "Seth is apparently in a cage on the other side of the wall of shadows the Dark King put in place to protect him."

A roar from the Dark King rocked the room as several abyss-guardians took shape alongside Bananach.

That's not a good sign.

"She's winning," Tavish said, rather unnecessarily. "I don't think we're going to be able to stop her."

The abyss-guardians looked from Bananach to Niall, but did nothing more than hover in the space near the two. Their loyalty was to the regent of the Dark Court, but that loyalty was compromised by Bananach's actions.

Which means she is a regent.

"Maybe we can at least contain her," Keenan started. "It's not ideal, but . . . it's better than letting her loose on the world."

"Good idea." Donia squeezed Keenan's hand and sent a spear of ice flinging toward War.

Bananach batted it out of the air without a moment's hesitation. "You're picking the wrong side, Snow."

"Not really." Donia set a sheet of ice to form under the raven-faery's feet. "You can't take another ruler's throne."

"But I did," Bananach crowed. "He's weak."

The Dark King wasn't wasting breath on words: he head-butted her.

Neither Keenan nor Tavish would be able to stand against Bananach: the abyss-guardians only appeared for Dark Court regents.

And only a regent can kill a regent.

That left Niall and Aislinn.

And me.

"I love you," she told Keenan—and then she ran forward and sealed a wall of ice around herself and the small space where Bananach and Niall fought, looking the three of them in a frozen cage. The Winter Queen concentrated on making the wall thick enough that even if Bananach did defeat both of them, the raven-faery wouldn't be getting out anytime soon.

Niall looked up and nodded curtly at her.

Through the ice, Donia could see Keenan clawing at the barricade. She turned her back on him.

"Tear it down." Bananach pushed shadows at the wall. Nothing happened.

"Doesn't work that way." Niall slammed his fist into Bananach's face. With his other hand, he raised an obsidian blade that he'd pulled from somewhere on his body and slashed toward her throat.

War dodged, and the blade glanced off her collarbone. A red gouge there showed that he'd at least made contact.

While Niall continued to fight Bananach, Donia crept closer.

She sent ice to wrap around the raven-faery. It started at the floor and covered her up to her hips, encasing her lower body in a miniature glacier, but between the wall around them and the ice used for fighting, the glacier wasn't as strong as it would've been if Donia had not expended so much energy already.

Niall continued striking Bananach even as she was unable to move. The Dark King was not in full possession of his court's powers, and War was in possession of her full strength *as well as* the rest of the Dark Court's strength. He needed every advantage he could get.

And I'm not going to be useful too much longer.

"Your death is inevitable if you continue to irritate me." Bananach pushed through the snow and ice as if she was wading through deep waters. "Perhaps *that* throne should be mine too."

The Winter Queen didn't see the need to engage in verbal barbs; she concentrated on collecting the remaining strength she had, pulling the deepest cold to the surface of her skin. She let the cold fill her, and she watched the fight.

Niall angled to block Bananach from Donia.

Steadily, Donia eased up behind Niall, extending ice in a thick blade from both of her hands.

"Bad idea," Bananach warned.

Donia ignored her. *One chance.* When she was within range, she raised her hands.

Just as she was ready to tell Niall to get out of the way, he was shoved to the side. In an almost simultaneous move, Bananach extended a sword of shadows and drove it clear through Donia's abdomen. "You've become too much of a nuisance, Snow."

Donia concentrated every remaining bit of Winter she could focus on the short blades of solid ice extending from her hands. Her legs gave out, so her weight was supported on the sword that War had buried in her body. The Winter Queen lifted both hands and tried to drive them into Bananach's neck.

"I don't think so." The raven-faery leaned backward.

War withdrew her sword, and as she did so it re-formed

as an ax. She swept her arm to the side. The shadow-made weapon was still taking shape as Bananach brought it down on Donia's chest.

"Donia!" Niall yelled, and it was the last thing Donia heard before she fell to the bloody floor.

CHAPTER 37

"No!" Keenan saw Donia through the ice, watched her fall, and could do nothing. Instinctively, he exhaled on the ice wall, but all that did was add to the already thick barrier. He slammed a sword into the wall. "Damn it, Don!"

He screamed, "Aislinn! I need help here. Please. Sunlight."

He dragged his hands against the wall in a futile effort to get to Donia, and tried to think of something he had to use. Ice was of no use against ice; swords and knives weren't going to chip away at a solid wall anytime soon enough to help her.

"Ash! Please!" He looked around, trying to find the Summer Queen. "Ash! Donia's down. I need your sunlight. Get me *in there. Please!*"

Beside him, Tavish clasped a hand on his shoulder. "Niall's with her."

"She's dying," Keenan snarled. *"Aislinn!"*

A blast of sunlight knocked a hole in the wall, and Keenan scrambled through it. Tavish didn't follow; he stayed behind, guarding the other side of the opening the Summer Queen had burned in the wall.

Keenan glanced at Niall, who was locked in the fight with Bananach, and then he gathered Donia into his arms and stood.

"Go," Niall barked out.

Keenan backed through the opening in the wall of ice and pulled Donia's motionless body with him. Winter fey were swarming over the remaining fights in the warehouse now.

"Close the hole," Tavish urged. "I can't stop her if she gets out."

Cwenhild raced toward them. As she reached them, she directed, "Freeze her wounds, and get her out of here."

The terror that was mounting inside Keenan made it difficult to speak. All he got out was: "She's . . ."

"Not dead yet." Cwenhild's tone was even, but her expression was worried. "She's my queen; I'd have felt it if she died."

Keenan looked down at Donia. "Where's Far Dorcha?"

. "Out there." Cwenhild pointed with a red-gloved hand. *Not a glove. Blood.*

"Keenan! The hole—"

"I can't. I'm sorry. I don't have enough to do both." Keenan cradled the unconscious, bleeding Winter Queen in his arms, and exhaled on her wounds. The ice he'd inherited from his mother felt like the greatest gift in his life just then.

Tavish stepped in front of him. "If Bananach gets out—"

"If Don dies, I don't care," Keenan interrupted.

"The court—"

"Get me to Far Dorcha," Keenan told Cwenhild as he stepped around his former advisor. "I don't care who you kill to do it. Now."

The head of the Winter Guard didn't hesitate. She raised her arm in some sort of signal, and winter fey flanked them. As they walked, Keenan concentrated on the Winter inside him. He exhaled on Donia's heavily bleeding wounds again, freezing them shut as best he could.

In only a few minutes—*which seemed too long*—they stood at the door of the warehouse. The ice wall that Donia had erected now stood in Keenan's way. He needed to get her to help, and he had no sunlight to melt this wall.

A cry of frustration spilled from his lips—and with it came a breath of frost.

Both hopeful and afraid, he leaned against the wall and attempted to draw the ice into him as he'd once pulled warmth into his body to try to resist the cold. He tried to ignore the thought of his body filling with ice, of shutting down as that cold poured into him as it had so often when the last Winter Queen was angry or punishing him.

For Donia. Even if it does feel like that . . .

He pulled the cold into his skin, but he wasn't a regent any longer. The wall softened in front of him, but it didn't vanish. A section of the wall was not ice but slush now, and Keenan pushed through it.

On the far side of the mostly still intact wall, the winter fey were strong enough that they were slaughtering those of Bananach's faeries who had remained in the street. A cadaverous faery stepped toward him and frowned.

Keenan backed away and clutched Donia tightly to him when he realized who the faery was. "No."

"You need not carry them to me. I can collect them without anyone's help. . . ." Ankou paused and sniffed Donia. "She's not dead yet."

The look Cwenhild leveled at the death-faery would've frightened most anyone, but Death was unconcerned. She simply walked away and resumed her corpse gathering.

Far Dorcha, however, was nowhere to be seen.

He can help. He will. He has to.

"Find the Dark Man," Keenan told the winter fey, and then he sank to his knees in the street.

Aislinn had heard Keenan's words to the Scrimshaw Sister and to Tavish, and at the edge of her vision, she had seen him carry Donia's limp body outside. *That leaves me and Niall.* She had no idea if Niall was still standing, or what the situation was. She could see a wall of shadows farther into the room, and she hoped that it was Niall who had erected it.

And that Seth is safe behind it.

She glanced toward the ice wall; on the other side of it,

a fight continued. Niall and Bananach were slashing at one another. On her side of the hole in the ice, the head of the Summer Guard waited. A Hound with an unsheathed blade raced toward her guard.

"Tavish!" Aislinn focused more sunlight in her hand—but then remembered that in this, the Hunt was on their side. She lowered her upraised hand just as Tavish looked her way.

"My Queen?" He came to her.

Around them, several more Hounds appeared and cut down Ly Ergs. The Hunt—which had been stretched thin only moments before—seemed to be everywhere at once. The tide had shifted against Bananach's faeries.

"What's happening?" Aislinn asked as Tavish arrived at her side.

"That." He motioned.

The Summer Queen followed her guard's gesture to the unexpected sight before them. Fey the likes of which she'd never seen were flowing into the warehouse. Water trailed in their wake as they gathered faeries into their embraces and departed. The newcomers wrapped amorphous bodies around Bananach's faeries, and then flowed back out the way they'd come.

One faery stood in the doorway; its hands were raised as if conducting a symphony. The faery's body seemed to be a droplet of water shimmering in the air, as if it would finish falling in another instant.

"What is that?" she asked.

The water-droplet creature turned its attention to her and said, "Ally. Of his."

"Yours?" Aislinn asked Tavish.

Her guard shook his head.

"Land king vow," the faery said, and then it continued conducting the other water fey.

"Oh." Aislinn shook her head. Between the Hounds, the rowan, the Dark Court, and now the water fey, the fighting had shifted to favor the united courts. Unfortunately, that didn't undo the fact that Donia was fallen—or that the faery who'd struck the Winter Queen was still standing.

The Hounds who had pushed the fight outside the warehouse were now returning—in part, it appeared, because of the reduction in the number of their opponents. The water fey didn't fight: they simply took prisoners and left.

Smaller areas of fighting continued, but the forces who opposed Bananach's fey were obviously going to prevail.

That leaves Bananach.

"I can either help Niall or leave the wall in place," Aislinn said softly. "Any advice?"

"He is not winning, and the one who would seal the wall appears to be unable to repair it," Tavish said. "If you can help him, do it. We are running out of options."

The Summer Queen exhaled, and the ice melted.

The flood of it rolled through the warehouse. The water fey pulled it to them, lifting it until a section of the room was underwater. It had the effect of a giant, wall-less aquarium. *Which is impossible.* The faeries that she had seen blended into the water. Some of the land faeries tried to swim in the vertical river, but it was futile.

And then, the water itself—and the whole of those contained within it—exited the warehouse in a rush.

Aislinn was left in a much less crowded warehouse. Hounds and rowan formed a line of defense behind Aislinn, and in front of her, Niall and Bananach fought on.

"Ash," Niall said. The Dark King was bleeding from more places than Aislinn could count, but he'd cut through the faeries and then stood against War while the rest of them barely made it to his side.

Or fell when we got here.

The Summer Queen took a steadying breath.

I would offer mercy if I could.

Summer is not made for murder.

But even as she reminded herself of those things, she knew too that Summer *was* deadly. Droughts and fires, storms and floods, mud slides and parched bodies—those were the domain of Summer as well.

We are past the point of mercy.

The Summer Queen concentrated the heat that radiated through her body and sent it as a single beam toward Bananach. The raven-faery couldn't knock away the sunlight, although she did lift a shadow-made shield. Some of the sunlight was absorbed by the shadows, but enough of it pushed through that it charred flesh and feathers.

Bananach glanced at Aislinn and snapped her beak-mouth in a wordless threat.

While she was turned away, Niall slashed at her with a short *sgian dubh*. Fresh blood dripped down Bananach's arm. Feathers clung to the wound.

"Your forces are defeated," Aislinn said.

"Not all," War crowed. "Not *me*. Snow is done. He"— she bashed Niall over the head with the shadow shield—"is faltering more by the moment."

"I am not faltering," Aislinn said softly. "I've energy to spare."

The derision in Bananach's eyes would've been daunt-ing once—*had been daunting*—but Aislinn wasn't a mortal, wasn't an unsure queen, wasn't anything to be daunted. She was the Summer Queen, the first faery regent in almost a millennium to be fully in possession of the strength that begged to escape her body now.

"Niall, shield. Now."

And without waiting but a moment, she exhaled sun-light; she pushed it from her skin; she sent it forward in a solar flare that set Bananach on fire.

In that split instant between Aislinn's warning and action, the Dark King had pulled his abyss-guardians to him. They tangled into a solid wall of shadows, shielding him from Aislinn's sunlight.

Vaguely, she was aware of his presence, of the faeries behind her watching, of Bananach's screams of pain. *Sun-light. Burn away the disease.* The Summer Queen walked toward the burning faery. Sunlight rolled ahead of her steps, a blazing forest fire contained in only a few feet. *Purify. Protect.* Aislinn glanced at Niall. She remembered him striking her once, threatening her. *Friend or not?*

Summer had no words to ask such questions. She stared at him, trying to remember if she should burn him away too.

"Ash?" he said. He was battered, limping, yet he stepped between her and the screeching faery. "I will finish this."

The Summer Queen shook her head. "She hurt Donia. She killed Evan . . . Irial. . . Gabriel, Tish, and she killed *my* fey."

The Dark King nodded. His shadowy guardians were watching, but immobile. Their bodies were illuminated by the flames.

Bananach shook off the fire, shed it and most of her wings in a horrific shudder.

"Move." Niall raised a sword.

"No." Aislinn let vines come to her hand. *Soil. Vines need soil.* So Aislinn drew earth to her in a great tug, heard the roar of it coming behind her, and watched as it rolled in on either side of her and covered Bananach.

The raven-faery's body was drowning in the weight of the now-boiling mud, tangled by the miniature white roses that sprang from the earth.

"She cannot kill now," Aislinn pronounced.

The Dark King stepped into the mud and drove a shadow-wrought broadsword into the earth up to the hilt.

"Blood feeds the magick," a corn-husk-dry voice said.

Aislinn turned to see Far Dorcha watching.

"Death feeds the soil," he added.

In front of them, Niall sat down in the mud. Despite his battered and bruised body, the Dark King was smiling. He looked at her and said, "Seth was right."

The Dark Man nodded. "He was."

Perplexed, Aislinn looked from one to the other.

With one hand, Niall still held on to the broadsword; with the other, he wiped blood and sweat from his face. "Seth said we could kill her without all of us dying. Wasn't sure if he was right."

Far Dorcha chuckled.

"Where is he?" Aislinn's poise faltered. "I looked during the . . . during . . . Is he? Where is he?"

"I put up a barrier to keep Seth safe when I got here," Niall said. "He's safe, Ash. Bananach couldn't reach him."

A strange look passed between Niall and Far Dorcha, but Aislinn wasn't interested in asking why. Later, maybe, but right now, she had two more pressing matters to tend to. She nodded at Niall and then called to the death-fey, who had turned away already. "Far Dorcha?"

He paused. His expression was no more readable than it had been when she'd met him, but she thought a flicker of sorrow crossed his face.

"You offered me an exchange when we met," she reminded him. "I know what I want."

"What do you ask?"

"Whatever Keenan and Donia need," she said. "If necessary, I will owe you a favor. Not a death, but I would put myself in your debt if I had to."

Far Dorcha stared at her, but he said nothing. Instead, he nodded, and then strode away.

CHAPTER 38

If he had it all to do over, the Dark Man didn't think he would change any of it. There was sorrow over the death of so many of the fey, but it wasn't the first time they'd been so destructive. In the past, their quarrels had bled into the mortal world. They didn't squander their immortality often, but they still made foolish—or brave—choices from time to time. The losses reminded them that they weren't impervious to some wounds.

Brutal wounds.

Steel-inflicted wounds.

Faery-made wounds.

He watched his sister collect the corpses, saw the shades gathering in the air around him, and shook his head. It was not joyous to have a sudden influx of shades to contend with.

I don't seek subjects.

Ankou stopped, frowned at him, and then gestured in

a wide arc around her. He stood invisible to faery eyes—just as shades were—and watched the former Summer King grieve.

The Winter Court could be his if Donia died. It was a natural order. The child of Winter would take his mother's court. He would grieve, grow bitter, and eventually his mourning would warp into something malicious.

Which would be tedious.

"Let's hope you make better choices than your parents did, Keenan," Far Dorcha said.

The Dark Man had offered all the assistance he could without being asked. He could aid the injured Winter Queen because of his debt to the Summer Queen, but there were still natural rules. *Some sacrifices must be made willingly.* He walked past the guards, and just as he approached the mourning faery, he made himself visible again.

When Death stood over them, Keenan wasn't sure whether it was to take Donia or not, but he wasn't going to give her up.

Not now. Not ever.

"Far Dorcha." Keenan bowed his head as reverently as he could with Donia clutched in his arms. "I need your help."

The Dark Man's expression was completely unreadable. "What do you have to offer?"

"I want to give her my Winter," Keenan said. "My life if she needs it."

Far Dorcha laughed.

"Mercy," Keenan begged. "I'll give everything I have if you save her."

"And if Bananach were to escape because of your choices? What of the court you've served? Of her"—he stroked a hand over Donia's bloodied shoulder—"court? Of Niall? Of Aislinn? What of all those who—"

"I don't care. Only Donia matters," Keenan insisted.

"If I offer you the choice between her life and all of theirs?"

"Hers," Keenan answered without hesitation.

The Dark Man gestured in the air beside him, and a stone altar, the top covered in thick furs, appeared. "Your immortal life or hers?"

"Take mine; take whatever you need." Keenan glanced at the altar.

Far Dorcha pointed at the fur-covered thing. "I mean her no harm."

Carefully, Keenan lowered Donia onto the altar. "What do you need?"

"Do you willingly offer your Winter and your immortal life for hers?" Far Dorcha asked. "If you say yes—"

"Yes."

"Perhaps wait to hear the terms?"

Keenan shook his head. "Doesn't matter."

The Dark Man shrugged, and in less than a heartbeat, Keenan collapsed to the ground. He felt like everything inside of him was being ripped out. As he stifled a cry of pain, a gasp escaped, and with it a breath of icy air stretched toward Donia.

"Could've listened to the terms," Far Dorcha muttered. He nudged Keenan with a boot-clad foot. "Scream."

So Keenan did. He let the sound of the pain inside him loose, and the frosty air that was extending to Donia grew thicker with each breath. As the Winter he'd been born with was violently torn from his body, it flowed into Donia.

He watched as it healed her, knit the tears in her flesh, and made her whole again. He saw her sit up, still blood-covered but uninjured. The horror on her face as she saw him on the ground screaming was almost enough to make him close his eyes, but if this was it, he wanted to see her as long as he could.

She struggled to get down from the altar, but couldn't. Her lips formed a word he couldn't hear but knew was his name. She turned her furious gaze to Far Dorcha and snarled something at him.

Keenan heard none of it. He felt heaviness descend on him, a weight unlike anything he'd ever known, and he couldn't open his mouth to make another sound. His eyes started to close, but he saw her as she jumped from the altar.

And then she vanished. Everyone in the street faded until he was suddenly alone.

So this is dying.

It wasn't as bad as he'd expected. The former Summer King closed his eyes and lay back on the street.

CHAPTER 39

The shadow wall in front of him was ripped aside, and Seth could see the remains of the battle on the ground for a moment. Then the room grew blindingly bright under the glow of the faery who strode through those remaining fights with no guards, no soldiers, nothing but her own sunlight to protect her. *Ash.* Seth watched his rescuer walk up to the cage—which was now a good forty feet above the ground.

Aislinn reached out and gripped the bars with both hands. The metal glowed as brightly as the fire poker had, and then broke. She bent the two bars toward her.

On the ground below her, Bananach's faeries attempted to evade Summer Court guards and Dark Court faeries. A Dark Court faery impaled one of Bananach's Ly Ergs with a morning star. The spike on the macelike weapon pierced the faery, and he screamed. His thread blinked out of existence. After so many threads had ended, Seth felt physically sick with the awareness of the losses. Lives were ending because of lies and machinations; the power-hungry Bananach had condemned both her followers and her opposition. *Deaths that didn't need to happen.* War was always contemptible, but war for no reason other than greed was unforgivable.

Seth didn't want Aislinn to see the horror in his eyes; did not know the words to speak of what he'd seen, how helpless he'd been. *How terrified for her.* She was here now, alive and apparently rescuing him. *With blood on her jeans.*

The silent Summer Queen extended her hands toward him, and Seth stepped into the seemingly empty air, trusting that she knew what she was doing. Until this moment, as far as he'd known, his girlfriend couldn't walk on air, but she obviously was doing it.

And holding on to me as she does so.

He suddenly felt like one of the cartoon characters who steps off a cliff, as if looking down would make him plummet. Despite that, he glanced at their feet and saw what looked like sunbeams under each of them. The sunbeams slowly lowered, and he and Aislinn were standing on the warehouse floor.

Seth saw Tavish outside the door. The Summer Court advisor held a thin sliver of steel that would look harmless to most mortals, but was deadly to faeries.

Tavish told Aislinn, "I will leave a few of our guards here with theirs to help look after Niall and . . . the others. You should go. We will tidy up the rest."

As Tavish spoke, Seth realized that there were words

the Summer Court advisor was studiously avoiding, and he wished that he could see threads that were currently invisible to him.

Aislinn looked at Tavish. "Donia?"

"She will survive. She has departed . . . *with* Keenan." Tavish looked heartsick for a moment. "Her guards have taken them both from here."

Seth couldn't tell what Tavish was hiding, but he didn't want to ask just then. Whatever grief Tavish was keeping from Aislinn would have to wait.

"She hurt you." Aislinn looked at the burn along the side of Seth's face and then directly at his eyes. "Are you . . . all right aside from this?"

Seth glanced at Tavish, who bowed his head with an unfamiliar degree of respect and stepped away to allow them some measure of privacy.

"My head feels like it's going to split from the things I've . . . seen," he started, but the temptation to tell her all he had seen—and could see yet—vied with the desire to do the very thing she'd asked of him when he returned from Faerie: let the world wait. "I want to tell you . . . I need to tell you, but . . . later."

She nodded.

Hand in hand, Aislinn and Seth walked through the warehouse; she didn't seem to even register the fact that vines entangled fighters as she passed them. Behind her, the ensnared faeries who had fought with Bananach's forces were killed by rowan and Hounds.

Just outside the warehouse, Far Dorcha stood with Niall. Ankou walked around, gathering the dead and placing them in a long black coach that was parked in the street. She sang softly to herself as she lifted bodies into her arms.

Far Dorcha nodded at them as they approached, and then his gaze returned to Niall and he beckoned with one finger as if hooking something and tugging it toward him. "Out. Now."

Irial's shade took form and stepped out of Niall's body.

Aislinn gasped.

The dead Dark King ignored everyone but the living Dark King. He turned to face Niall. "You're as stubborn as ever."

"But not insane," Niall said.

"True." Irial lifted a hand as if he would touch Niall's battered face. "You defended our court admirably. I knew you were meant to be the Dark King."

Niall shook his head, but he was smiling now. "You aren't ever satisfied, are you? You were *right*, Irial. They are mine. The court is mine." Niall held up bloodied hands. "I will kill or die for them."

"And they for you," Irial said.

"There has been enough killing today." Far Dorcha's words drew all of their gazes to him. In the midst of the bruised and wearied faeries, Death alone seemed untouched. He folded his arms over his chest and looked at them.

"In all of forever, this has not happened. She"—the Dark Man paused and motioned toward the warehouse—"was

one of the first of two. Said to be unkillable without damn-
ing us all. There must be balance." The Dark Man's gaze
flickered to Aislinn. "You have first right."

Aislinn's hand tightened on Seth's. "No."

"And you?" Far Dorcha's attention turned to Seth.
"Would you fill the vacant role of Discord? By right of your
mother's heritage, you are entitled to fill this. Your Sight is
already in place; you travel between the worlds. You walk in
the four courts and as a solitary. Unless you are planning to
keep your new role . . ."

Seth glanced at Niall. "I don't suppose the consequences
of *not* being who I am would be good."

Far Dorcha shrugged, but made no comment.

"I'll pass." Seth might not be able to see his own future,
but he saw—and suspected that Far Dorcha saw—the
increasingly probable futures of several of the faeries around
him. Irial and Niall still had choices to make. Seth was all
but certain what those choices were, but the decisions still
must be made manifest.

There are always choices.

Far Dorcha continued as if nothing was certain. "Niall?
Your sword ended her."

"No. I am the Dark King." Niall stared at Irial as he
spoke. "I didn't fight for my throne, bleed for the court,
only to step away." Then, with visible effort, Niall pulled
his gaze from Irial and asked Far Dorcha, "The role must
be filled, right?"

Far Dorcha sighed. "It must, and as much as it pains me

to offer it to the one who *avoided* dying . . . Irial?"

The shade of the dead king did not even glance at Death—or at anyone there. As if no one else stood with them, he asked Niall, "Are you sure? I could stay. . . ."

"Dead?" Niall snorted. "An eternity of you in my head isn't exactly ideal for either of us."

At that, Irial glanced at Far Dorcha. "Are there other options?"

"You can remain as you are now, unconnected to the live king; you can resume your possession of him; or you can assume the vacant role." Far Dorcha scowled at Irial. "If you are not this, I need to find another to fill it. There will be balance. Discord is—"

"Right." Irial waved his hand as if brushing words away. "If I am unconnected, will they see me?"

"Not unless I am near or they are dead too," Far Dorcha said.

"So possession, absence, or War." Irial turned his back on all of them again. "Niall? I can stay, help mind the court, advise you; being tied to you means that our dreams are real."

"I don't want you to be a shade," Niall said. "War belongs in the Dark Court, and . . . This is what I want."

"Not War," Far Dorcha corrected. "She was Discord— just as her twin is Order. Bananach forgot what she was. The aim of Discord is not solely one of violence. To do your work, you will be able to walk through the veil to Faerie as well. I will remedy that problem: the veil will be open to you . . . if you are Discord."

"Discord." Irial flashed a wry smile at all of them. "I'm sure I can stir up some discontent."

The Dark Man snorted, but said nothing.

As they all stood there, Irial grew serious. He reached out with an insubstantial hand that hovered over the Dark King's forearm. "You can't trust me after this. Not the same way you do now."

"I don't tr—" The words Niall attempted to say became unpronounceable. "I don't want you dead, Iri. I can find a new advisor. . . . Tell him yes, so we can get to work setting things in order."

"Discord doesn't generally work at putting things *in* order." Irial's smile returned.

Far Dorcha shook his head. "No one else has ever tricked Death, so I suppose it's fitting that you fill the unkillable role."

"I never have been much for rules." Irial's insubstantial form became solid as they watched. "You have to admit that it was a good loophole."

The incredulous look Far Dorcha gave him made quite clear that he wasn't going to admit anything, but as the Dark Man turned his back to Irial and Niall, he winked at Seth.

As Seth watched, threads became steady and stretched into the future.

Death was smiling as he walked toward Ankou; Niall's tension seemed to vanish as Irial murmured something too softly for anyone else to hear.

Then Aislinn leaned her head on Seth's arm. "Let's get out of here?"

He had unresolved business with Niall, but given the option of dealing with Niall or being with Aislinn . . . there was no choice. He tightened his arms around her, but before they took two steps, the Summer Court's advisor cleared his throat.

"If I could borrow you for a moment, my Queen?" Tavish said as he joined them. "I will handle what's here, but I need you to make a few decisions before you depart."

The Summer Queen looked at Seth. "Give me a sec?"

He nodded.

Tavish led Aislinn a few steps away, and Seth was left standing with Niall and Irial.

With a smile, Irial turned to Niall. "Far Dorcha deserves just a little more discord in his life. See you inside?"

After a grateful look at Irial's departing figure, Niall turned to face Seth. They stood in silence for only as long as it took to assure that no one overheard them.

"I was angry," Niall said.

Seth folded his arms.

The Dark King rubbed a hand over his face. "If Ash had been killed, you would've been unwell too."

"That's a *reason*, not an excuse." Seth gestured at the burn on the side of his face. "You were going to burn my *eye*, man. That's so far from forgivable."

"I didn't."

"Because Leslie stopped you." Seth stepped closer. "You considered letting Far Dorcha kill me."

"I didn't offer you to him," Niall said.

"You told me last year that you didn't want me to see the ugly part of the Dark Court, that you didn't want the whole bastard thing"—Seth paused, weighing the words, trying to balance hurt and logic—"to affect me . . . that I wouldn't see you the same if I did."

The hope in Niall's expression was at odds with the battered state he was in. "You told me I was wrong."

"You were *right*." Seth stared directly at Niall. "I don't see you the same way."

"I'm sorry," Niall said.

"I'm not an idiot. I knew what you were. Objectively, I got it. If you weren't capable of horrible choices, you wouldn't be a faery. If you weren't capable of doing those things, you wouldn't have been able to be the Dark King."

"You mean horrible like keeping secrets that lead to deaths and violence and chaos?" Niall snorted.

"And caging your friends? And getting unthroned by War because you're unbalanced and acting like an ass?" Seth clasped the Dark King's upper arm. "I don't see you the same, but I can live with what I do see. You're my *brother*."

Niall pulled Seth in for a brief one-armed hug. "For what it's worth, I'm glad you still have both eyes."

As Seth stepped away, he shook his head. "Next time? Direct the bastard thing elsewhere."

"Or what?"

"Seriously?" Seth grinned. "I had a little time to think while I was in my *cage*. . . . The voice of reason is pretty lacking on this side of the veil, and unless my mother and the Shadow Court decide to remove the veil, you all might need to have the occasional reminder here."

"You declaring yourself a king, little brother? Bit presumptuous, isn't it?" Niall's tone was more curious than anything.

"I watched you become more balanced when I came to you, and when I decided to do . . . whatever it took to balance you, I felt it. I felt *you*, Niall. I hung in the cage where you put me, and I watched Bananach come into your court and take it from you, and I accepted the inevitable." Seth understood the rightness of what he'd had to do, but part of him mourned it. "I am Sorcha's heir. I'm the *only* faery in the mortal world who *can* be your balance. I am the Order to your Darkness."

"So you're what? The King of Order?" Niall watched him with a mixture of pride and sorrow.

"No. I'm not king of anything. I suspect I'll get enough of court structure and pomp in Faerie." Seth rolled his eyes at the thought of trying to be a king. "I'm your balance, though."

Niall smiled.

Seth continued, "It wouldn't be bad to have the solitary fey know there's someone they can talk to if any of you all get stupid again. My two brothers head the Dark Court and the Shadow Court. My mother is High Queen. My"—Seth glanced over to where Aislinn and Tavish talked—"Ash is the Summer Queen. I can see the future; I can go between the two worlds; and I can reason with the faeries I love, the faeries who are family, and the faeries I call friends."

The expression on Niall's face became utterly unreadable. "You think you could stand up to her? No conflict of interest—"

"You're sharing your house with *Discord*," Seth reminded him. "And I'll be damned if I believe he's not going to play favorites."

The faery in question walked past Seth. "Well, seer, luckily *your* future sight wouldn't encourage you to play favorites, sacrifice people, gamble with courts. . . ." Irial paused and withdrew a cigarette case and lighter from Niall's pocket. He extracted a cigarette, glanced at Seth, and drawled, "Say, like letting me die for your agenda."

Silently, Niall took the cigarette from Irial, lit it, and inhaled.

Seth shrugged. "Who's to say I didn't see the end result? You're not addictive to mortals. *Either* of you. You're back at odds, where you like to be. Bananach's dead . . . and Leslie is sitting in your house, where all three of you hope she will eventually stay."

At their stunned expressions, Seth paused. "Of course, there were other outcomes that were a lot less positive for you, but . . . a lot of things worked out because of your death."

"You may do all right at this balancing thing, boy." Irial

shook his head, and then turned his attention to Niall. "Our Shadow Girl waits at the house."

"Leslie waits at our *home*," Niall corrected.

And Discord smiled.

Seth smiled too as he watched them walk away. The threads he could see for the two faeries were woven tightly together, and in many of the possible futures, he saw Leslie's not-quite-mortal, not-quite-fey thread wrapped with theirs. She wasn't anywhere near ready to stay with the Dark Court, but there were more than a few possible futures for her that brought her into a happy future with the two faeries who loved her and each other.

As he looked at their entangled futures, Seth felt a surge of envy. He wasn't sure what the future held—if he was about to lose Aislinn, if he had an eternity of trying to accept her relationship with another faery—but he did know that he'd wasted time with Aislinn because of his fears.

No more.

He walked over to her, and with a comfort he hadn't felt in months, he took her hand. Sunlight flared from her skin. She might not be his forever, but after what had just happened, she was going to be his tonight. Whether he was staying or going, he was going to spend tonight in her arms.

CHAPTER 40

After washing the signs of the fight away from both of them, the Winter Queen had tenderly lain Keenan in the bed they'd shared. She'd done everything she could to keep him safe, and it hadn't worked.

It's not fair to finally have a chance at forever together and have it taken away. She glanced at his motionless body again. *Maybe we were never meant to have forever.* She'd spent more than an hour of pacing anxiously. Now, she was alternating between weeping, stroking his face, and talking to him.

"You're an idiot," she whispered tearfully.

Finally, he opened his eyes and stared up at her; by then, she had moved on to stroking his hair *and* crying. She sat beside him on the edge of the bed, trying very hard not to bump him or let her cold tears fall on his bare chest and arms.

For a moment, he blinked at her. Then he asked, "Are you dead too?"

"No." She leaned in as carefully as she could and brushed her lips over his. *How do I do this?* She sat back and examined his lips for frostbite.

"Don?" Keenan's face crinkled in a frown. "I don't understand."

He's here. That's the important part.

"You're alive."

"And you are." Keenan struggled to sit up. He frowned briefly. "I guess giving up my Winter left me weaker than I thought it would. I feel . . . wrong."

The sob that Donia intended to hold in escaped.

"Don?" He tried to pull her to him, but she resisted—and he couldn't move her.

Despite her resolve, frozen tears raced down her cheeks and onto the sheets. "I'm so sorry."

"For what?" he asked. His voice was almost the same, but it sounded different enough that every word he spoke reminded her of his changed state.

"Getting hurt. This." She pointed at him in the bed.

He caught her hand in his. "I'm alive . . . with *you* . . . in your bed. What do you have to be sorry about?"

"You're mortal," she blurted. *Graceful, Don.* She opened her mouth to try to say more, but he was laughing.

There were a lot of reactions she'd considered while he'd lain unconscious in her bed, but laughter wasn't one of them. He held her hand and laughed until she was a bit worried. Then he shook his head. "Well, that's new."

"You don't understand—"

"Don?" Keenan tugged her to him, and she let herself be pulled into his embrace.

Careful; no frost, no ice.

"I'm here with you. I don't care about anything else." Keenan stared at her with something like wonder in his very mortal blue eyes. "You're alive, and I'm here with you."

"But—"

"I *love* you, and I'm here with you." He slid his hand over her cheek. "Nothing else matters."

"You'll *die*," she protested.

"Not today." He covered her mouth with his and kissed her just as thoroughly as he had when he was a faery. His arms slid around her, and he pulled her down beside him.

The fear of hurting him made her cautious, but he had no hesitation. His hand was at the buttons of her shirt. Mortality hadn't erased his deftness with clothing removal either.

He leaned back for a moment to tug her shirt down her arms, with the same wicked, lovely smile that had first stolen her breath years ago.

"You know," he said, "after centuries, there aren't too many things I can think of that I've wanted to try but haven't."

"Oh?" Cautiously, she slid her hands over his chest.

"Mm-hmm." His fingertips traced her collarbone and down her arm, while his other hand unzipped her skirt.

She lifted her hips for him to remove her skirt.

"What did . . ." she started, but her words vanished as he

leaned over and kissed her hip.

A few moments later, he whispered against her skin, "You know what I've never done?"

Absently, she realized that while he had distracted her with one hand, he'd used his other hand to remove the pajama pants she'd put on him. With effort she forced her eyes to stay open and meet his gaze. "What's that?"

"Made love as a mortal." He breathed the words against her stomach. Between kisses and caresses, he asked, "Do you suppose you could help me? Be my first? My only? My till-death-do-we-part?"

"Keenan . . ."

He kissed his way up her stomach and chest until he was stretched out on top of her. "I will love you every minute of every day of my life."

Tenderness they'd shared before; passion they'd shared before; but the desperation she felt was new. His words broke her heart. "I don't want you to die," she sobbed. "We just—"

"I'm here with you in your bed, Donia. Neither of us died today." He kissed the tears from her cheeks. "Make love with me?"

When she didn't answer, he said, "Unless you want to wait until after the wedding . . ."

More tears slipped from the corners of her eyes even as a small laugh escaped her lips. She reached up and cupped his face in her hands. "No."

He looked nervous for a moment. "But you *are* going to

marry me, aren't you, Donia?"

"I am," she promised. "But I don't really want to wait until after the wedding. You already have my vow. You had it years ago when I promised you forever alongside a hawthorn bush."

"And you have mine. I'm yours for as long as I live. Only yours. My vow on it." He lowered his lips to hers, and they celebrated the life, the moment, the time they had together.

CHAPTER 41

As Aislinn and Seth reached the parts of Huntsdale untouched by the violence of the day, the Summer Guards stepped away. They looked at Aislinn expectantly. One of them, a Summer Girl Seth had never seen looking anything other than giddy, nodded. "We will handle what remains to be done here."

"Run with me, Seth." Aislinn squeezed his hand in hers, and then before the next breath, she took off.

Unlike when he was mortal, Seth could run without holding on to her now, but he would hold on to her forever if he could. So he held tightly to her hand, and together they sped through the snow-covered streets of Huntsdale.

Once they crossed the threshold of the area where Summer held dominion, more rowan guards stood waiting. They looked at her with a new intensity, and Seth knew that the question that had stood between them was about to be answered for better or worse.

Faeries were filtering into the park around them. As they passed Aislinn, many of them touched her, a brief brush of fingertips over her arm or her hair. They didn't speak, but their expressions relaxed at the sight of her.

Aislinn kept hold of his hand, but with her free hand, she motioned for him to wait. "You've kept secrets from me."

"Only one," Seth said.

"You see the future."

"Yeah." Seth gave her a wry smile. "But not the parts I wanted to see."

The Summer Queen looked up at the sky, and a warm rain shower began. The Summer Court faeries raised their arms and let the rain wash away the dirt and blood from their skin. Flowers and grass grew in vibrant waves of color across the ground at the Summer Queen's feet. Her clothes were clinging to her body, and her hair was hanging in wet tendrils.

Like a pagan goddess.

As faeries began to dance slowly, she looked not at Seth, but at her court. "I told you we would revel once the danger was past. We are here, alive, and your fallen family would not want tears."

A faery queen.

"How do we remember?" Aislinn called.

The faeries around them caught hands, entangled arms and legs, and watched their queen. They answered:

"In joy."

"In living."

"In celebrating."

Aislinn sighed, and the heat of Summer rolled out over the park. "Rejoice as Summer should." She smiled, and rainbows arced over the assembled fey. "Chase away sorrow by living."

Then she turned to Seth and added, "Celebrate."

After the horrors of the past days, the fight with Bananach, the time in Faerie, being caged by his friend, seeing—*and feeling*—the loss of so many faeries, he wanted the joy that the Summer Court was allowing themselves. Drenched faeries cavorted around them, almost frantic in their revelry, as if they were taking pleasure for themselves and for their fallen brethren.

"Will you stay with me tonight?" she asked.

And Seth caught her hand in his again. "Yes."

Vaguely, he was aware that summer fey were cheering, but it seemed distant. Everything was distant, except for the faery holding his hand.

My reason. My everything.

Part of him wanted her to say the words, but the rest of him couldn't care less. If he had to let her go tomorrow, he would, but tonight she was his. Silently, he followed her away from her faeries, across the street, and to the loft.

Aislinn opened the door to the building. "Be welcome in my home, Seth."

He stilled. "Pretty formal."

"Things have changed." She smiled enigmatically and walked inside.

He reached out to grab Aislinn's hand again, but as he did so, she was already at the top of the first flight of stairs.

She leaned over the railing and smiled. "You're awfully far away."

Vines raced along the railing and burst into flower. Lilac petals rained down all around him as he stared up at her.

"Once you asked me to stop running so you could catch me," she said. "Do you remember?"

"You were mortal then." He started up the stairs, not running, but skipping stairs as he went.

She watched him. "So were you."

"And now?" He was only a few steps away from her.

She laughed and ran up the second flight of stairs.

Seth followed, not as fast as she was, but fast enough that she hadn't opened the door yet. He put a hand flat on the door and leaned close to her. "So am I to chase you, Ash?"

"When I was mortal, you told me that you'd waited for me." She wrapped her arms around his neck. Vines threaded down from her hair and twisted behind him. "Lately, I've been the one waiting."

"Losing you would destroy me." He breathed the words against her neck. He'd thought about her while he was Niall's prisoner, thought about never holding her in his arms again. "But I love you, and tonight I need—"

"Ask me. Ask me to choose."

"Tonight, it doesn't have to matter. I'm here either way." Seth didn't want to speak his fears; when he'd thought he would never see her again, he couldn't remember why he'd wasted the nights they could've had.

"*Ask* me, Seth," she urged.

And he didn't need to ask the question. He saw that in her eyes, felt it in the way she was wrapped around him. *Here. Now.* He covered her mouth with his and kissed her the way he had when they first fell in love. When he pulled back, he asked, "And the Summer King?"

"There is no Summer King." Aislinn reached behind her and opened the door. "He gave up his court."

"He . . . *gave it up*?" Seth echoed. Of all the things he'd thought she might have told him, Keenan giving up his court wasn't anywhere on the list. "He . . . How? When? Why?"

"When I told him that I'd made my choice, he left." Aislinn looked at Seth. "We both want to be with the ones we love."

He'd imagined hearing that she was truly his, dreamed of it, but in that moment, all he could do was kiss her. Seth lifted her into his arms and crossed the threshold from the hallway into the loft with her.

When he lowered her feet to the floor, she backed away, out of his arms, out of reach. "The Summer Court is strongest when its regent is happy. Do you know what makes me happy?"

When he tried to step forward, vines tangled around his legs. He glanced down at them.

She waited for him to look at her and said, "*You* make me happy, Seth. Always. Only you. For eternity."

Seth pulled free of the vines that twisted around his ankles as Aislinn laughed and ran from the room.

Faeries chase.

He caught her in the hallway, and she stayed still long enough for him to kiss her breathless before she twisted away again, slipping from his grasp as if she was sunlight darting away.

"Catch me, Seth," she invited.

He paused.

"Faeries chase," he said, and then, with a flirtatious smile, he turned away, but before he could take a second step, she was behind him, arms around him, lips pressed against his neck.

"I seem caught," he murmured.

The Summer Queen whispered, "Me too."

And they fell together into the bed of flowers that now covered the floor.

EPILOGUE

A YEAR LATER . . .

He knelt before her.

"Is this what you freely choose, to accept winter's chill?" she asked him—the faery she'd fallen in love with so many years ago. She'd dreamed that they would be together forever, but not like this. It was so strange and beautiful that she couldn't look away.

"It's what I want," he assured her again.

"You understand that if this doesn't work . . ."

He paused, glancing at her with pain in his eyes. "I'll still be here. If you don't want to risk it . . . I'm still here either way. We don't need to do this if you aren't sure."

"Keenan—"

"But *I* am willing to take the chance if it's what we *both* want," he said quietly. "I would spend eternity in the Winter with you, even if it means being your subject." He paused before adding, "Irial and Niall say it should work."

Discord says it's a good idea. That's comforting.

Donia pushed back her fears. "But if they're wrong . . ."

"It's what I freely choose," he repeated.

She walked over to the hawthorn bush they'd planted together last year. The leaves brushed against her arms as she bent down and reached under it. Her fingers wrapped around the Winter Queen's staff. It was a plain thing, worn from the countless hands that had clenched the wood.

Please let this work.

She stood and held it out to him; he wrapped his hand around it.

He clutched the Winter Queen's staff—and she hoped. For a moment she thought they were wrong, as she watched him falter. She felt the tendrils of Winter slide into his skin, the shards of ice fill his veins. The staff was an extension of her, and she felt the pain of it all over again as Keenan's body was remade.

With icy tears sliding down her cheeks, she knelt beside him and called his name: "Keenan!"

"My Queen," he breathed reverently as his eyes filled with snow.

Unlike her, he was born of winter, so he wasn't aching with the pain of the cold. In truth, he was more stunning in that instant than he'd ever been before.

"My *consort*," she whispered.

He took her free hand in his. Bands of ice began to wrap around their arms, binding their wrists together.

"Will you be my forever, Donia?"

"Yes. Will you share my life? My court? My forever?"

"Till death, my Queen." Keenan sighed the words against her cheek; frost formed in her hair.

She pressed her lips to his, relishing the cold that lifted from his skin.

And the Winter Queen and her consort covered their winter garden with a fall of white snow.

THE END

"Send the messengers for the Faery Courts. This is the end."

LOVE. DESPAIR. BETRAYAL.
ARE YOU READY FOR THE ASTONISHING FINAL ADVENTURE?

Use your phone to take a picture of the bar code below or text DARKESTMERCY to READIT to prepare for the thrilling conclusion of Melissa Marr's breathtaking Wicked Lovely series.

http://melissamarr.mobi

- Download the 2D bar code reader software with your phone at http://melissamarr.mobi/reader
- Take a photo of the code using your phone's camera.
- Experience the enchantment.

Text **DARKESTMERCY** to
READIT (732348) for more!

U.S. Residents Only. Message and Data Rates May Apply.